THE STUART SAPPHIRE

THE STUART SAPPHIRE

Alanna Knight

CHIVERS

British Library Cataloguing in Publication Data available

This Large Print edition published by BBC Audiobooks Ltd, Bath, 2006.
Published by arrangement with Allison & Busby

U.K. Hardcover ISBN 10: 1 4056 3828 1
              ISBN 13: 978 1 405 63828 9
U.K. Softcover ISBN 10: 1 4056 3829 X
              ISBN 13: 978 1 405 63829 6

Printed and bound in Great Britain by
Antony Rowe Ltd., Chippenham, Wiltshire

For David Shelley

ACKNOWLEDGEMENTS

In the third of Tam Eildor's time-quests through history, the following books have provided invaluable sources of information.

The Prince and his Pleasures by Andrew Barlow; *The Encyclopedia of Brighton* by Timothy Carder; *Prince of Pleasure* by Saul David; *The Regency Underworld* by Donald A Low; *Maria Fitzherbert: the Secret Wife of George IV* by James Munson; *George IV, The Grand Entertainment* by Stephen Parissien; *Caroline and Charlotte* by Alison Plowden; *A Prince's Passion: The Life of the Royal Pavilion* by Jessica Rutherford.

My grateful thanks to son Kevin and daughter-in-law Patricia for their tireless guided tours of Brighton and Lewes and boundless enthusiasm for my many visits. My love to them and to Chloe, Julia and Woody, as always.

Chapter One

Voices . . .

It was their voices, the stink of their breath and sweat that aroused him. He had made contact.

'Boots—by God. Look at them. New!'

'And see the shirt on him, that's fine linen.'

'And the breeches. Leather—we'll have those off him.'

A coarse laugh. 'He'll not need them where he's going.'

Was he dead? Had he died in transit, was that it? But rough hands dragging off his boots—he felt that. He was alive, the stench all around him was real enough. His face in semi-darkness did not interest them and he opened his eyes cautiously.

Screams and moans issuing from somewhere below. A moving floor—the creak of wooden timbers . . .

That other smell—the sea. He was on a ship!

Something had gone seriously wrong with his time-quest.

The men were cursing, trying to drag him upright to remove his clothes.

Wherever he was in time and place now made little difference. He had to escape and what his captors didn't realise was that Tam

1

Eildor from the twenty-third century could move much more swiftly than any man alive in the year 1811. Future science had conquered both time and space, and with space went gravity and weightlessness.

On his feet in one bound, before his captors could regain their balance, he cracked their two astonished heads together. Before they fell, moaning and cursing, he was off leaping away, thankful that they hadn't got him below decks in this accursed ship.

He ran, considering his escape route. To his certain knowledge this was the first time he had been aboard a ship at sea. In less dangerous circumstances he might have relished this as an exciting new prospect to explore.

Pausing in his flight, he considered the gently swaying masts above his head. Devoid of sails, it didn't look as if this particular ship had been at sea for a very long time and the deck, with its air of neglect, of dirt and decaying timbers, confirmed his suspicions.

Cautiously he leaned over the rusting ship's rail. In the gathering darkness pinpoints of light indicated landfall. This massive ship, with no sails, was at anchor and Tam was relieved to see that the distant shore was within swimming distance.

Behind him the swaying deck was still deserted. His captors obviously had not yet regained their equilibrium, but he could still hear the screams and moans from below, his stomach retching at the stench as he realised the appalling truth of his present circumstances.

Something had indeed gone awry with his time-quest. By some serious miscalculation he had landed in what was obviously the right period but in the wrong place. Instead of Regency Brighton, his destination, he was marooned offshore somewhere along the English south coast on a particularly unpleasant vessel. At a guess, transportation accommodation for convicts about to be shipped off to the Colonies or Van Diemen's Land.

He moved swiftly, taking great care around the ship's rail. He was sad about the boots, but should he have to swim for it, he would be better without them. Far below there was a heavy cable leading to the submerged anchor, and attached to it a jolly-boat—presumably to ferry the jailers across to the delights awaiting behind those far-off shore lights.

That would do for him too, he decided as angry voices and scurrying footsteps indicated that his captors had recovered their senses and raised the alarm.

Not a moment to lose. He was about to swing over the side using the cable to reach the boat when he noticed a small figure crouched nearby.

A child's face looked up at him, a terrified

face, boy or girl, he didn't know which. An instant of recognition and then it was gone.

'Please help me, sir. Don't leave me here. They'll kill me.'

A language he understood and with relief he recognised that if this child was a captive then his calculations were right and that distant hump of greyness was the English coast.

The footsteps were nearer now, the shouts angry.

'Come along, then,' he said.

A twelve-year-old boy in breeches, a coarse shirt many sizes too large for him, an unruly mop of fair curls. He stood up, trembling.

Tam pointed. 'See that boat down there. That's where we're heading.'

The boy shuddered, drew back from the rail. 'I cannot—I cannot swim.'

The voices were too close for comfort. In another moment they would be seen. He didn't care to dwell on what the captors would do then.

Tam made an impatient gesture. 'Hang on to me. I'm going to jump.'

'No!'

'All right. Stay and be killed.'

No time now for the niceties of a tidy descent via the cable. And with a stifled moan he took for assent, Tam seized his feather-light human burden and jumped into the water.

They emerged gasping for breath, several

4

yards away from the ship, swaying massively at anchor, and with the boy still clinging to his neck. Tam reached the side of the boat that hid them from the view of the men who were now searching for them, staring over the side of the ship's rail far above their heads.

At his side, the boy was crying softly. Tam whispered, 'Be quiet and keep your head down. Hang on while I swim round and get the line loose. We'll be safe soon.' (That was a lie, but he could do without a snivelling child on his hands at the moment.)

Fortunately the thick rope didn't look as if it would be too difficult to untie. He swam back to the boy.

'Is it all right? We'll get away—won't we?'

All that Tam could reply was, 'I hope so,' reassurance he was far from feeling.

The boy sighed and was about to climb into the boat.

'No,' said Tam. 'We must wait—'

'Wait?' wailed the lad. 'I'm freezing.'

'Better be freezing than dead,' was the grim reply. 'We must wait until it's completely dark.'

'Why? When will that be?'

'An interesting question.' Even as he said the words, Tam would have given much to know the time of day and whether the heavy black sky above their heads heralded growing darkness or an approaching storm.

'If they see the boat drifting away, they'll

know we're on it,' he continued patiently. 'Then we'll either be recaptured or shot. Which would you prefer?'

A stifled sob was the only response.

Carefully Tam scanned the ship's rail high above them. The faces gone, he would take a chance that their captors were now extending their search to the far side of the ship.

'Very well. You can get aboard. You're small, so you can hide under that tarpaulin.'

'But—'

Tam's patience was running out. 'Stop arguing and do as I say.'

The boy scrambled into the boat, and stared down at Tam. 'What about you? Where are you going? You're not going to leave me here, are you?'

Tam wished with all his heart that he could do just that. It was going to be hard enough to escape even with the dark sky indicating nightfall and trusting that the missing jolly-boat would not be spotted until morning.

He could have managed it on his own, but with a terrified child to deal with the odds were against him. 'I'll be close at hand,' he said. 'Right here.'

'In the water. You'll freeze.'

Tam decided not to argue, aware that once inside the boat he would be trapped. In the water, he could swim, still have a chance and sniffing the air was encouraging. At least he had landed at the right season.

6

The water was still warm, suggesting the close of what had been a hot summer's day on land. He was quite comfortable and he obviously didn't have the boy's problems with feeling the cold.

Taking his bearings, he was thankful there was no moon. If his calculations were right, it might soon be completely dark, safe to steer the boat towards the shore.

And while they waited he had better think out very carefully his next move and what had gone wrong. As excellent as the maps of the past were in his own century, they had not taken into account some form of coastal erosion, and that the Brighton shoreline had vanished under a mile of sea, or whatever was the nautical measure.

While he was deciding on his next move, the scenario changed dramatically, confirming his worst fears; that the blackness above them was not only approaching all-concealing night but something less welcome and considerably more dangerous. Heavy raindrops and the distant rumble of thunder hinted that the ship was in the path of a rapidly approaching storm.

The sea recognised the signs with a sudden respectful heaving and swirling of waves in what had been millpond smooth around them.

'You had better come aboard.' The small white face peered at him from under the tarpaulin. 'You're getting very wet,' was the

7

added somewhat obvious comment.

Tam looked upwards as lightning snarled across the sky, throwing briefly into tremulous life the massive ship, its timbers creaking above their heads, sending up spray and agitating the surrounding area. Now clinging on to the jolly-boat brought the added danger of being dashed against the ship's side.

Again he glanced upwards. The ship's rail seemed deserted. No doubt their captors, or whatever guards normally patrolled, had taken refuge from the storm and were now below decks.

He decided to take the boy's advice.

Shivering, he scrambled aboard, under the tarpaulin held by the boy who said, rather triumphantly, 'You're the one who's freezing now. See that jacket on the bench—too big for me. You should put it on.'

And Tam was aware for the first time that he was cold, more from the icy rain than from the sea's rapidly cooling temperature.

He could just make out the braid of some kind of naval uniform. It smelt of sweat but not too badly, he thought, as he struggled into it, wondering as he did so why it had been left in this small boat. No doubt stolen with some felonious intent, perhaps to sell to a French spy.

'Are we going now?' asked the boy plaintively as the ship swayed ominously above them.

'Going where?'

'You said we'd row away, escape when it got dark,' was the reproachful whisper.

'Dark, yes, but I hadn't bargained for a storm.'

'They wouldn't see us in this. We'd be safe,' said the boy encouragingly.

'Are you quite mad?' demanded Tam. 'We'll have to wait until this blows over. And can you handle an oar?'

The boy thought for a moment. 'I—think so.'

'And I hope so. Because it'll need both of us to reach the shore.'

If the child was afraid, he now had it under control. Just as well, thought Tam, as deciding on his next move became increasingly difficult by the minute. A certain confusion of thought occurred which he recognised again as the requirements of the time-quest; that present memory links with his own century faded quite swiftly once contact was made with his chosen time period.

Soon the last vestiges of his familiar world would disappear, abandoning him to the past world he had chosen to visit, taking nothing with him apart from the clothes he was wearing. His only contact was a tiny microchip inside his wrist, the last emergency.

Suddenly he was curious about the child so silent at his side, and above the noise of the storm he asked: 'What were you doing up

9

there—on the ship?'

The boy sighed and turned his head towards the once handsome man o'war, battle-scarred and proud, that had in antiquity sunk so low.

'It's one of the hulks, a convict ship,' was the whispered reply. 'You know—'

'I don't—you tell me!'

'We're waiting to be transported to the Colonies.'

'And what had you done to deserve such a fate?'

'I—I stole some bread. I was starving.'

The present situation was now becoming clear. In the course of his fascination with the past, Tam had read about the dreaded prison hulks without the least intimation of the horror of finding himself on one.

The few minutes he had spent above decks was enough of that experience to reassure him that however off-course the judgement of his landing, at least he was in the right century.

A period when London's criminal population seriously threatened to outnumber its law-abiding citizens and with no police force yet invented to deal with crime, prisons were overcrowded, murderers mixed indiscriminately with unfortunate men and women incarcerated for small debts. And children, like the lad before him—for stealing a loaf of bread.

England did not believe in prisons. What England wanted was to rid itself of the

10

problem by sending overseas any who escaped the gallows. The dumping grounds were originally the plantations of Virginia and the other American colonies. During the War of Independence all available ships were otherwise occupied and someone came up with the plan to imprison convicts awaiting transportation—to Botany Bay or that dreaded place of no return, Norfolk Island—in the hulks of two old ships moored in the Thames, where wrong-doers could be gainfully employed cleansing the river by raising sand, soil and gravel 'for the benefit of navigation'.

The idea immediately caught on of converting ships no longer seaworthy in to crude prisons, which cost far less than building new ones, and this idea became so popular that it extended beyond London to mooring places off the south coast where these hulks were also convenient for housing French soldiers and sailors who were prisoners of war.

Conditions were unspeakably horrific, with unwashed men and women packed together very closely on three decks, breathing putrid air. At night, the hatches were screwed down and the convicts left in darkness. New arrivals were stripped of their clothes and any other possessions before being thrown down in to the hellhole, as the lowest deck was known. In due course, if they survived death by jailfever, they progressed to the middle deck with its sickly and diseased occupants. Then at last to the upper deck, for either transportation or to await and pray for the unlikely miracle of a reprieve.

And that, Tam decided, was where he and the lad came in. The fact that the jailers were stripping him of his clothes meant that he was recognised as a newcomer to be speedily assigned to the lowest deck. The lad too must have been awaiting their grim attentions.

He was about to ask his unwelcome companion for confirmation of this fact, when he realised that the storm had lessened, the sea no longer boiled around them with waves like the giant white fingers of some angry sea-god.

'I think it is time to make a move. Ready?' And so saying, Tam, after a cautious look at the still empty ship's rail, inched forward and, after some anxious moments, managed to undo the heavy rope linking boat to ship.

Pushing aside the tarpaulin he nodded towards one of the oars. 'Take it.'

'I'll try,' was the uncertain reply. 'It's very heavy.'

'That will be all right once we are moving, the sea will keep it afloat,' said Tam with a confidence he was far from feeling.

The departing storm had left not the inky darkness but the steely twilight of a long summer evening in which they would be clearly visible, an added danger to their

12

escape, thought Tam, should any decide to stroll on the deck.

However, a glimpse of candlelight from an upper-deck cabin window brought faint sounds of drunken laughter, indicating that the jailers were off duty and too busy with their noisy leisure to notice any sounds from beyond the ship.

Tam looked at the boy struggling with the oar. 'Steer away. We'll be safe soon. What's your name, lad?'

'Jem, sir. Is it far?'

Tam thought it would be easy, rowing steadily towards the shore. But distance was deceptive, those white cliffs further away than he had imagined.

'Is it far?' the boy shouted again.

A difficult question to answer. Even as he thought of a plausible statement that would not reduce his companion's spirits—or his somewhat ineffectual rowing, the boy screamed and dropped the oar.

Tam saw it floating away and cursed him steadily.

'Why did you let it go? What did you do that for?'

'My hands—they're sore. Look at my blisters.'

Tam had no desire to see his wounds; he could have cheerfully added to them by strangling him, but instead he was considering a more urgent problem: how the prevailing

13

offshore wind might help them reach land with only one oar.

Suddenly, like some miracle of prayers answered, the horizon was no longer deserted as the dark shape of an approaching ship loomed into view.

A three-masted frigate was heading rapidly in their direction.

The boy stood up, regardless of the effect on the balance of the boat, and yelled:

'Help! Help!'

'Sit down, you idiot. They can't hear you. And you'll have us in the sea. Do as I say.'

The boy sat down wearily, nursing his hands and sobbing quietly.

'Stop that—when they get nearer, then you can start shouting and they'll see us and hear us.'

Tam was not, however, totally confident about that either and wished he had something, a lantern, any kind of light to show the ship bearing down on them where they were.

It was certainly gaining on them, moving very rapidly, and a feeling of horror added to their danger. This was no longer a frigate homeward bound but a crippled and dying vessel, masts dangling, sails ripped. What concerned him most was that although the tide and the prevailing wind were driving it towards the shore—and them—the crash of breaking timbers indicated that it was also sinking rapidly.

Chapter Two

Thanks to the deft use of his telescope by the captain of a small merchant vessel on its way along the Channel, the fishermen of Brighton had been alerted to the plight of a Scottish frigate, the *Royal Stuart*, adrift and heading landwards.

This promising drama had succeeded in summoning George, Prince of Wales, newly created Prince Regent in his mad father George III's sad decline, from the arms of his latest conquest, Sarah, Marchioness of Creeve, presently sated and asleep in his bed.

Attired in one of his more spectacular naval uniforms, chosen at random, he had joined other spectators in the fading light of a summer evening where a canopy had been hastily erected on the promenade to protect the royal viewers from the townsfolk's vulgar gaze.

This measure also offered protection from the thieves who inhabited Brighton's ever-growing underworld which, like fleas on a dog, had now settled happily in the area surrounding the Marine Pavilion.

A royal court meant royal pickings and twilight was their friend, with enough illumination to assist cutpurses in such an audience of eager spectators, yet enough dusk to make sure they slipped away unobserved. For all knew the price of capture, the gibbets chain-rattling their burdens on high ground above the town, a grisly testament to the cost of failure.

As for the royal courtiers, the solemn sight of a sinking ship had already ensured a brisk trade of their own. Bets on how long it would take the ship to sink beneath the waves, and whether there would be any survivors and most of all how many might be expected to reach the shore alive. An entertainment that was considerably more exciting than watching fowls or animals tearing each other to pieces, or even the bloodier, brutal human boxing matches. True, the latter had a certain secret appeal to many of the court ladies as a more stimulating experience than the daily boredom of gown-fittings and Court gossip.

Here was novelty indeed, a new kind of entertainment with many human lives in hazard, and an air of excitement prevailed as, for those addicts to gambling on anything and everything, there was already a clerk seated in his carriage busily taking promissory notes.

Amongst the more fervent, the prince had challenged George 'Beau' Brummell: '100 guineas against the ship sinking within the next half hour.'

The response: 'Give you 200 guineas against

any survivors.'

His Royal Highness's sporting tastes were not shared by his fifteen-year-old daughter Princess Charlotte, stammering protests at his side.

'I—I—Do you think Papa, co—consider—such—m—m—matters?'

Prince George regarded his only legitimate offspring, heiress to the throne of England, with distaste. Aware that he had never liked her from the very day she was born, repulsed by the sight of 'an immense girl' and remarking before witnesses who had long memories: 'We would have hoped for a son.'

And that was it, the fact that gnawed at his guts through the passing years, the gross unfairness that even the power of Divine Right of kings did not extend to producing a son—and securing the future dynasty of England.

Wearily he turned his back on Charlotte, seeing a parade of all the women he had slept with since he was a lad of sixteen. The latest and very voluptuous Sarah Creeve was also mistress of his younger brother Frederick, Duke of York, which gave the affair a certain extra titillation. Last seen and heard snoring as he crept out and looking less like the 'Kitten' (so-called for her slanting green eyes) than a fat tabby cat, with a passion for jewels to enhance her nakedness.

He sighed. Even the poorest peasant was

17

welcome to his favours, his proud boast that satisfaction of his lust merely required a tolerably pretty woman with full breasts: 'a bright wench and clean straw.'

It was unfair that Fate had been so grossly unkind. Considering that his scattered seed could have populated a small town with a multitude of largely unacknowledged (but still eternally clamouring) fine, healthy sons, on more than one occasion he regarded Charlotte closely.

He would have liked to prove that she had not sprung from his loins. God only knew how many lovers his wretched Princess Caroline of Wales had taken to her bed in the sixteen years since their marriage. But seeing the girl's face reflected beside his own in the mirror left him in no doubt over her legitimacy. She was unmistakably his daughter.

The miraculous product of an arranged marriage, hideous to him, and from only two copulations with his unsanitary foul-smelling bride. The first on their wedding night heavily reinforced with wine. Rising from the floor where he had slept as dawn crept through the window of their bridal chamber, he had slipped between the sheets and performed his dynastic duty. And again with equal reluctance some days later when this most unlikely princess had been spawned.

After her birth he could have, should have,

tried again, fought back his nausea for his bride's unwashed body: 'fore and hind parts indescribably filthy,' he whispered to his intimates. And although his manhood could normally be guaranteed to rise to the occasion, ready and eager when required, even fortified by large quantities of stimulants, it remained limp and flaccid in his lawful marriage bed with his lawful or, as he most frequently referred to her, his 'awful' wife.

Charlotte was clutching his arm, stammering her protests, whining that she was cold, she wished to go indoors. He signalled to her governess whose curtsey did not quite conceal a look of disapproval.

He watched them head back towards the Pavilion and sighed deeply. He must marry the girl off without delay. There were plenty of royal families in Europe hovering in the wings anxious and eager to negotiate an alliance with the future Queen of England.

An arranged marriage to a royal prince, such as William of Orange, had a certain appeal to the Prince Regent. Candidly he cared not to whom, and refused to listen to Charlotte's protests that she did not want to marry for years and years and, when the time came, that she would choose her own husband. Her future, such a small matter of whether she would be happy or not, did not concern him, his only reason for the hustle was the hope of male issue. The nearest he would ever get to securing the throne for a grandson of his own dynasty.

'It's sinking, Sire. Only minutes now . . .'

'It's going down . . .'

A panic-stricken rush to the clerk's carriage with hands eagerly waving promissory notes ensued. The prince rewarded, to his gleeful satisfaction, with a baleful glance from Brummell who had just lost 100 guineas, gave permission for a return to the Pavilion.

Back to bed? His thoughts returned with little enthusiasm as he remembered how early morning light could render exceeding tawdry the naked, bejewelled body of Sarah Creeve eagerly awaiting his return.

He sighed deeply, in sore need of a devotion less demanding as from the direction of Steine House, home of Mrs Fitzherbert, candles gleamed in the upstairs window. Maria Fitzherbert, commoner and Roman Catholic, twice widowed, whom he had married secretly in 1785 and whom he still regarded as his legal wife with undying affection, although not with undying faithfulness. Maria had never reproached him, always aware that a dynastic royal marriage was inevitable, and she pretended, at least, to understand that gratification of lust had little to do with impeding the course of his true love.

Another glance towards that inviting

candlelit window and with a whisper to his equerry, a cloak thrown over his uniform, he could still hear the cheers for the lost ship echoing as his carriage headed across the Steine.

*   *   *

'It's going down,' shrieked the boy.

It was indeed. Tam shouted: 'Hang on, whatever you do.'

A mile offshore and Tam, aware of the deadly danger, was using the one remaining oar to steer their tiny boat out of the path of the sinking ship.

They were too close. If it hit them they were doomed. They would go under with it. And avoiding that, as it sank the swell in its wake would break their frail craft like matchwood and carry them to the bottom of the sea.

Where was its crew? Dead or drowned, for its deck seemed deserted of all life. Then with an almighty tearing sound, the groan of a dying giant, sails ripping, a shriek of timbers, the masts were ripped from their moorings.

Tam and the boy hung on grimly as the wreck vanished beneath the waves. Seized as if in some sea-monster's relentless fist, helpless, they watched as an enormous wave sped towards them, lifting the boat, heaving them up into the air, holding them on its crest before hurling them back down again into the sea.

Gasping for breath, Tam surfaced first, looked for the boy. Saw a white face, a thin arm and grabbed it.

'Hold on!'

A piece of mast, strong and sturdy, surfaced and drifted by.

'Seize it!'

As the boy did so, Tam's worst fears were realised.

That boiling frothy sea in the momentum of the ship's last moments had carried them further away from the distant shore, where pinpoints of light were now barely visible.

There was only one solution. He pointed. 'Swim for it! You can swim, I take it.'

He wasn't sure whether the answer was yes or no, so he shouted: 'Hang on to the spar, it'll carry you in. It's not far off.'

'Look! There's another ship!' shouted the boy.

Turning his face from the shore, Tam saw a small cutter rocking across the waves towards the spot where the ship had gone down.

'We're saved!' And the boy so saying began to wave and shout for help.

Tam could see figures on board, leaning over, watching. They certainly seemed to be looking in their direction.

A fishing boat—what a piece of luck, he decided as it turned towards them.

'We're saved,' the boy sobbed. As the cutter

22

loomed above him, Tam realised that while he would be glad to have seen the lad to safety, the more dominant part of his mind demanded, what next?

After having helped him escape from the dreaded hulk and transportation, and the worse fate of near drowning, once they were set ashore on dry land together, would conscience allow him to abandon this youngster without a qualm to take his own chances of survival? Ruefully, Tam decided that Jem had already displayed all the symptoms of being totally unable to survive an uncertain future.

At the same time, the very last thing he wanted or needed on his time-quest was having a scared young lad hanging on to him. Such were his thoughts as the men, huddled in cloaks, leaned over and held out an oar for the boy to seize.

As they pulled him aboard he laughed. 'Thank you, sirs, thank you. You saved our lives.' Dripping wet, the boy did not forget his manners. Turning, he looked down anxiously at Tam, who, pushing aside the spar, seized upon the oar and waiting to be heaved aboard, held out his hand.

His hand was ignored.

'Only the boy. Not him—he's a law officer. See the uniform.'

'Push him back into the sea.'

'We'll do more than that.'

A coarse laugh. 'Aye, make a good job of it—one less to cope with.'

And the oar that was to be his lifeline, now struck out at him. Instinctively he ducked as violent contact was made with the side of his head. His sudden agony darkened the sky and a deadly flash of insight brought too late the realisation that their rescuers were not fishermen.

They were smugglers, carrion searching the seas for anything of value drifting from the wreckage.

His last thought as he sank beneath the waves, eager to swallow him once again, was that the uniform jacket labelling him as an excise officer was to be his shroud.

Chapter Three

At five o'clock in the morning two anonymous black carriages left the royal stables and crossed the short distance to Steine House. The door opened and a corpulent well-muffled anonymous-looking gentleman descended the steps and entered the first carriage which headed towards a secluded part of the seashore.

A journey of great discretion, although few were about in Brighton at such an early hour. But such was the rule on those occasions when the Prince Regent visited Maria Fitzherbert and stayed the night at Steine House.

A rule which caused some suppressed merriment and cynical remarks in the royal household. However, even the fact that they were never in the slightest danger of being taken unawares by Princess Caroline, resident permanently in London since the royal separation, a strong sense of morality and discretion prevented Mrs Fitzherbert from sleeping under the ornate roof of the Marine Pavilion with the prince whom she piously regarded as her legal husband in the eyes of God.

The prince emerged into a bright morning and at the seashore, apart from a few pieces of floating debris littering an otherwise delightfully calm sea, nothing remained of yesterday's violent storm or the wreck of the *Royal Stuart*.

At the water's edge the prince's bathing machine waited, a wooden changing-room on wheels to be drawn into the water by a patient horse. Distinguished by the imperial crown on its roof, once inside, its royal occupant was quickly divested of his outer garments and assisted into a lavishly striped bathing costume by his attendant, a heavily built, moustached gentleman with a permanent frown of anxiety and exceedingly strong arms—the marks of his trade—and needed on more than one occasion to rescue nervous gentlemen sea-bathers from disaster.

Jack, son of 'Smoaker' Miles, the prince's favourite bathing assistant, honoured by being regularly received at the Marine Pavilion and having a racehorse and a race named after him, stayed close to his royal charge who resembled a young whale as he floated, gasping and puffing and blowing, and thoroughly enjoying this almost daily health-giving routine, the remarkable discovery of Dr Richard Russell.

The learned physician from Lewes had successfully established the future of the fishing village of Brighthelmstone as a spa, and put Brighton on the map, via his learned 'Dissertation on the Use of Sea-water in the Affection of the Glands'.

In due course this had fallen into royal hands and on a visit to his uncle, the Duke of Cumberland, young Prince George had been enthusiastically advised that as well as being drinkable, the waters had other benefits, and that daily sea-bathing would work exceedingly well as a cure for his tiresome swollen neck glands. Glands which he hid under the high starched neckcloths which had set the fashion and become *de rigueur* in high society.

No longer floating but being dipped vigorously in and out of the water as was the custom by Jack Miles, the prince was secure in the knowledge that there were no other bathers in the vicinity. Not only did Brighton seem to be his alone, but even the sea was Canute-like at his command.

But not for long. Today was different.

An upsurge in the calm waters, waves where there should have been none, and Jack Miles, alarmed, had his royal charge immediately upright as an interloper was washed into this peaceful scene.

A man's body had been spotted a few yards away on a raft floating shoreward and heading fast in the direction of the bathing machine.

To the prince's anxious enquiry, Miles replied: 'From that shipwreck, Your Royal Highness, a dead 'un, I expect.' And hastily assisting the now flustered, thoroughly irritated prince out of the water, Miles added soothing statements that this would be taken care of.

The incident had already been spotted by onlookers from the second closed carriage, by servants filling in the time with a game of cards and the prince's physician, who accompanied these morning outings in case of accident. They were already rushing down towards the shoreline when the raft, propelled by a particularly large breaker, reached the pebbled beach in unison with the prince's bathing machine.

Consumed as he was by anger and frustration at having his daily routine cut short by this human flotsam, the prince was overcome with curiosity and excitement.

If this was indeed a survivor then George Brummell owed him 200 guineas and, poking his head out of the machine, he asked: 'Is he dead?'

The men bending over the body moved slightly aside to allow the prince a heartening glimpse of a uniform jacket. Definitely from the ship.

In answer to his query, a moment's hesitation, then his physician stood up, bowed. 'He is still alive, Your Royal Highness—' a shake of his head. 'But barely so. Considering that he must have been in the water, exposed to the elements for several hours—if he lives, it will be quite miraculous.' A sigh and another shake of the head indicated that he thought this miracle highly unlikely.

A survivor. The prince beamed. But there was no time to be wasted. The 200 guineas were almost in his purse, but aware of Brummell's untrustworthy nature—indeed, he had been more than a little trying of late—he realised that this survivor, whose life hung by a thread, must be taken at once to the Pavilion and delivered to Brummell as evidence that he had won their bet.

The order was given and Tam Eildor, more dead than alive, was carried into the closed carriage and transported across the short distance into the royal residence.

His sopping uniform jacket was replaced by a thick blanket and, restored to full consciousness by some foul-tasting liquid being forced down his throat, the events of the night after he had been struck over the side of his head by the smuggler's oar were hazy indeed.

He shared the physician's belief in a miracle that he had survived but, as a drowning man clutches at straws, so had Tam in similar condition grasped at a floating board from the wreckage of the *Royal Stuart*.

Once a cabin door from the doomed ship, it did admirable service as a raft.

*　　　*　　　*

Pulling himself aboard, he had tried paddling with his arms, but the effort was too much for him. He collapsed from pain and exhaustion, his fatal mismanaged time-quest over as well as his life, or so he thought when the emergency microchip in his wrist had failed to respond.

His rescue and arrival at the Pavilion were similarly hazy but he recognised with gratitude that even in his weakened condition he was no longer aimlessly adrift in a merciless sea, but alive and on dry land. And unless there were further dangers lurking, rapid recuperation might reasonably be expected.

He looked around cautiously and found his surroundings remarkably opulent. This was undoubtedly the Marine Pavilion, a neoclassical mansion, bearing not the slightest resemblance to the original somewhat dilapidated farmhouse belonging to Thomas Kemp, MP for Lewes. In 1796, aware that the Prince of Wales was searching for a permanent residence in Brighton, Kemp leased it to him on condition that he would rebuild it. Henry Holland, the royal architect, was commissioned, and completion resulted in a large mortgage which the prince urgently required to raise an annuity for Mrs Fitzherbert. Difficult to imagine anything as commonplace as cows, sheep and geese amid such splendour, Tam thought, as a flunkey summoned him with the words:

'His Royal Highness the Prince Regent wishes to see you as soon as you feel able. Your name, sir?'

A short while later, hastily clad in a borrowed shirt, breeches and shoes, apparently from the servants' wardrobe, which fitted tolerably well, he was escorted into the breakfast room where Prince George, attired in the quilted banyan or Eastern dressing gown made popular in the eighteenth century, was poised before the table, about to break his fast. Such was his custom returning from sea-bathing, and before going to his wardrobe to be dressed in one of his many uniforms appropriate to the events of the day.

Introduced by the lofty flunkey, a regal hand gestured Tam to be seated. Judging by the number of chafing dishes he realised that this daily routine was likely to take some time.

A servant hovered by his chair and after a courtly bow and a murmured thanks to his royal host, Tam needed no second invitation to address himself to the said array of covers and, unaware of the real reason for his presence, namely 200 guineas, the payment of a gambling debt, he was puzzled to know why he should have been honoured by this informal meal with the future King of England.

True, the circumstances of his rescue were dramatic, but was the prince given to impulses of picking up ship-wrecked mariners and bringing them to the Pavilion? Was an almost childish impulse the solution to this little mystery?

Surreptitiously glancing at the royal diner whose frame overflowed the chair, he considered the face emerging from the high neckcloth above several chins, and suddenly Tam could see exactly what the forty-nine-year-old Prince Regent had looked like in childhood. The now corpulent frame and overblown features were a clear indication of the solemn warning (that had gone unheeded): 'What are follies at twenty are vices at forty.' But from a lifetime devoted to wine, women and sundry debaucheries, there remained the ghost of a once handsome infant. Curls now vanished had been replaced by large quantities of false hair, but the tendency for merry laughter lurked in the pouched eyes while pouting, petulant lips hinted at grim determination to have his own way from a very early age.

Tam shrugged, unlikely to ever know the answer to this particular mystery, and, hard-pressed to remember exactly when he had last eaten anything, the prospect before him was enticing. Roasts of pork, beef and lamb jostled with pigeons, quail and a display of kidneys, liver and a further array of colourful but anonymous side dishes. Nor had the prince's appetite for sweetmeats been forgotten. All in all a meal future centuries would regard as a celebration feast rather than an everyday repast.

Tam was heartily glad that the prince now applied himself solidly to the gargantuan task of satisfying his royal appetite in comparative silence, broken only by sounds of munching, crunching and the odd belch and fart, from which Tam realised that the consumption of food was a single-minded event, a solemn ritual from which his presence, apart from an occasional glance in his direction, seemed to have been forgotten.

But he had misjudged his host. Prince George was shrewder than Tam imagined and already those casual glances were making a rapid assessment of this guest at his table.

There seemed little doubt, judging by the

rescued man's hearty appetite, that his survival was guaranteed. However, he must be kept here in the Pavilion for a few hours or until Brummell chose to reappear. That 200 guineas must not be allowed to slip through the royal fingers by being unable to produce evidence in the person of the young man who sat opposite.

A very personable young man indeed, this Mr Eildor. He was tall, above six foot, and enviably slender, about thirty years old with fine features that hinted at a class above the peasant. As if to confirm this, his teeth were excellent, which suggested a good lifestyle, a fine diet. It was a matter of regret to the prince who was fastidious in his bodily, if not his moral, habits, that so many otherwise beautiful young men and women were ruined by decaying teeth and bad breath as soon as they opened their mouths.

Another firm glance made note of a pale complexion at odds with what he would have expected as a sailor's weather-beaten countenance. A well-shaped mouth and firm chin, thick black hair. The prince's once youthful pride in his own natural curls had set the fashion for men to wear their own hair, with wigs abandoned, thanks to a tax on hair powder (usually made of flour). However, ear-length hair, short and straight, seemed a strange choice among seagoing men, who normally wore their hair ponytailed.

Perhaps fashions were different in Scotland. He must ask Mr Eildor about such matters. This very personable young man's most remarkable feature was undoubtedly his eyes. The prince had not seen their like before, their colour dark but indefinable and of such a strange quality, so luminous in their depths.

At last a word to a passing servant. Tam heard the word: 'Brummell' and then with a final belch, the prince leaning back in his throne-like chair, and regarding Tam benignly said: 'Well, sir, tell us about your ship?'

A difficult question but in the slight pause, the prince said: 'The *Royal Stuart*, was it not?'

Tam agreed eagerly and the prince continued: 'A Scotch ship?'

Tam agreed once more, thinking quickly, wondering how all this might give him a lead into some plausible account of his appearance in Brighton.

'It would seem that you have been exceedingly fortunate, sir—that you were the sole survivor of the ship's crew,' said the prince, doing another quick calculation. If there were more survivors than this one young man, then there was a heartening possibility of extracting more guineas from Brummell, at 200 per head.

'I was merely a passenger, Your Royal Highness,' said Tam, 'travelling from Leith.' And a sudden inspiration. 'I am an Edinburgh lawyer.'

34

The prince's eyes gleamed. 'Ah, a Scotchman on board the *Royal Stuart*. How appropriate. What became of the crew?'

Tam shook his head, looked appropriately sad. That was a poser, a question for which he had not the least idea of an answer.

'We were pursued by a privateer and a sudden storm swept us into its path.' (That sounded feasible, at least.) 'We were boarded and the crew taken off, pressed into service, I suspect.'

The prince frowned and Tam continued hastily. 'As I am a very bad sailor, I knew little of this and had retired below for the entire voyage. They looked at my papers and, deciding I was useless, left me there to go down with the ship. I staggered on to deck at the last moment and jumped into the sea. From there I was rescued only to find myself aboard a smuggler's craft. They took exception to my presence.' (That at least was true.) 'I was hit on the head and thrown back into the sea as an excise man—they were deceived by an old naval jacket someone had given me while I was being so violently ill.'

The prince tut-tutted a great deal and shook his head but looked constantly towards the door and much to his relief, Tam realised that the improbability of what he was saying was fortunately not getting the prince's full attention. He was listening with only half an ear, his mind clearly on more important

35

issues.

At that moment the door opened and the servant reappeared. A murmured conversation of which Tam heard only a few of the words. Brummell, it appeared, was not on the premises, could not be found. None knew where he had gone or when he would return.

The prince's face flushed scarlet. Brummell's arrogance was beyond belief. He was a personal attendant, sartorial advisor and boon companion of his youth, but, as the prince tended to tire of even his closest friends, so had Brummell—the acclaimed dandy adored by men and women alike—fallen from grace, with one more score to settle in a growing list.

Now the prince looked in imminent danger of apoplexy as he shouted: 'Then you are to find him, dig him out wherever he is, tell him he is commanded—aye, commanded to our presence immediately—and that we will not tolerate the slightest delay or excuse.'

The servant bowed, scuttled off. The prince's attention returned to Tam once again. 'It would please us to have you remain here for a short while—before continuing your journey—to fully recover from your recent ordeal. We have ordered a room to be prepared for you.'

Tam had expected at most to be dismissed and left to his own devices. But a room? He was expected to stay. What on earth for? He had fully expected the prince's gesture of hospitality to end with a royal breakfast, certainly not to be extended to a room in the Pavilion.

He could hardly refuse a royal invitation as, with a brief nod to Tam's bewildered thanks, the prince stood up indicating that the audience was over.

Tam bowed and, in the look they exchanged, the prince, with a flash of insight he was to remember later, decided that this was a man who was to be trusted, a loyal friend—or a deadly foe. And watching him follow the servant out of the room, he noticed how lightly he walked, almost as if his feet glided across the floor, his borrowed shoes leaving no echo of footsteps on the polished floor.

The prince frowned, shrugging aside the thought that before Mr Eildor continued his journey and his own purse was the richer by 200 guineas, during what promised to be a very short acquaintance he would have little chance of finding out more about this peculiarly enigmatic young man.

The room seemed suddenly very empty and with a sigh he realised that he could now return to his bedroom and commence his daily toilette, happy in the knowledge that royal whores were strictly reserved for the night's entertainment only.

Tam's exit was also witnessed by Princess

Charlotte. He bowed politely, her unprepossessing appearance suggesting an upper servant or lady-in-waiting. He was quite unaware of the turmoil his presence had raised in the fifteen-year-old's bosom.

Unloved by either parent and passed from one to the other, a pawn to be manipulated in the royal separation, a chance to score points, Charlotte was extremely sensitive to the reactions of her mother Princess Caroline in Carlton House, where a grown daughter was an embarrassment among her many lovers. As for her father, he had never liked her from the day she was born and had made that clear by never forgiving her for not being the male heir he craved.

Not particularly pretty, a little top-heavy and cumbersome, Charlotte's already over-ripe body poised on rather too-small feet, she was acutely aware that every man with a title who paid her lavish compliments, which her appearance did nothing to justify, was looking at a point beyond her to the English throne which she would eventually inherit.

No one, it seemed, could ever love her for herself alone, except perhaps an ordinary young man, handsome but hopelessly ineligible, whose ambitions must fall short of advancement.

Her eyes followed this intriguing stranger briefly set down in Brighton by a shipwreck—and wasn't that romantic!—with nothing to gain.

There was something in his bearing, different from any of the titled lords and princes, something indefinite, mysterious and appealing that put him in the frame of the lover she yearned for.

And so poor Charlotte fell in love with Tam Eildor, romantically shipwrecked, at first sight.

Chapter Four

As Tam was led along a corridor, guarded at frequent intervals by soldiers in the uniform of the prince's own Hussars, he realised these were the king's private apartments. The servant ushered him into a handsome room overlooking the Pavilion Gardens, and with a bow, since he had had no further instructions regarding this unusual guest, left him to his own devices.

Tam sat down on the four-postered bed which was exceedingly comfortable and regarded his opulent surroundings. To his delight there was even a tiny dressing room with a basin of warm water, towels, even a razor for shaving had been remembered, plus a rather ornate hip bath and that rarest of all luxuries, a water closet.

What a blessed relief. But what was he doing

here, receiving such treatment? What was the purpose of this extended invitation, more or less under the royal eye, when surely even more illustrious visitors than himself would have been shown to the guest apartments somewhere in the rear of the Pavilion?

With a sigh he decided he might as well make the most of what was currently on offer, while thinking about what was to be his next move, and where in Regency Brighton lay his time-quest.

As he regarded his unshaven face in the mirror and considered the razor with some trepidation, he thought about the boy he had rescued, the boy whose name was Jem, sentenced to transportation for stealing a loaf of bread.

Where had the smugglers taken him? He avoided thinking of how such a pretty young lad might fare at their hands. Wherever he was now, Tam hoped he would be safe and far from Brighton, their paths unlikely to cross ever again. Doubtless the lad's poor abilities as a thief would be extended dramatically and directed into bigger and better crimes.

His thoughts returned to that moment on the hulks when he had opened his eyes in the year of Our Lord 1811 and had seen the boy crouching nearby.

A prisoner like himself. Tam frowned. There was something odd about that, something he should have recognised.

He took a deep breath and was contemplating the razor poised above his chin when suddenly the silence around him was broken by a shout and the sounds of running footsteps in the corridor outside his room.

The prince had climbed the stairs a short while after Tam, hopeful at least that the insatiable Sarah, Marchioness of Creeve, no longer occupied his bed. He had given her plenty of time to realise that he had been unavoidably delayed after the drama of the sinking ship.

The chiming of some very handsome French clocks that were his pride and joy signalled the time as eight o'clock, time for her to have tactfully withdrawn by what looked like a continuation of the decorated walls, but in fact hid a secret staircase leading directly from the royal bedroom to an unobtrusive exit from the Pavilion. A step across the garden to a door where a carriage waited to carry her back the few miles to Creeve House and her own domestic problems.

Some bore a bond-making similarity to the prince's own. The thankless defiant young stepdaughter who had left Creeve House a month ago after a bitter disagreement with Lady Sarah. One of many, but sufficient for her to run off to her grandmother's London house.

It seemed, however, that the girl had failed to appear. She had never arrived, and a few

41

half-hearted attempts by her father, the Marquis, to track her down were abandoned. Her stepmother, singularly lacking in maternal feelings, especially for the girl she declared 'a mere annoyance', had long since done her duty and produced the required son to inherit the title.

And that she decided was all that any decent husband could demand, considering herself free to live her own life. Which she did—to the full and brimming over.

In London at the opera, she had caught the eye of Frederick, Duke of York, George's younger brother. This mutual eye-catching had swiftly led to his bed and six months later, to the Marine Pavilion and one step higher into the bed of the Prince Regent.

As he approached the bedroom door, such were the Prince's thoughts. From their earliest days Frederick had been his rival, marked down as the declared favourite son of their father King George. To Frederick went all the love and affection their father was capable of, and so there had been a certain piquancy in secretly sharing the favours of Sarah with the blissfully unaware Frederick.

Now that the novelty was wearing thin, as was the case with all George's many amours, he had to admit he was finding Sarah somewhat trying in her passionate embraces and her addiction to jewellery. Giving jewels was the regular expected payment for

42

favours, and in this too the marchioness was proving insatiable. Her addiction to wearing diamonds, rubies and sapphires during their lovemaking had at first seemed stimulating, but now seemed dashed tawdry. Odd how the most precious jewels in the kingdom could turn to glass worn on a woman's naked body in the cold light of dawn.

The prince sighed as he passed through the withdrawing room, acknowledging Lord Henry Fitzgeorge, Groom of the Bedchamber, who favoured him strongly in looks and in demeanour. The unacknowledged product— so he claimed—of an early affair with an actress, there were hints also unacknowledged that he was Maria Fitzherbert's son.

Taking a deep breath he opened the bedroom door. The bed curtains were partly closed but the jewellery hastily piled on the small table indicated that Sarah had tactfully withdrawn. On closer inspection it was with considerable annoyance he saw she had not removed herself after all. She lay there much as he had left her at the conclusion of their rumbustious and exhausting lovemaking.

He looked down on her with distaste, lying in a very indecorous position, naked except for the long string of pearls, which were her own, around her neck.

How extremely disagreeable of her. The agreed arrangement was to tug the bellrope connected to the stables, summoning a carriage which would be waiting in readiness to tactfully remove her before his return.

With the bed curtains still only partially open, he coughed loudly.

Sarah did not move. He approached the bed and reaching out a hand to stroke that fleshy wrist, the next instant he realised why there had been no response to his touch.

Sarah would no longer tempt him again, or his brother, or any other man.

Sarah, Marchioness of Creeve, was dead. Dead in his royal bed.

With a shout of terror, he rushed out, having the presence of mind to slam the door shut behind him as a thousand terrible images went through his mind in rapid succession of the appalling inconvenience of such a frightful discovery.

In the withdrawing room Henry had been joined by Lord Percy Wellsby, the second groom. They sprang to their feet.

'There's—there's been an accident—' The prince threw open the bedroom door, pointed to the bed. 'She is—dead!' he shrieked.

The two grooms followed him warily. Lord Percy, who was squeamish, retired hastily to be sick. Lord Henry who was made of sterner stuff merely averted his eyes and stood firmly by the prince's side. Percy returned and together they awaited instructions while their royal master, moaning and sweating profusely, stumbled to a chair. He sat down, his eyes rolling wildly.

What to do next? God only knew! He had never in his life, never in his wildest dreams, encountered such a situation as this.

A dead woman in his bed. A corpse who was the wife of the Marquis of Creeve and—perhaps even worse—the current mistress of his younger brother. What a scandal. He was shivering, he had not the slightest idea what to do in such circumstances. How fortunate that his father, mad King George, would never hear of it. As for his mother—he shuddered, returned to the state of very naughty, misguided and wilful child, his unchanging image in her eyes for almost fifty years.

Lord Henry took the initiative, came forward. Eyes that were identical in colour to the prince's own stared down at him.

'Are you ill, Sire, shall we summon Dr Bliss?' he asked gently.

The prince stared at him. 'How can he help me? Are you mad?' How could a physician help?

Except to whisper to all the world the dreadful secret that lay behind his bedroom door. Stumbling to his feet again, he opened the door into the corridor and hastily closed it again on the group of guards who, perhaps aware of a disturbance within, lingered alert and at the ready on the threshold.

'Get rid of them,' he said. 'Tell them—everything is well. Anything, but get rid of

45

them. No one must know,' he babbled. 'No one—it must go no further than this room. Do you understand?'

Henry, bewildered, exchanged a glance with Percy and did as he was told. The prince leaned his head against the slightly opened door and moaned, listening to murmurs about a slight accident. His Royal Highness, it appeared, had fallen and hurt his leg. There were shakes of the head, sympathetic nods, knowing that the prince was a martyr already to gout, deuced painful too.

'What are we to do?'

The grooms, not surprisingly, frowned and tried to look as if they were giving the matter intelligent thought, nervously averting their eyes from the royal bedroom from which the prince had emerged like a bat out of hell.

Suddenly the prince lost all control, threw up his hands and sobbing, burst out of the royal apartments to the astonishment of the guards, accustomed as they were to the unexplained tantrums and shrieks of their royal master.

At that moment, Brummell chose to make his appearance, his high heels clattering along the polished floor, his attire a little awry. He was in an ill humour, controlling with difficulty his extreme displeasure at this untimely summons from a very satisfying night in one of the flash houses, those brothels disguised as gaming houses in Brighton's less salubrious areas.

Simultaneously, like a scene from a very bad play by Mr Sheridan, Tam Eildor also appeared from his room at the other end of the corridor to see what the disturbance was all about.

There the curtain rightly should have fallen on this particularly dramatic moment, but alas the curtain was about to rise on Act II: Confusion.

With considerable difficulty the prince took control of the situation.

'Ah, Brummell, there you are,' he snapped, taking refuge in the obvious.

'Sire,' said Brummell, bowing stiffly.

As the prince took Tam's arm, ushered him forward, Tam realised that he was shaking, his terror communicated itself as he said:

'This is Mr Eildor, sole survivor of the *Royal Stuart* which sank last night. As you will no doubt recall, now that you see the living evidence before you, we will be pleased to accept the 200 guineas that you now owe us. You have our permission to withdraw.'

But Brummell was in no hurry. Taking up his quizzing-glass in leisurely fashion, he examined Tam closely, while Tam realised there was something more to do with the prince's white-faced anguish than winning or losing a bet.

Curious by nature, eager to find some new topic of gossip, Brummell also was aware of

47

something amiss as he gave this survivor of the shipwreck his full attention. He did not look in the least like a shipwrecked mariner and, suspicious by nature, Brummell's reaction was that he was being tricked by the prince into parting with 200 guineas.

He bowed to Tam. 'My congratulations, sir. Perhaps you would be so good as to honour me with your company, in order that I might hear more of your ordeal, over a glass of claret—'

'We cannot allow that,' the prince interrupted. And showing remarkable sensitivity, 'To relive such—such moments.' And seizing Tam's arm. 'Can you not observe how shaken this gentleman is by his experience?' he demanded.

Tam regarded this outburst with faint amusement seeing that he was by far the calmer of the two and it was the prince himself who might have emerged, sweating and pale, from the ordeal of shipwreck. At the same time he was understanding the reasons for his regal treatment, a splendid repast and a handsome room. He was merely the object of a royal bet.

It was also obvious, since the two men displayed such signs of disagreement, that there were cracks in the once boon companionship, that chilly royal stare the eventual bottom line for those who briefly enjoyed their hour of glory.

And Brummell had lasted longer than most. He had seen numerous men with more claims to nobility than his humble origins, rise and slide back into oblivion, while he eyed their dismay with slight contempt, secure in the certainty that such would never be his own fate.

But Brummell's popularity spelt his own downfall. Adored by men and women alike, venerated as a royal dandy, he was viewed by Prince George with increasing jealousy, soured by an incident at Belvoir Castle in which Brummell, out riding in a fur pelisse, was mistaken by the great number of people who had assembled and saluted—this arrogant son of a clerk—as the future King of England.

It was intolerable and worse was to follow. His antipathy towards Mrs Fitzherbert—the feeling was mutual—and his constantly disparaging remarks concerning her dress sense and her ample figure soon found their way back to the prince's ears, his fate sealed by the public declaration (presumably relating to sartorial matters): 'I made the Prince of Wales what he is and I can unmake him.'

There were obviously more scores to settle than a gambling debt, Tam decided, as Brummell's quizzing-glass remained fixed upon him. Regarding him narrowly, and in direct disobedience to the royal command, Brummell said: 'Perhaps you will join me for a glass of claret, before you resume your journey to—where was it?'

Tam pretended not to hear and bowed. 'I will be delighted to accept your kind invitation, sir,' he said, realising that he would be hustled away from the Pavilion at the earliest and have no chance of further encounters with Beau Brummell who, receiving a dismissive wave of the royal hand, glared angrily at his former dearest friend and, turning on his heels, clattered back the way he had come.

'Thank you for your kindness, Your Royal Highness, but as I am now quite restored to health and strength, have I your permission to leave,' asked Tam, 'to resume my journey?'

Even as he said the words, he wondered where on earth he was supposed to be going.

The prince's eyes rolled heavenward as he remembered the scene he had just left. He glanced wildly at the three men before him. Who could he trust to dispose of Sarah's corpse? His son, Henry—Percy perhaps, and then turning his gaze to Tam. But who better than Mr Eildor?

Mr Eildor was an Edinburgh lawyer, after all. He was also, more importantly, a stranger.

The prince's mind worked rapidly. A stranger sent by some miracle to relieve him of a dreadful situation. And since he had been presumed lost on the *Royal Stuart*, his purpose served, he was also conveniently disposable.

50

He made up his mind.

'Follow me, Mr Eildor.' To Henry and Percy he said, 'Remain here, within call. We are not to be disturbed.' And with a stifled sob, he threw open the door of his bedroom.

Chapter Five

Although the curtains were still drawn Prince George was heartily glad that he had thrown a sheet over Sarah's corpse. Even then he had to admit that a naked female body wearing nothing but a string of pearls was a sordid sight.

Again he thought how extremely disagreeable it was of her to die in his bed, especially with the Masque Ball at Creeve House that evening. Frederick would be there. Suddenly he felt very cold indeed as he motioned Tam toward the bed.

Tam who wasn't squeamish in the least regarded the body with distaste.

'Dead, ain't she. That's for sure,' said the prince in a hollow voice.

'She is indeed, Your Royal Highness, no doubt about that. And not only dead, I'm afraid she has been murdered.'

'Murdered! That cannot be! There must be some mistake. Who would dare?'

'Someone dared.' And Tam pointed to the

rope of pearls which had been wound very tightly around her neck.

'Could it have been an accident?' asked the prince clutching at straws. Tam moved the body so that he could see that the pearls had been twisted to form a garrotte.

The prince leaned against the bedpost. Dead was bad enough, getting rid of a corpse, but a murdered corpse!

He sat down heavily on one of the gilt chairs which gave a creak of protest. He had never experienced anything like this—this *lèse majesté*—a murdered woman in his bed, the wife of the Marquis of Creeve and, even worse, the mistress of his brother. Now all would be revealed.

He shook his head from side to side, groaning like a wounded beast.

'Dear God, dear God. What are things coming to? Is no one safe? Murders like this don't happen in royal residences in the nineteenth century. They call this the age of enlightenment. This sort of thing belongs to less civilised countries, to those vile Italians— the Borgias.'

Tam glanced at him. The future King would be well advised to pay close attention to books recording English history, where it would soon become abundantly clear that palaces and castles were extremely popular settings for getting rid of kings and their royal offspring.

The prince looked up at Tam. 'But who

could have done this to us? We have never harmed anyone.'

A somewhat sweeping and naïve statement since Tam guessed that a litany of the prince's misdemeanours, of young women ruined and men's lives destroyed, might have quite comfortably filled several volumes of rather boring reading.

'Who has had the audacity to incriminate us in such a fearful act?'

Tam gave the prince a searching stare. It was noteworthy, he thought, that none of this chronicle of self-pity included any sorrow or regret for the untimely death of the woman who had shared his bed last night. She had become an embarrassment in her life and worse than that, death had turned her into a terrifying liability, a dreadful source of guilt.

The prince waved a dismissive hand towards the two grooms lingering by the doorway, their faces pale, their expressions shocked and anxious.

Tam would have given much to read their minds, certain they were familiar with the morals or, more correctly, lack of them in the Pavilion. But the naked corpse of a woman was not something they encountered with any regularity in their royal master's bed. In this instance, not only dead but murdered, she must present a new experience.

He presumed that the prince could rely on their discretion as the door closed and,

53

turning to Tam, he cleared his throat and said: 'As an Edinburgh lawyer, Mr Eildor, I expect you have dealt with crimes of this nature.'

Hardly, thought Tam, and took refuge in a vague smile.

The prince leaned towards him earnestly. 'Will you help me in this matter, sir? I would be most grateful for your assistance.'

And through this somewhat bewildering appeal a light began to emerge, as suddenly the whole reason why Tam had been invited to partake of this sordid sight became evident. Who better than a lawyer, a stranger passing through Brighton with no friends? There was something vaguely sinister in all this and Tam did not care for it at all. He scented danger.

Sensing hesitation, the prince said: 'You will of course be paid. Handsomely, sir, one hundred guineas to assist you on your journey.'

Tam did some rapid calculations. Half of the bet the prince had won from Brummell for producing him as the sole survivor of the shipwreck of the *Royal Stuart*.

'Very well, Your Royal Highness.'

Grunting an acknowledgement, the prince turning quickly cannoned into the small table. Tam helped him steady it and looked down on the huddle of coloured stones from which all the magic of rare and exquisite gems had been also removed. Historic and ancient, Tam did

54

not doubt, and worth a king's ransom. Now they looked worthless and tawdry beside an extinguished human life.

The prince, his hand shaking, pointed to the pearls around the Marchioness's throat. 'They—they are her own.'

'May I know the lady's identity, Your Royal Highness?' Tam asked delicately.

The prince gave him a suspicious glance as if this was an intrusion of the royal privacy. 'Sarah, Marchioness of Creeve, of Creeve House, Lewes.' An embarrassed throat clearing. 'A recent acquaintance.' With a sharp look to see how Tam was taking this audacious statement with all its implications, he went on hurriedly:

'Do you wish to inspect the room, see how the murderer gained access?'

'Indeed, yes, and I should like to make some notes.'

Handsome notepaper and pens were produced as Tam walked round looking for means of entrance rather than exit.

'Would Your Royal Highness care to give me an exact account of the events of last night, so that we can properly reconstruct the scene?'

The prince closed his eyes, cleared his throat and leaned back as if such remembrance threatened to be painful. 'We left the marchioness at eight o'clock. We know the time exactly since that was when your sinking ship was spotted on the horizon.'

'The marchioness did not wish to accompany Your Royal Highness.'

'Not in the least.' An embarrassment she had spared him, he thought bitterly, and stayed here in the warm luxury of his bed instead to get herself killed.

'And when Your Royal Highness returned again?'

'We did not. Instead we stayed with our wife—' a lowering of brows, rather threatening this time—'Mrs Fitzherbert at Steine House. We left her at five o'clock when our carriage called as usual to take us for our morning bathe.'

'Your Royal Highness and Mrs Fitzherbert?'

'No.'

And Tam realised there was to be some further confusion added to the case by the use of the royal 'we' as the prince continued: 'We then returned to the Pavilion where you, the sole survivor of the shipwreck, were brought to us. After breaking our fast together, we came upstairs immediately—and found this—' he said with a disgusted shudder.

Tam thought. So the murder could have taken place any time during the last twelve hours.

'These are our usual morning arrangements before beginning our toilette for the day. We were taken aback to find the marchioness here since, er, any invited guest usually takes her leave of us around seven o'clock. We were

56

horrified—yes, horrified to find her still here—and—'

The prince paused, gulped, cast his eyes heavenward, whispered: 'And—dead! There is a bell pull,' he pointed towards the bedhead. 'It connects with the stables and should have summoned a carriage to return her ladyship to her home in Lewes.' He did not feel it necessary to mention her convenient apartment nearby, or that she was only returning to Creeve for the Masque that evening.

'What about her maid, surely she does not travel alone?'

'In this instance, yes,' was the stiff reply.

'This is the usual procedure?' asked Tam.

How could the prince explain that the delicacy of the situation concerning his brother, York, required the utmost secrecy and discretion. Mere paid servants, however devoted, were subject to bribes, and quite out of the question.

Closing his eyes, he groaned. And now it would all come out. How on earth could it be avoided?

'Yes.' He closed his mouth, firmly aware of Tam's searching glance.

'Does she not require assistance with her toilette?' Tam asked delicately, aware that he travelled in an age when women of substance were helpless even to dress themselves.

Was it possible that the Prince Regent had

hidden talents as a lady's maid, he wondered, when suddenly he was hearing the solution to such a problem.

'Her ladyship merely wears her sable cloak—over the chair there.' Clearing his throat, he added: 'Nothing under it.' A naughty twinkle and an arch look at Tam. 'You understand me, sir. We are both men of the world and such a prospect, you must agree, is daring in the extreme and most stimulating.'

Men of the world they were, thought Tam sourly, but of two entirely different worlds. Separated from the Regency by four hundred years of decadence, and without being in the least 'holier than thou' he was beginning to dislike his royal host exceedingly.

He glanced around the room. 'How does the lady make her exit? Does she not proceed through the withdrawing room under the close observation of the grooms?'

The prince laughed at his naïvety and shaking a finger said: 'That would never do—utmost discretion and all that.' As he spoke, he walked over to one of the elaborate painted panels on the walls and touched a piece of the ornate dado, which responded as a secret door invisible from the walls of the room. It slid open to reveal a steep narrow stair.

'Down there,' whispered the prince, glancing nervously over his shoulder as if in danger of being overheard. 'Down there—a door built into the exterior walls—ivy-covered, can't be seen. Leads out across the garden to a gate in the Steine where a carriage awaits in readiness.'

He seemed very pleased and nodded excitedly as if expecting approval for this piece of architectural ingenuity. Obviously, thought Tam, the sinister implications had not occurred to him, that anyone who knew this secret, one that the marchioness and doubtless many before her were privy to, realised that the door could also be opened from inside this room giving access to the interior of the Pavilion.

Indeed the staircase would be a perfect hiding place for an assassin, Tam thought grimly, whose target, the Prince Regent, might subsequently be found dead one morning, not a mark upon him, having been smothered while he slept. Before the birth of forensic medicine, death dismissed as heart failure would not be received by the populace as any great surprise, considering that he was grossly overweight and his lifestyle threatened perpetually by over-indulgence.

Deciding to keep this dangerous observation to himself for the time being, Tam said: 'Might I suggest that Your Royal Highness confirms that no message was received by the stables from this room at any time during the last night or the early hours of this morning.'

The prince considered the matter, frowned, nodded and hastily made his exit, leaving Tam to his own devices.

The marchioness had been murdered. The evidence was there. All that was needed was the identity of her killer. How had her assignation with death been achieved? Was it the result of an insatiable woman's lust for some exotic lovemaking to fill in an hour of boredom? If so, what had gone wrong?

The prospect of a transient exciting experience with a new young lover—yes, he would certainly need be young and naïve too, Tam decided, to put any faith in the affections of this royal whore.

From the little that Tam had been told about the marchioness, and what he had seen—he shuddered, all too much—he did not feel that her morals were in very good repair, and greedy and acquisitive by nature, blackmail might not be beyond contemplation should the need arise. Only a frightened young man, his whole future at stake should she betray him to Prince George or Prince Frederick, had seized upon that rope of pearls so conveniently around her neck as the only way out of a particularly nasty dilemma, of ruin posed by exposure to the royal displeasure.

Glad to turn his back on the now decently covered corpse in the prince's bed, Tam walked around the room reconstructing the scene from the dead woman's angle. There were no signs of a struggle. Quite the opposite, and, bearing in mind the implications of the secret door, he was fairly certain that the marchioness had not been taken by surprise. The scene suggested that she might already be on terms of intimacy with her killer, since she had not considered it necessary to cover her nakedness, the natural reaction before an interloper.

Tam rubbed his chin thoughtfully. What had she to gain apart from an hour's titillation and the risk of discovery? And a measure of paying the prince back for abandoning her to look elsewhere for his pleasures—the novelty of a shipwreck as rival to her voluptuous charms.

Whatever this crime, it had not been planned, that was for sure. It was a crime of passion and anger, of terror and doubtless somewhere in the Pavilion at this very moment, the killer sat trembling at the consequences of exposure, and the dreadful payment for his dalliance with the insatiable marchioness.

While Tam was still walking round the room, picking up and laying down objects, deep in thought, the prince returned. 'You were quite right, Mr Eildor. No message was received at the stables, no carriage summoned. The bell pull was silent all night.'

Tam nodded. He would have been surprised

at any other information. 'May I ask Your Royal Highness, who else has access to this room—in your absence?'

'During the day, servants and so forth. But from the hour when we take our evening repast at eight o'clock until five in the morning, when we depart for our sea bathe, no one—absolutely no one—is allowed access beyond the Grooms of the Bedchamber who are on constant alert. Beyond their quarters in the withdrawing room, guards of the Tenth Dragoons, our own regiment, sir, are on duty patrolling the corridors approaching our apartments.'

A pause for Tam's reactions, and he continued: 'All these measures, you will realise, are of vital importance for the safety of our realm since several attempts have been made on the life of our royal father, especially during the last year when he has so unfortunately declined in health and spirits.'

So the killer had to come from within the Pavilion, someone known to the duty guards who would go unchallenged. Someone aware of the prince's daily sea-bathing and that he was absent watching the shipwreck. Which put an end to any theory that the fatal assignation was prearranged.

'London is not Brighton, Your Royal Highness,' Tam pointed out tactfully and was rewarded with a scowl.

'Is it not, sir, is it not? Upon my soul, we

62

have to inform you that the conclusions you have drawn are quite incorrect. Remarkably so! Brighton is no longer the genteel spa where we chose to build a retreat far from our capital city.' Pausing, he shook his head sadly. 'During the last few years, our residence here has become a magnet for the activities of that vile underworld which has followed us down from London.' And with a sniff of disgust, 'Encouraged, we do not doubt, by the wicked and false insinuations of our former wife, the Princess of Wales.'

Allowing a moment for Tam to digest this interesting piece of information regarding his domestic life, the prince continued: 'We have narrowly escaped with our lives on two occasions in the past few weeks since we were created Regent. Out riding on the Steine, as is our habit, shots were fired at our person. But before the criminal could be seized and identified, he vanished into those narrow lanes and alleys, seeking the protection of a thieves' kitchen, which few of our law officers dare to penetrate. We expect it is there you will find the monster who committed this dreadful deed.'

Tam had his own reasons for considering that extremely unlikely as the prince boomed:

'The Watch will give you any assistance that you require, although they are notoriously lacking in able-bodied men. We have as yet no force to equal the Bow Street Runners who take care of such matters in our capital under the admirable supervision of Mr John Townsend. If you fail to make an early arrest, we shall summon his assistance to track the villain down.'

Tam detected a little reluctance in that suggestion as the prince continued: 'Well, sir, and what are your conclusions now?'

Tam bowed, sought refuge in: 'Without having access to all the facts, one must not be too hasty, Your Royal Highness, but be assured that I am giving the matter careful thought.'

A secret entrance, invisible and inaccessible from the outside, that could, however, be activated from within the Pavilion, and no signs of a struggle, were facts whose significance he was unwilling at this stage to share with the prince, or the obvious indication that his marchioness was playing him false. Further, that the identity of her killer was well known to her, would possibly be received with anger and astonishment by her royal lover.

Suddenly the room seemed unbearably oppressive. This sordid scene, the smell of stale human sweat, stale perfume—and death.

Tam felt badly in need of some of the sunshine and fresh air that filtered in from the gardens deep in birdsong. For a glimpse of the sea, which he was certain would be an undiminishing blue line stretching to the horizon. A whole new exciting world waiting to be explored.

An insect trapped in the window pane buzzed frantically seeking an escape route. The prince glared at it angrily and, rising to his feet with a creaking that put in jeopardy the future of the frail gold chair, he indicated that Tam should follow him.

Chapter Six

In the withdrawing room the two grooms sprang to their feet, their countenances registering embarrassment, and Tam decided he would have enjoyed being a fly on that particular wall. What were those two polite scions of the nobility—one a royal bastard—making of this latest conclusion of an episode in the prince's love life?

Tam paused. 'With Your Royal Highness's permission, I should like to ask these two gentlemen a few questions.'

The prince frowned, stared from Henry to Percy and back again, as if the request was a matter requiring intense deliberation. Tam thought he was about to refuse, then with a brisk nod he said:

'Of course, of course. Proceed. We will leave you to it, Mr Eildor.' And to the grooms, 'And when Mr Eildor has completed his enquiries, you will attend us in the salon. We have our duties to attend, our appropriate uniforms of the day to consider,' he added sternly.

'Life must go on,' and with a shake of the head, that wry philosophy completely inadequate to the occasion, he quit the room, leaving Tam to explain that he was an Edinburgh lawyer and that, as such, the prince had asked him to look into the night's events. The two grooms looked increasingly uncomfortable, frowning sternly at their well-polished Hessian boots as if such elegant footwear might be expected to provide reassuring answers to the problem.

Endeavouring to put them at their ease, Tam said: 'Won't you please be seated, gentlemen,' and indicating the table nearby he took the seat opposite.

'This is a very unpleasant business,' he said in what he hoped would pass for a good imitation of a member of the legal profession. 'And as both of you gentlemen were on duty in the vicinity at the time of death,' he continued gently, 'I have to ask—did either of you have cause to leave this room unattended during His Royal Highness's absence?'

Uneasy looks were exchanged, then Lord Henry spoke up, keeping a sharp eye on the closed bedroom door as if it might suddenly spring open and reveal its fearful contents. Then, clearing his throat in an exact imitation of his royal father, he whispered: 'We went upstairs—just for a short while, to see how the shipwreck was progressing.'

'There's an excellent view from the windows,' Percy explained. 'We wanted to see what was happening—not to miss all the fun, y'know.'

A well-directed kick under the table alerted him to the insensitivity of such a remark, as Henry interposed quickly:

'We are delighted, sir, fortunate indeed, that you survived such a disaster.'

Tam nodded, thinking how fortune had misdirected him into what had all the elements of a worse one. Already the path was lined with lies and deceit and a situation which promised to be increasingly difficult to escape from.

He said to Henry: 'You mentioned that you were absent for a while—can you be more exact—about how long would you estimate that to be?'

Frowns and looks between the two indicated that calculations were being exchanged. 'Until it got too dark to see anything more of significance,' said Percy. 'Of the ship's final moments, you know,' he added in tones of disappointment. 'We understood that bets were being taken—'

A scowl and a cough from his more sensitive companion who said: 'We were absent for about half an hour, sir.'

Tam made a mental note and asked: 'When

you returned did you by any chance hear any sounds suggesting a disturbance in His Royal Highness's bedroom?'

'None at all, sir. But then there never are any sounds—the walls are exceedingly thick in this part of the house.' Percy tried and failed to restrain a raised eyebrow, an arch look, indicating that it would never do for such intimacies of the royal love life to be overheard.

'And in the corridor—out there?'

'Four household guards. Tenth Dragoons, sir, on duty all night.'

'I shall have a word with them. Thank you, gentlemen, for your assistance.'

Relief was so clearly indicated on their countenances, the door opened for him with such alacrity, as they followed him out, he was left wondering whether it was merely an unpleasant interview over or if they had something to hide, some vital clue withheld.

As Henry was making the introductions, explaining to the guardsmen that Mr Eildor was an Edinburgh lawyer, Tam caught a glimpse of the grooms' faces in the mirror. Bland, innocent faces in this nest of corruption and iniquity, as they bowed out to mull over his questions, their answers and, he did not doubt, the many worrisome speculations that their imaginations might invent.

They could not be much younger than

himself in years, but catching sight of his own reflection, he felt intensely old at thirty, as if too many of the world's past sorrows, inhumanities and follies had been thrust upon his shoulders.

He turned his attention to the four guardsmen who regarded him with carefully suppressed curiosity. Standing at attention, politely awaiting his questions, identical as painted tin soldiers who had leapt from a child's toy box, their fresh young faces clean-shaven and helmeted, the only difference being that the weapons they carried were primed and ready for instant action.

'There was an incident last night while His Royal Highness was absent watching the shipwreck, and he has asked me to ascertain the whereabouts of everyone in the vicinity of the royal apartments at that time.'

Puzzled anxious looks were exchanged. Clearly they did not know the nature of the incident and nor was Tam about to enlighten them.

Finding their unmoving rigid presence a little intimidating, he indicated that they should be seated.

'Perhaps I might start with you, sir,' he said to the one sitting nearest to him, who had been introduced as Warren and was the senior officer.

'I was here, all night, sir. And I can vouch for these three fellows.'

His gaze was quite direct, no cautious exchange of doubtful glances with his comrades here. All perfectly correct and right.

'As a matter of fact, sir, we were playing at cards—our usual evening pursuit when we are on duty. The hours can seem very long and very boring.'

Nods of approval from fellow officers.

'Where do you sit?'

'At the table, right here, as we are now.'

Tam looked round the table with its direct unbroken view. The players would be alerted instantly to anyone approaching the royal apartments, unless their powers of concentration were absorbed by a losing hand and the probable financial loss involving a large bet.

'So you would observe anyone coming or going?'

Warren nodded. 'We would indeed, sir. But there rarely is anyone but ourselves. And,' he added confidently, 'there is an outer ring of guards downstairs any interloper would have to get through first.'

A nod from the guardsman sitting next to him, whose name was Toby: 'Very strong security, sir, particularly since attempts on His Royal Highness's life—'

A delicate cough, the suspicion of a warning nudge from Warren and, clearing his throat apologetically, Toby subsided.

Tam said: 'You mentioned that there never

was anyone—usually.'

Again Warren nodded. 'Last night Lord Henry and Lord Percy went upstairs to watch the shipwreck. They gave us the nod and we promised to keep an eye on everything.'

'And when would that be?'

'Before nine o'clock. They were only gone for half an hour.'

'And that is absolutely all? There was nothing unusual during their absence?'

Looks exchanged, heads shaken. 'Nothing in the least unusual,' said Warren.

'Unless you would consider it significant for one of our fellows from downstairs,' prompted Toby, 'walking along the corridor, inspecting the condition of the light sconces.'

Warren nodded. 'There had been complaints.'

'And who was this fellow?'

Warren shook his head. 'One of our lads, wearing a uniform jacket, a bit casually dressed,' he added rather severely, 'but the light was too dim to make out any details. But he knew us, greeted us by name, gave us goodnight.'

'He forgot to salute, which he should have done to his superior officers,' said Toby severely.

'We don't make too much insistence on such details,' Warren interrupted hastily, 'not during the night. Keep it informal, we're not in battle rank ready for inspection.'

'Did you see this officer return again in the direction of the stairs?'

Again heads were shaken. 'We weren't watching him every moment, sir. We were somewhat involved in our game—a crucial stage—'

'So you presumed he had completed his inspection.'

'That is so, sir.'

'Without actually seeing him leave?'

A frown from Warren. 'Exactly so, sir. Is it important?'

It was important, but Tam, feeling that he was on the road to nowhere, thanked them and took his departure.

The interview had been something of a revelation and had yielded the first clue. This genial guardsman who had forgotten to salute his superior officers was most probably also the murderer. In a borrowed uniform, causing a diversion about the lights, he had managed to distract the guards' attention. Knowing that Henry and Percy were absent he had taken the opportunity to slip into the royal bedroom and murder the marchioness.

A more daring and brazen approach, carefully planned and timed with the possibility of an accomplice, cancelled out Tam's original theory regarding the secret entrance to the royal bedroom.

For a moment it all sounded plausible enough, but closer thought revealed a

72

multitude of holes that needed filling in, a host of improbabilities. And the greatest of them looming heavily upon the horizon was the missing key to the solution of any crime. Who had most to gain; find that and with it you unlock the answer.

Tam shook his head wearily. With someone as enigmatic and dissolute as the marchioness, there might be in the Pavilion itself quite a queue lining up of gentlemen, or ladies for that matter, who had their own reasons for wishing to see the back of her permanently. Her husband the marquis, at home in Lewes, with a carefully prepared alibi, might well head the list.

The trouble was, how did this person or persons unknown manage to fit it all so neatly into the time when the grooms were watching the shipwreck? Surely a stroke of luck, a heaven-sent opportunity.

Tam shook his head and returned again to the most plausible solution of the crime. The secret door and the possibility that the marchioness might not have been murdered during the grooms' absence but at any time before the prince's expected return.

As he prepared to return through the withdrawing room, Warren said sternly:

'We have instructions from Lord Henry and Lord Percy that the royal apartments are to be left untouched and unentered awaiting further orders from His Royal Highness.'

Tam nodded. 'I believe I am an exception, gentlemen, as I am in charge of this enquiry.'

'Can you tell us more, sir, is it serious?' asked Toby.

Tam shook his head gravely. 'I am afraid you must obey royal orders and I must also request your silence and your discretion. Doubtless you will be fully informed in due course.'

Leaving them, he hurried towards the bedroom, averting his eyes from the sheeted corpse. How much longer could the prince keep the presence of the dead woman in his bed a secret? Had he already activated some plans for her discreet disposal? And what of her family?

None of these delicate matters, he was thankful, were any of his business, he thought as, repeating the prince's action, he touched the decorated dado and the secret door slid open, revealing the narrow staircase, lit by narrow slits in the outer fabric of the wall which, if noticed at all, would be taken for some sort of ventilation.

Had this been the entrance for the marchioness's unknown visitor or had the genial guardsman attending to the lights been her killer, Tam wondered, as a steep descent ended at a closed door.

Turning the lock, a moment later he emerged into the brightness of summer sunlight and an unmistakable smell of horses, indicating, along with the cobbled road, the presence of the royal stables, their exit on to the Steine marked by double gates in a solid wall. Letting himself out by a tiny door for pedestrians within the gates, he was in the vast grounds which enclosed the Pavilion.

He smiled delightedly. Until he had a clearer indication where this particular time-quest was leading, he intended to enjoy the less sinister aspects of nature as characterised by the ornate gardens surrounding him. Flowers, shrubs and a handsome grove of elms framed arbours with secluded seats, all dominated by a circular glass dome, an outdoor salon used for musical evenings, for masques and social gatherings.

It was all extremely elegant, music to his ears to hear in the middle distance the refreshing sounds of a normal world. Raised voices of street vendors, children playing, a baby crying, a couple quarrelling, the rumble of coaches and horses trotting nearby, the raucous cries of seabirds wheeling above his head and the salt-pure smell of the sea. The everyday sounds of lives that existed side by side with the claustrophobic Pavilion and its extraordinary inmates from which he had temporarily escaped.

He inhaled deeply, and the air was good. Good to be alone without having to measure each sentence, each word, knowing that a false step could leave him floundering in that slough of deception and corruption.

But he was not alone. Someone else was of like mind. Was he never to escape, not even for a few minutes? He groaned as he saw approaching rapidly in his direction the now familiar figure of Lord Henry. He was accompanied by the buxom girl he had glimpsed earlier who had beamed upon him so coquettishly as he was leaving the prince's breakfast room.

A maid or lady-in-waiting, now again smiling broadly in his direction, waving her hand. How very tiresome. He bowed.

A moment later they were face-to-face and he saw that Henry bore a remarkable resemblance to the girl on closer inspection. They could have been siblings—which indeed they almost were.

Henry was making the introductions and Tam found himself in the embarrassing situation of being presented to the unprepossessing young female as Her Royal Highness, Princess Charlotte, England's future queen.

Chapter Seven

Tam would have found this disclosure even more embarrassing had he realised that Princess Charlotte had been eagerly tracking him down since their first—almost—

encounter in what had appeared to him as a brazen attempt by a serving wench to strike up an acquaintance.

As for the princess, her immediate demand was to find out who he was and what such a divine young man, so unconventionally attired in the habitually overdressed court, was doing at breakfast with her father.

For answers she turned as usual to Lord Henry. He had always been her friend, her natural half-brother, and as he was also close to her father, as she had never been, she managed to waylay him and lure him into conversation about the mysterious stranger.

When she learned that he was the sole survivor of the *Royal Stuart*, her eyes closed in ecstasy. What a cloudburst of romance! How could any girl fail to lose her heart to such a gallant godlike creature?

What were his intentions, how long would he remain in Brighton? Henry could give her no answers to that. A pity that she had also to endure the presence of her governess, Lady de Clifford, tenacious as an extra limb.

Determined not to lose sight of her royal protégée, Lady de Clifford managed this task admirably with an ability, when necessary, to melt into the background and make herself invisible. As she was growing rather deaf, Charlotte being out of earshot was not a formidable problem, but as the possessor of an excellent memory, no incident was too small to be dismissed as insignificant.

She had been around the court long enough to recognise that Charlotte was at a dangerous age, already exceedingly vulnerable to possible romantic encounters. Most regretfully it was becoming strikingly obvious that she had not only inherited her father's looks and physique, but also his amorous propensities, an unfortunate tendency that would require her governess to have the vigilance of a hawk, since the princess was already exhibiting alarming signs of indifference to convention and royal protocol.

Sometimes Lady de Clifford awoke in the middle of the night with bad dreams. What if the princess, while under her care, slipped the leash for an hour or two and became—(she gulped)—*enceinte*?

She had not missed the predatory gleam in the princess's eye as she had raced down the path with Lord Henry to force an encounter with this very presentable young man. Watching him bow deeply, she shuddered. There could be no trail of royal bastards for the future Queen of England to legitimise in the traditional manner of past English kings.

'Ah, Mr Eildor,' said Charlotte, breathless with eager anticipation. 'A pleasant day for a stroll, is it not?'

Tam, smiling politely, thought regretfully that it had indeed been a very pleasant day, full of promise until that moment, as the dark-clad middle-aged woman trailing at a respectful distance behind the princess and Lord Henry, moved forward protectively.

'My governess Lady de Clifford,' said Charlotte. 'You may leave us now, Henry.' Her hand raised in a dismissive gesture was an exact copy that could only have been inherited from her royal father.

Henry bowed and with a look of relief turned on his heel, heading back along the path to the Pavilion.

The governess acknowledged Tam with a frigid curtsey while the princess wagged a teasing finger at him.

'Mr Eildor is a lawyer from Edinburgh.' She smiled, showing excellent teeth, and rather a lot of them. 'We—we have—have heard all—all about you, Mr Eildor. Henry has informed us that you were—were a—a passenger on—on the ship that went down—sank last night. The sole survivor—how very fortunate.' All this speech was delivered in a shrill voice hampered by a stammer while nervous glances in Lady de Clifford's direction invited encouraging comment. The governess regarded Tam sternly.

'Fortunate indeed. Ship sank—all hands lost, we understood,' she added in a sepulchral voice exactly matching her gloomy appearance.

Tam bowed politely, hoping that this was also the end of the conversation, that escape

79

was imminent and that the tiresome encounter would also be allowed to sink forgetfully into the ground.

But that was not Charlotte's intention. Under that royal stare, Tam felt uncomfortably that his appearance was being assimilated inch by inch. It was all quite unnerving, as she continued to regard him, bright-eyed and eager, occasionally licking her rather thick, red lips—a disconcerting habit, like someone watching a particularly strange and exotic insect through a microscope.

Suddenly she shivered. 'Be so good as to recover our shawl and our book. We laid them down—somewhere—while we were looking at the latest art acquisitions—our royal father's weakness.'

Although she addressed her governess, she did so without yielding her gaze from Tam's countenance as if he might choose that moment to escape from her.

With a sigh, she watched Lady de Clifford hurry back across the gardens. Unable to conceal a gleam of satisfaction, another broad smile awaited Tam's approval. This was followed by a convincing shiver, rubbing her bare arms, a gesture which brought an unfortunate reminder to the observer that the fashion for white muslin gowns reaching down to the ankles, but extreme décolleté even in daytime, was less than flattering to ladies, however young, with overample bosoms. The flowing empire line had its origins in France and it struck Tam as curious that all female attire seemed to have been designed for a tropical climate of eternal summers, despite the fact that the climate of England was totally unreliable, with snowy winters exceedingly harsh and long-lasting. True, shawls were an essential accessory, the mark of the lady of fashion, to wear with grace.

'Are you to stay in Brighton for some time, Mr Eildor?' she asked.

As Tam did not know the answer to that one himself, he smiled and said: 'Until my plans are made, Your Royal Highness.'

Charlotte giggled, and let a plump hand linger on his arm. He felt its warmth through his borrowed shirt.

'Please—please—you may call me—Charlotte, if you wish.'

Tam did not so wish and she saw too late that he was no doubt embarrassed by the thought of such intimacy with a royal person.

Aware that she was moving too fast, she removed her hand, her gaze becoming more intent as she did so, a myopic staring deeply into his eyes. Her breath touching his face, she laughed.

A deep, throaty and rather coarse laugh in one so young. Fourteen, fifteen—Tam wondered, perhaps girls grew up quickly in royal residences where loose morals were constantly in evidence, and his thoughts flew momentarily to the sight he had left in the royal bedroom, as with a suppressed groan, he heard her say:

'When we know each other better—' she hesitated. 'What do your friends call you, Mr Eildor?'

'My name is Tam.' He bowed.

'Tam? Why, what an interesting name. Scottish, is it not? From your accent—'

Tam agreed. They had at least found something safe to agree upon.

'Where were you journeying—when the ship—went—went down?'

'To London, Your Royal Highness.'

'Please—please—Highness will do adequately, if you must—for the moment,' she added with a flutter of pale eyelashes.

'Very well, Highness,' was the reluctant reply.

A pause. 'I know London well. It is—my home—my—my mother lives at Carlton House. This is a brief—brief—visit only—to my father. We rarely see each other.'

Tam was quick to detect sadness, a certain loneliness and resentment too, as she said: 'You have—have friends in London? We might meet—'

'I have legal business—that is all,' said Tam, dousing that hopeful suggestion.

Charlotte smiled, waiting patiently for more information. As there was none forthcoming, she eyed him coyly, head to one side, and said:

'Your wife—in Edinburgh—she will miss you.'

And while Tam was considering a suitable comment, she continued: 'Your wife and family will be heartily rejoicing that you have been spared from the shipwreck.'

Tam's mouth twitched at this further probe into his private life from this royal minx. He shook his head.

Exact recollections of his life in the year 2250 already had a dreamlike quality, part of the condition of a time-quest, but he did remember that matrimony, as former centuries recognised it, had now become almost extinct.

Partners were chosen, male and female, male and male, female and female, for as long or as short a time as the couple desired. It was not completely unknown for a relationship to last for life, with children if one wished, and ultimately grandchildren, from the union. There were no hard and fast rules, only the human heart and its inclinations existed for each individual.

'I have no wife,' Tam said, and instantly regretted that automatic response, since he could not at this moment honestly recall any details of his own category.

How the princess's eyes gleamed.

Damn, thought Tam. That was a mistake. He had thrown away a refuge—or would the off-stage presence of a wife have made any difference? Perhaps only to make him more desirable, a challenge, seeing that matrimonial vows seemed of equally minor importance to royal houses as those of the world he had temporarily left. Here, where marriage existed purely for territorial or dynastic purposes: 'An heir and a spare' was the rule.

'Tell me about Scotland,' said Charlotte. 'We intend to visit Edinburgh immediately after our coronation.'

Tam gave her a sharp glance. Anticipating that her grandfather, mad King George III, would die imminently, she obviously did not think, or hope, that her father would long occupy the throne.

'Loyal subjects will wish to see their new queen and we will wish to reward them for their devotion. We are told that Edinburgh Castle is rather chilly and that the Palace of Holyroodhouse is even worse. We understand,' she added in a horrified whisper, 'that one of our ancestors, Queen Mary, murdered her husband there.'

Before Tam could correct this popular is misrepresentation of Scottish history, no doubt taught in English schools, the governess hastened along the path towards them, clutching a shawl and two moderately large books, while from the opposite direction Beau Brummell made a leisurely approach.

Tam observed that he was more immaculately clad than at their first meeting, having given due attention to his toilette.

84

Bowing to the princess, who received this polite gesture with what could only be regarded as a look of annoyance, he turned to Tam:

'Ah, Mr Eildor, what a pleasure to see you again—I was hoping we might meet and continue our most interesting conversation.'

Tam bowed, aware that Lady de Clifford's firm hold on Charlotte's arm was indicating that they should leave. But ignoring both her governess and the newcomer, Charlotte addressed Tam:

'We are heading to the circulating library— over there, Mr Eildor,' she pointed across the park towards the promenade. 'Please join us there, when you are free.'

She managed a smile but looked mutinous, cutting Brummell dead, angry that her encounter with Tam had been interrupted and not quite sure whether she should vent her displeasure on her governess, Mr Brummell, or both.

As was clearly evident from Brummell's audible sigh of relief and a certain measure of ice in his polite greeting, a state of mutual dislike existed between the two.

As for Tam, he watched them go, feeling trapped as well as wondering why on earth the princess should need to borrow books, and if he might be in more danger from Brummell's curiosity than the princess's flirtation.

'The library, did I hear aright?'

At his side Brummell laughed. 'The library, did she say? Allow me to interpret your thoughts, dear fellow. Why should Her Highness consider a circulating library, says you, when there are enough books in the royal library to furnish most of London with reading matter?'

A pause. 'Shall we walk?'

This was Tam's first chance to view from the Steine the exterior of the dramatic and somewhat bizarre Marine Pavilion with its two oval-shaped wings, an addition to the original and more conventional dwelling that had replaced the prince's rented farmhouse.

Alas, the search for a suitable excuse for escape was no longer possible, as Brummell continued: 'Our circulating library has other attractions than books. There are gaming tables and it is the haunt of fashionable society during the daytime. Having one's name in the subscription book is a passport into Brighton society. Indeed the Master of Ceremonies visitors' book is the first port of call for new arrivals wishing to find out who else is in town.

'Allow me to escort you there, dear fellow, a little later perhaps. Meanwhile I have a humble lodging at North House but I am sorely in need of refreshment, as I imagine you are too. So let us adjourn to the Old Ship Inn.'

Tam's mind remained obstinately blank of

any suitable excuse for declining this invitation, as Brummell led him out of the grounds across the Steine towards a less imposing huddle of buildings. Houses, taverns, market and shops, dwelling places of those whose daily bread and employment depended on their proximity to the royal court, as well as the now numerous petty thieves and criminals who preyed upon the advantages such a situation offered.

As they walked, Tam was amused to see that his companion's appearance created quite a stir in the narrow lanes. Ladies curtseyed, simpered, fluttered fans, while gentlemen bowed gravely.

The interior of the Old Ship suggested that its roots were well established long before Prince George or even Dr Russell of Lewes, for that matter, discovered the restorative powers of the waters of the humble fishing village as a potential health spa.

There were many dark corners which suggested secret meetings and hinted at darker days as a favourite haunt and safe haven for smugglers, bent on the lucrative and illegal exchange of taxable goods from the Continent. The royal dandy was obviously someone of great importance and, it seemed, was well liked and respected, and not only for the cut of his clothes and the snugness of his breeches. A condition, Tam decided, which must be quite a thorn in the abundant flesh of the Prince Regent who regarded this man as a serious rival and a danger to his own jealously guarded popularity, with an elegance to which he could no longer aspire, trapped forever in the gross flesh of decades of over-indulgence.

As they took their seats Tam observed the elaboration of Brummell's neckwear that had become *de rigueur* in high society. The shirt collar was worn upright, the two points projected on to the cheeks kept in place by a neckcloth, either in the form of a cravat or a stock. Some dandies were alleged to spend a whole morning in the arrangement of their cravats and in happier days the young Prince of Wales had been Brummell's most apt and eager pupil.

Comfort fell flat on its face and bowed to fashion, since such neckwear made it difficult, if not impossible, to turn or lower the head, which contributed to the dandy's apparent imperturbability and hauteur.

Tam saw that Brummell was warmly welcomed by the landlord, a popular and esteemed customer who might also be treated with some measure of informality. Without any words being spoken, a flagon and two crystal goblets of excellent French brandy wine, most probably smuggled, were placed before them. This was followed by the mouth-watering smell of a plate of steaming hot mutton pies, and Tam needed no second invitation to join in what Brummell was pleased to describe as a humble repast.

'Humble fare, indeed, but a pleasant relief to one's stomach after the rich daily fare at the royal table. As many as sixteen courses, dear fellow—such a trial sometimes,' he sighed, and dusting aside the crumbs with an elegant lace handkerchief, he took up his quizzing-glass once more and said:

'Tell me more about yourself, Mr Eildor. I am eager to hear about your destination in London. I have a house and you would be most welcome as my guest. It is even possible that we have acquaintances in common.'

Tam's vague nod doubted that exceedingly as the Beau continued: 'But tell me about Scotland—and Edinburgh and what business brought you to our southern shores, if you please.'

Tam did not please, but he did not relish trying to deceive this man who was, he suspected, considerably more intelligent than his languorous appearance suggested.

But help was at hand. The door opened to admit an officer in the uniform of the Tenth Dragoons. Looking around he spoke earnestly to the landlord who indicated Tam and Brummell.

He came over, bowed and said: 'Mr Eildor. His Royal Highness requests that I am to escort you back to the Pavilion immediately.'

Brummell gave an exasperated sigh. He looked exceedingly annoyed at this

89

interruption but there was little he could do in the face of a royal command.

Chapter Eight

George Augustus Frederick, twenty-first Prince of Wales, Prince Regent and heir to the throne, was a very unhappy man. He sat in the withdrawing room of his apartments, unable to face what continued to lie in his royal bed, his most urgent need to get rid of the dead woman before someone else made the discovery.

Tears or sentimental regrets were quite absent from his thoughts, since the marchioness had ceased to be a human being, with whom only twenty-four hours ago he had fancied that he was hopelessly infatuated and was on the most intimate terms. Death had turned her into a nuisance, an aggravation, a monstrous burden presenting diabolic and insurmountable problems quite beyond his normally rather dull imagination.

At his side the faithful Lord Henry quietly informed him that servants were curious at being denied access to the bedroom.

'Let them be curious!' boomed the prince.

'Sire, they wish to attend to daily matters regarding your ablutions, changing bed linen, lighting fires and so forth.'

Henry had already observed that something must be done, and quickly. As the hours passed in his preoccupation, the prince was increasingly in need of a shave. Henry regarded him anxiously, toying with the bright idea of summoning the royal barber to the withdrawing room, on the pretext that His Royal Highness was in too great haste to take this matter in his accustomed leisurely fashion, surrounded by hot towels and the usual luxuries.

Henry, it so happened, was full of bright ideas. Indeed, that had been almost the whole story of his life since the age of fourteen, when he had become aware of being yet another royal bastard. Far from despising or hating the prince for this unfortunate label, he had become obsessed with his idol.

According to well-spread rumour, his mother was an actress and one (of many) of the prince's first loves. Basking in the happy accident of his resemblance to the prince, there was nothing Henry would not do to stay in that blissful royal orbit, especially as Mrs Fitzherbert's affectionate regard and attention over the years suggested that his parentage might be a more dangerous secret.

On more than one occasion since he had grown to manhood, he had stood in as alibi for his royal father, and borne the full displeasure of some irate noble husband whose noble wife he had saved from being taken in adultery with the prince. A dead mistress in the royal bed was quite another matter, as the prince said:

'You delivered our message to the stables? Exactly so—it does break our heart to miss a fine race but how can we leave at such a time? We are trapped—trapped, Henry, in our own residence. What are we to do?' he moaned. 'We cannot go on like this indefinitely.'

So much was true and obviously so. Henry was sympathetic about the term indefinitely. It was a hot August day outside and the corpse would not stay fresh for much longer. Already he thought he heard the buzzing of flies beyond the door, but hoped that the prince's hearing and sense of smell was not as sharp as his own to detect the significance.

Returning from the stables, where he had informed the grooms that His Royal Highness most regretfully had to cancel his afternoon visit to the racecourse at Whitehawk, where he was to have seen his own horse Orbis take part in one of the most prestigious events in the racing calendar, he had encountered Charlotte. She seized upon him immediately, hoping that her father had confided some details about the young man who had occupied her thoughts since seeing him leaving the breakfast room.

Henry was sympathetic. He and Charlotte had shared many innocent secrets through the years. In the capacity of elder brother, Henry accepted her avid interest in this newcomer good-humouredly, recognising that young girls of fifteen or so frequently imagine themselves infatuated by older men. As Tam Eildor was not destined to remain long in the Pavilion, a passing stranger, there could be no harm in indulging Charlotte in this whim, by sharing with her the little he knew of the Edinburgh lawyer.

*   *   *

'What are we to do?' the prince repeated.

Henry waited a moment said respectfully: 'Sire, I have thought of something—'

'You have! Out with it then. Out with it—'

'Yes, Sire. This might just work. Percy could ride swiftly to Lewes and bring back her ladyship's maid—with suitable attire,' he added, aware that Lady Sarah wore only a fur cloak as she scuttled across from her nearby apartment and through the secret entrance to the royal bedroom.

'Impossible, Henry. How do we know she is to be trusted?'

'Sire, please hear me out. The maid Simone is on—er, intimate terms with Percy. She will do anything for him. I understand that she did not expect favours from her mistress and merely obeyed her wishes, keeping silent— since she was well paid to do so,' he added grimly.

93

'And—' demanded the prince who was losing patience rapidly. Of course, Percy had seen the dead marchioness but was he to be trusted? His father had been a faithful equerry until his untimely death but Percy kept his own counsel. Unlike Henry, he was a married man with a young family and a wife to whom he was constantly unfaithful. He had never resented, or indeed expected to share, the prince's affinity with his natural son.

'Sire, it would be to your advantage to pay Simone well,' Henry persisted.

The prince sighed. 'If you are sure she is to be trusted. Very well, see to it.'

Henry withdrew and returned shortly afterwards, having been so sure that the prince would agree to this desperate plan that he had sent Percy off on the swiftest horse in the stables an hour ago.

Without asking permission, he sat down opposite the prince who groaned and bit his lip, taking deep sobbing breaths.

'The plan, Sire, is that we can smuggle her ladyship down the private staircase, into a sedan chair and across the garden—'

'How—how?' demanded the prince, vaguely aware of what might be happening through the wall and that only a warm day could have prevented rigor mortis with consequent difficulties of negotiating a corpse down a steep and narrow staircase.

Henry smiled. 'It could be managed with

94

ease, Sire, simply by the use of a roll of carpet.' So speaking Henry tapped the handsome Persian carpet beneath their feet.

The prince followed his gaze wide-eyed. 'You mean—roll her—in that.' A present from a visiting high dignitary, its colours had failed to impress and it been banished to the withdrawing room.

'Exactly, Sire. Transport her across the garden into a closed carriage and speed her on the way back to Creeve House where, as prearranged, she will be found in the garden by Simone during the Masque this evening, a glass of some intoxicating spirit at her side, the victim of a heart attack.'

For the first time, the prince relaxed. The muscles of his face were so set in anxiety that a smile was something of an achievement. Leaning over, he patted Henry's knee. 'By Jove, Henry, you are an excellent fellow. Quite exceptional. Well done, well done, indeed.'

The barber was admitted and, after watching the prince expertly shaved in absolute silence, Henry saw him leave and said consolingly, 'Percy should be back soon with the maid.'

But that was not to be. Percy had been unable to find Simone, who had taken advantage of her mistress's absence to visit an old aunt—or so she had told the other servants. An old flame was more likely, thought Percy suspiciously, since no one knew

95

where this aunt lived. He was very angry.

As for the prince, he was also angry and sunk in despair once more. Beyond the simple questioning of how Percy, on even the swiftest horse possible, could have made the journey to Lewes and back in such a remarkably short time.

The carpet had seemed a lifeline, the maid finding her mistress in the garden of her home the perfect way out. While being shaved he had composed a note of condolence to her husband, the marquis, and to her lover, his brother Frederick. Now it had all fallen through, and he was back at the beginning with a dead woman, if not exactly on his hands, still lying on his bed.

Percy had departed at Henry's suggestion, to sulk over Simone's infidelity, his part in the drama ended.

'What are we to do now?' the prince wailed. 'All is lost. All is lost, Henry!'

'Not quite, Sire. We still have the carpet. I will drive the carriage, it is safer that way. The fewer people who know the plan the better.'

'What about Percy? could he not be driver?'

Henry shook his head. 'No, Sire. That would not be advisable. As a frequent visitor to Creeve House, he might be recognised by some of the servants. They don't know me and I will keep a hat well down over my eyes, a scarf about my chin.'

The prince looked at him, realised he was

enjoying the excitement of such a role. He nodded approval as Henry continued:

'There is one problem. We are lacking a maid and we must have someone inside the carriage with her ladyship—in case of accidents. To see her safely into the grounds and the gardens at Creeve House where she will be left for someone to find her.'

These were desperate measures indeed and Henry avoided concerning himself or drawing the prince's attention to natural questions regarding the marchioness found dead in the garden at the Masque, naked but for a fur cloak.

That would take some remarkable feats of imagination by way of explanation, but hopefully might rest on the assumption that the marchioness was well known to be somewhat eccentric in her habits.

As for the prince, once the marchioness left the Pavilion, her discovery was no longer his concern. Only when the news reached him that she had been found dead on her own territory, would he breathe freely again.

And as both turned their thoughts towards the production of some discreet person other than Percy who knew all the facts and could be trusted, Henry said: 'I thought perhaps Mr Eildor—might be willing.'

'Excellent, quite excellent, Henry. You have hit the nail on the head. Mr Eildor is the perfect choice. A small favour—and the deed successfully accomplished, what would you say to a handsome purse to speed him on his way to London? That is the last we shall see or hear of him,' the prince continued gleefully. 'What a stroke of good fortune that he should have been rescued from the sea and at a time when he should be of such use to us. Capital, Henry, absolutely capital.'

The moral issues about finding out who had murdered the marchioness no longer troubled the prince's conscience and he was so overcome, almost tearful, at the expected happy outcome, that Henry was sent immediately to summon Mr Eildor to the royal presence.

There was some unexpected difficulty. Mr Eildor was not in the quarters set aside for him. He had been seen talking to Princess Charlotte in the gardens and was last reported walking across the Steine with Beau Brummell.

The prince, his good humour vanished, almost snarled with displeasure at the thought that the so-very-useful Mr Eildor had fallen into the hands of two of the people he despised. One his tiresome daughter and the other a man he actually feared.

'Send for him. Immediately!'

Chapter Nine

Summoned to the royal presence, the delicate situation explained, the purse temptingly offered, the prince and Lord Henry eagerly awaited Tam's response.

He did not care for the idea in the least. What a disappointing ending. He had hoped that he would have had a chance to solve this particular crime. Instead his time-quest was to end in a carriage escorting a murdered woman back home to Lewes.

Except that it couldn't end there.

Grimly he remembered that the only way he could return to his own time was from the exact spot where he had landed—on a convict ship anchored somewhere off the south-east coast near Brighton in the year 1811. How he was to find it again was a problem that would no doubt require not only his own ingenuity but also the contents of the royal purse he was being offered.

'You will do it, Mr Eildor? Oh, excellent, excellent,' said the prince happily.

It was all arranged. His Royal Highness sent a messenger with apologies for his regrettable absence from the Masque, owing to a severe attack of gout, and Tam returned to his bedroom, where he would remain until summoned later that evening, and looked at the costumes set out for his approval.

Nothing too memorable, but wearing masks would admit them without question to Creeve House. Nor would the anonymous closed carriage from the royal stables draw unwelcome attention.

*   *   *

Lord Percy's assistance had been invaluable according to Henry. He was familiar with a convenient path leading off the main drive, wide enough for a carriage. This led past stables and kitchen premises, towards the gardens, a place of assignation with the marchioness's maid, Simone. There they would deposit their burden on one of the stone seats and return again by the same route to the main drive.

Henry made it sound easy but Tam already had qualms about the success of such an enterprise, having wisely dismissed the idea of that rolled carpet as too difficult.

Were there any windows overlooking the secret exit from the royal bedroom? he asked.

'Of course not. That's why it is secret!' was the scornful response.

Then was it not much simpler to carry her wrapped in the fur cloak directly to the carriage?

This proposal was considered and met with approval but Tam was far from enthralled at the prospect of sitting inside the carriage, even masked, with the dead woman propped up beside him apparently enjoying a peaceful sleep.

As for the prince, he was ecstatic, totally confident, beaming on them both, without entertaining a moment's doubt on the plan's success, satisfied that having shifted the burden on to someone else, it was no longer his responsibility. At his most genial, Tam guessed that he had already washed his hands of the whole gruesome episode.

Thinking ahead, as a light supper was served to him by a silent footman, Tam could envisage that when the prince heard of the dramatic discovery of the dead marchioness in her garden, he would genuinely believe the story of the heart attack, and would banish from his mind entirely that she had been murdered in his bed in the Pavilion, on the night he watched the sinking of the *Royal Stuart*.

Tam finally decided what to wear, a black cutaway coat and breeches, a modest outfit that might suggest a lawyer or a minister with white bands, plus a dark, enveloping cloak and, once he attached the mask to the wide-brimmed hat, a sinister stranger stared back at him from the mirror.

He shook his head sadly at his reflection. The more he thought about the plan the less he liked it. Candidly there were too many loopholes, but he saw no way of refusing to participate in such a mad exploit, fraught with unseen and unimaginable dangers.

By eight o'clock it was already growing dusk when he presented himself at the royal bedroom. The prince was not in evidence, but he was relieved to see Percy waiting for him by the concealed door and glad of their immediate exodus. There seemed to be an abundance of flies buzzing about, angry at having been deprived of a dainty morsel.

As he followed Percy down the stairs, he was informed that they had wrapped her ladyship in her fur cloak, and that she was at present propped up in a sedan chair at the gate where Henry, driving the closed carriage, was waiting for them.

Percy smiled as he talked and seemed to think of it all as rather a good jape. All thoughts of the murder that had necessitated this grim task seemed to have slipped by him too.

It was no easy task settling the dead woman into a corner of the carriage. Even with Tam seated alongside, she tended to slump sideways in his direction and he realised with a sense of horror that keeping her upright and propping her up would require his constant attention during the miles ahead.

At last Percy waved them off. The window blinds were drawn, and being in charge of a corpse in semi-darkness promised to be an even more unpleasant experience.

As they drove along the Steine, Tam raised a corner of the shade and peered out cautiously. The hilly countryside north of the Pavilion seemed deserted and it was not until they were well on to the Stanmer road that other carriages, more handsome and distinguished, were in evidence, heading for Creeve House.

Leaving Brighton behind, Henry called down that, on Percy's instructions, they were to depart from the main route and proceed by a less-frequented faster road. It was also less comfortable inside the carriage as the twisting road narrowed alarmingly along the edge of an embankment, with a belt of trees sweeping from far above them towards the steep slope, and a rider approached out of the dusk.

Riding alongside he peered in the window at Tam. 'Excuse me, sir,' he panted, 'I am for Brighton but I seem to have got on to the wrong road.'

The carriage had slowed down and Tam tapped on the roof. 'Coachman, can you direct this gentleman, please.'

Explanations and directions were given by Henry, still heavily muffled, and repeated by the traveller who looked in at the window to thank Tam once again, and politely saluting the motionless figure beside him said: 'Your servant, ma'am.' Then with a sigh of relief they were steadily on the move again and, occupied with the business of supporting his inert companion, Tam thought he heard Henry call out, something like—a warning!

The next moment the carriage jolted to a halt, with the sound of horses jingling harnesses, and Tam raised the blind to be confronted by four masked men.

Travellers for Creeve House who had also taken the fast route and lost their way, he decided. His offer to lean out and offer reassurances was cut short as the door was flung open and a pistol flourished before his face.

He sat back with a groan. Not guests but highwaymen, he realised with a sinking heart. Before he could take in the full measure of this unexpected inconvenience to their progress, let alone recognise the probable fatalities of such an encounter at night on a lonely road, with a pistol still at his chin, he heard Henry being told to dismount and unharness the horses.

Brutal laughter from the men. 'Save the horses, we'll have them for a start. Aye, plenty of life in fine beasts like them.'

Even as he wondered how they were to continue their journey without horses, he heard Henry yell—a thud and the sound of a body—Henry's—hitting the ground.

If he was still alive, he must try to rescue him. But how? Unarmed, Tam could do nothing. His natural reaction was to leap from the carriage by the other door. He knew he could outrun most men, and by the time they got their pistols cocked he could have been out of sight down among the trees, but what about Henry?

The carriage swayed horribly towards the edge of the embankment as the horses were released from the shafts. He heard the men's voices outside, realised what was about to happen and wondered why they were not interested in the two passengers. Apart from that pistol being flourished as a warning, the highwayman must have observed that there was also a lady passenger, apparently asleep, wearing a handsome fur cloak, and a fine rope of pearls about her neck.

Now the carriage jerked and jolted nearer the edge of the slope, Tam realised almost too late what was about to happen and as he prepared to jump out a pistol smashed down towards his head.

Only the gathering momentum of the swaying carriage which hurled him to the floor saved him from what would have been a certain death blow, as the carriage trembled for an instant on the edge of the embankment. Then, gathering speed, it seemed to leap into the air, hurtling downwards, crashing into trees and shrubs which shattered in its path, stones and boulders flying.

So this is death, was Tam's last thought. No longer able to cling on to anything substantial, as doors and windows disintegrated, he tumbled out and rolling helplessly downhill landed heavily, with his head hard against a tree trunk.

The world around him faded and was lost.

*   *   *

He opened his eyes painfully, groaned and wondered how long he had lain there and how great were his injuries from the steep fall. Time had passed for it was darker now, but not yet nightfall.

Struggling cautiously to his feet, at least there were no bones broken, but he suspected bruises and scratches in plenty. All around him lay the scattered remains of the carriage, reduced to unrecognisable matchwood. Wheels, doors and seats had vanished down the slope.

Scrambling up the slope, he noticed a large, furry shape, the outline of a dead animal, lying a short distance away.

Tam shuddered as he realised without further inspection that the marchioness had found an unplanned resting place. Making his way painfully back to the road, there was as he expected no sign of highwaymen, horses—or Henry. All had vanished into the twilight dusk.

Shaken, he sat down gratefully on a boulder, rubbing his bruised knees, thankful that his injuries were no worse with the prospect of a long walk back into Brighton, and an unavoidable confrontation with the prince regarding the disastrous end of their plan. In the circumstances, he could see all prospects vanishing of the promised purse to continue his mythical journey.

As he began walking, his confused thoughts became more ordered.

Where was Henry, was he still alive? The highwaymen had taken the horses. Was Henry also a hostage, had he been their main target? Some sinister plot involving the natural son of the Prince Regent was at least a feasible explanation.

At that moment, a stifled groan reached his ears and gave him the answer to what most concerned him—having to return to the Prince and tell him the dread news concerning Lord Henry. No need now, for Henry was very much alive, trussed up and gagged and tied to a young sapling by the roadside.

Tam rushed to his assistance. Henry seemed surprised to see him. Dazed, he murmured thanks while Tam untying his bonds observed that they were neither aggressively restricting nor even very efficiently tied at all, considering the desperate nature of highwaymen. In fact, had he been their victim, he would have found it not too difficult to wriggle out and escape from their confines.

Helping Henry to his feet again, his tearful gratitude was an exact replica of the prince's and emphasised again his remarkable resemblance to his royal father.

'I can never thank you enough—I thought—I thought you must be dead.' A pause as if expecting reassurance from Tam before continuing. 'I saw the fiends push the carriage down the embankment. I heard the sound of it breaking into pieces, and I thought how terrible. Poor Mr Eildor. No one could survive such a disaster.' And regarding Tam in amazement, 'But you did—'

Again he paused. 'Is—is she—'

'Yes, down there among the wreckage.'

'What rotten luck.' Henry sighed and went on cheerfully. 'Well, it does makes it a lot easier from our point of view. I expect someone will find her ladyship's body sooner or later—an unfortunate accident—and nothing to connect her to recent events,' he added in a whisper.

Tam gave him a hard look. Henry was taking it remarkably lightly, smoothing over inevitable questions that the discovery must raise. Where had she come from, for instance, and why had she been travelling in only a fur cloak and pearls? And had this been an accident, where were the coachman and horses?

'Ah yes,' Henry continued happily, 'the highwaymen saved us a journey to Lewes and, quite candidly, between ourselves, I was not all that convinced that we would be successful in staging her ladyship's sudden death in the garden of Creeve House. That was Percy's idea,' he added in a tone of self-righteousness.

'Was it his idea that we should take the short cut?'

'Indeed it was, just as I told you,' said Henry somewhat huffily.

'Not very clever, I'm afraid. But Percy is very impulsive—I could tell you many examples—'

But Tam was no longer listening. His thoughts were elsewhere. There was something not quite right about their attackers who did not behave in the characters of highwaymen.

Why had there been no 'stand and deliver,' the usual demands for jewellery and valuables from a handsomely clad sleeping lady, in valuable furs and wearing a rope of extremely valuable pearls around her neck?

Why had they shown so little interest in the occupants of the carriage? Their only intention seemed to be to destroy the carriage—and himself—not with a bullet but with a blow from a pistol that would fracture his skull and look as if he had suffered that fatal blow when the carriage was wrecked.

No longer listening to Henry, he was thinking about the original plan involving the return of the marchioness's body to Creeve House and the more ingenious plan that had taken its place.

There was something else, of even greater significance. At the moment when the carriage lurched towards the slope, the cloak had slipped from the arm of his assailant, the highwayman wielding the pistol. And Tam had seen a flash of a red and gold uniform sleeve, which he recognised as the uniform of the four guards he had interviewed in connection with the marchioness's death. The uniform of the Prince Regent's own regiment, his Tenth Dragoons.

This revelation confirmed his suspicions that their attackers were not highwaymen at all and certainly had not been adequately schooled in how to perform such roles.

'Are you quite unhurt?' He was aware that Henry had repeated the question, somewhat bemused that Mr Eildor was still in one piece and had suffered so little damage in what Tam realised was intended to be recorded as a fatal carriage accident. The disposal of the marchioness—and himself, as a mysterious stranger who knew too much of the events that had led to her murder . . .

'I am quite fit. And you—'

'Just some rope burns, rather uncomfortable.'

'But you are fit enough to walk back to Brighton?' asked Tam.

At his side Henry chuckled. 'A longish way, but there is no need for us to walk anywhere.' And so saying, he withdrew a handsome timepiece from his pocket. Had the highwaymen troubled to search him, and relieve him of that, Tam thought, they would have reckoned they had earned a substantial reward for any night's activity.

Holding it close to his face, Henry smiled.

'There is just enough light for me to see the time—it is almost nine o'clock. And do you know,' he added in tones of surprise, 'the stagecoach that goes through Lewes to collect passengers for Brighton and the coastal towns, comes along the road here in ten minutes precisely. What an excellent piece of good fortune!'

And for Tam, that piece of information had a significant role to play in the night's events. There was no way the driver could have missed seeing Henry tied to a sapling by the roadside in the twilight of a clear summer's night. He decided not to share his thoughts with Henry after all, in common with the glimpse of a dragoon's uniform sleeve under a dark cloak.

Or the fact that the highwaymen had completely overlooked their life's work and daily bread, of robbing frightened travellers on lonely roads.

Henry with his gold timepiece, the female passenger with fur cloak and pearls . . .

Unless they knew that she was dead already and robbery was not their commission.

As for himself, why had they omitted to strip him of any valuables he might be carrying, such as a sword or pistol, with which gentlemen frequently armed themselves against possible attention from highwaymen, especially if there were female passengers, wives and daughters, to protect?

It was not unknown for rich ladies to receive rough treatment and lewd handling if their persons did not yield expected items of jewellery. As a precaution many carried 'bad purses', containing some coins or perhaps a pair of earrings, to divert attention from more valuable items.

And as they waited for the appearance of the stagecoach, Tam realised the true nature of the false highwaymen's attack.

He had been considered expendable, his death part of that prearranged plan. Henry's astonishment at his survival seemed genuine. Percy certainly had a minor role. But was it the prince himself who had masterminded operations for his faithful Dragoons, alias four desperate highwaymen?

Chapter Ten

Tam and Henry alighted from the stagecoach on the Steine after a crowded, noisy, but mercifully short journey. Most of the male passengers—and some of the females too— were very drunk and noisy, genially passing round bottles and inclined to hilarity which neither Tam nor Henry were inclined to share. Especially as every one of them, thanks to close confinement for several hours on what had been a hot August day, smelt abominably.

While realising that his escape from almost certain death on the Lewes road a short while ago was nothing short of a miracle, Tam was now feeling the full effects of his bruises which stiffened up during the drive, and was thankful that he had sustained no serious injuries to his legs and arms. After the fetid atmosphere inside the coach, he was grateful to be able to breathe fresh air again.

The gentle evening breeze with its faint perfume from the Pavilion garden's aromatic flowers and shrubs was welcome indeed, and as they walked towards the building, its windows shone with the brilliance of a hundred candles lighting their path. A full moon drifted lazily through the clouds, and couples walked or dallied, the ladies' white muslin gowns glowing moth-like in the darkness. Emanating from the rotunda strains of Handel played by the prince's expert group of resident musicians contributed an element of romance, with the faint susurrus of the waves at high tide, silvered by moonlight, enhancing the scene.

The guards at the door saluted Henry, who, on the threshold, hesitated for the first time. Observing that he had kept his own counsel since leaving the coach, fully preoccupied with his own thoughts, Tam decided cynically that he might make a shrewd guess at what was troubling Henry.

A poor actor, he was doubtless nervously rehearsing which version of the abortive carriage ride to Lewes he was to present as most readily acceptable and believable to his royal father. As for Tam, he smiled to himself in the darkness. He was looking forward to being present at that particular interrogation.

It was not to be. As they climbed the stairs and approached the royal apartments with its Dragoon guards on duty along the corridor standing to attention and saluting smartly, Henry turned quickly to Tam and said:

'I will not delay you further, Mr Eildor. You have had a very dangerous and painful experience and I am sure that you wish to adjourn to your apartment, to wash and refresh.'

This was not at all what Tam wished, in fact, he was bitterly disappointed but as no argument was possible, he acknowledged what was hopefully intended as a kindly, thoughtful gesture.

'We will meet tomorrow morning, I trust,' Henry continued, 'before you resume your journey. Until then, I will bid you goodnight. Rest well.'

With frustration added to his physical aches at this forced retiral from what promised to be a most interesting and illuminating interview,

Tam went into his bedroom. Removing the dark clothes he had been wearing, now sadly in need of attention and repair after his fall down the embankment, he was pleased to see the silent footman bearing a ewer of warm water and fresh towels and even more gratified at the appearance of a jug of wine.

Pouring a large glass of what tasted like the best vintage from the royal cellar, for a moment he considered the nightshirt spread neatly on the bed. His bruises plagued him, he was exhausted, yawning, but he sternly resisted the temptation to lay his head on the soft pillows and close his eyes on the day.

With the faint hope that he might yet be summoned by the prince to give his own version of the encounter with the highwaymen, he dressed once more in the clothes he had been given on his arrival and consoled by a further glass of wine, he sat down on the bed to await events, deciding that bodily discomfort was easier to ignore than uneasiness of mind.

Over and again he returned to the intriguing question of what Henry was whispering to the prince concerning the carriage accident and the unexpected disposal of the marchioness's body. But what troubled him most was whether or not the prince had been party to the plan.

He had not long to linger with his dismal thoughts, busy as rats trapped in a cage. A tap at the door announced a guard who looked in with the command:

'Mr Eildor, I am to escort you to His Royal Highness's apartments on the instant.'

*   *   *

Outside the royal bedroom, Percy sat alone, his glum expression showing his disappointment at being excluded from the interview within. His brief nod in Tam's direction gave nothing away as the guard opened the door.

Henry was present and Tam observed that he too looked less than happy. He summoned a weak smile and, after a polite question regarding Tam's recovery, he came to the point of the interview, and bowing to his father he said:

'Perhaps you would be good enough to give an account of our journey to His Royal Highness—'

That one swift glance at the prince's grim expression suggested to Tam that Henry's return and his tale of the misadventures with the highwaymen had not been well received. Was that nervous gesture of dismissal of the subject one of guilt?

His suspicions however were wrong. In fact it was doubtful if the prince heard more than the first sentence of Henry's account.

Tam had been summoned for quite a

116

different reason.

There had been a second disaster.

*   *   *

It had been a terrible evening.

Since pressures of age-old daily domestic routine concerning bed linen, fires and so forth in the royal apartments could not be ignored indefinitely, the prince had forced himself to return to his bedroom and remove all traces of the marchioness's presence.

That included the jewellery she had worn. The task filled him with distaste and loathing. To lay his hands on the glittering jewels in their untidy heap on the small table was to touch cold stones fouled by death.

Replacing them in their individual caskets, only one remained empty.

The box which contained the Stuart Sapphire, the marchioness's favourite adornment, always her first choice for decoration before their lovemaking. With a shudder he remembered that only yesterday he had clasped the jewel held by a belt of diamonds about her slender waist.

He looked around, fell awkwardly on his knees and scrabbled under the bed. Perhaps the sapphire had slipped off unnoticed and rolled away when Mr Eildor helped him steady the table. It was not there and he sat back on his heels reeling in horror from the full significance of the missing jewel.

Eagerly he had awaited Henry's return, dismissing the events of the journey in a casual manner that quite shocked the young man. Henry had expected praise, dramatic sighs. Instead it seemed as if the prince had already forgotten all about the murdered marchioness and that bizarre carriage ride to return her body to Lewes.

Or, as it transpired, its tumble down an embankment for someone else to make the gruesome discovery, at a safe distance from any association with her recent fatal visit to the Pavilion. Known to be eccentric in her habits, perhaps some member of the marquis's staff would come up with a satisfactory explanation of why she was naked under her furs.

But that was no longer of the least concern or interest to the prince, and Henry found himself instead of receiving praise and adulation for his brilliant idea, being bombarded with questions about the missing jewel.

It was all very trying. Over and over he tried to listen politely, repeating no, he had not seen the Stuart Sapphire when he and Percy were preparing the marchioness for transport. She was wearing only her own pearls, and her cloak had no pockets, he pointed out tactfully.

Too late, the prince realised, it had never occurred to him that dreadful morning, with so many horrors on his mind, to check that no jewels were missing.

What about Mr Eildor? Was it possible that he stole it? Possible but hardly likely. Only someone who knew its value would have taken it. A thief would have taken one of the glittering diamonds. And again the prince groaned, tapping his fingers in an agitated rhythm on the arm of his chair.

What of Percy, he demanded. Was he to be trusted? Was that the answer?

Henry was shocked. 'Percy is your most devoted and most loyal servant, Sire. Such a theft by him is beyond belief.'

'Is it now?' And the prince wagged his head sagely. 'But there could be other issues at stake, political issues in the making that we know nothing about. When that is the case, even the most trusted servants are not beyond bribery, we can assure you.'

Pausing he sighed heavily. 'Indeed, we might even stretch a point to include those nearest in blood,' he added darkly at which Henry, outraged by a suspicion that the royal glance also included him in this vile category, felt dangerously near to tears.

But he was safe. The prince groaned, struggled up from his chair to pace the floor.

The Stuart Sapphire, the most valuable, the most precious of the royal jewels was missing. Already the thought was looming in the back of his mind, whoever stole it had also

119

murdered the marchioness.

'It has to be found. Has to,' he said. 'The future of England is imperilled. Don't you see?'

Henry didn't see. His feelings had been hurt and he decided that the prince was indulging in a slight exaggeration and that the future of his own reputation would have struck a truer note.

Then he had another of his brainwaves.

Perhaps Providence had meant that Tam Eildor should not have been eliminated and that he should survive the disastrous accident on the Lewes road. Perhaps Providence in the unlikely shape of the Prince Regent intended him for higher things, this Edinburgh lawyer who was used to investigating criminal activities.

'Sire, I have an idea,' he said.

*   *   *

And so it was that Tam found himself listening to the disaster of the stolen jewel in somewhat bizarre circumstances, which included the origins of the Stuart Sapphire from the Crown of Scotland. Part of King James the Sixth's baggage when he became James I of England in 1603, Prince George would wear it when he was crowned King George IV.

An event, considering the condition of his

poor mad father, that was hopefully not too distant, and the prince was already well-rehearsed in the bliss of that future scene, proudly seeing himself wearing the Stuart Sapphire, together with the diamond saltire worn by Charles I at his Scottish coronation in 1633, and inherited by his ill-fated great-grandson Bonnie Prince Charles Edward Stuart who wore it on his return to Britain from exile in 1745.

Both the Old Pretender, James II, and his son the Young Pretender had passed into history, the Jacobite cause lost forever on the battlefield of Culloden in 1746, leaving disappointed Scotsmen to murmur over their whisky and toast the King over the Water while the Stuart Sapphire passed into the hands of the last surviving son of James I.

Henry, Duke of York, styled by his supporters King Henry IX, was not only a cardinal but unlike many of his saintly colleagues, Henry practised the morality he preached and thus childless, the Jacobite claim to the British throne perished with him in 1806. At the time of his death he was receiving a generous pension of £4,000 from the English Crown, and as a mark of gratitude King George was offered the Stuart Sapphire.

'It has to be found—immediately! There is not a moment to lose!' the prince ranted on while Tam listened patiently having decided, rather triumphantly, that he now had the vital clue as to why the marchioness was murdered. Logically it had to be for possession of this particular jewel, since diamonds, emeralds and rubies, more valuable in monetary terms, had been ignored.

With the reason for the crime, all Tam needed now was the killer's identity. Logic immediately suggested someone inside the Pavilion, familiar with the prince's intimate habits and his daily routine.

Would that hopefully narrow down the list of suspects? he wondered, as the prince continued: 'I have already sent for John Townsend, our good friend and a marvellous thief-taker. He has been with the Bow Street Runners for thirty years and knows all the tricks of the trade. However, his arrival may take a day or two and we cannot afford to lose any time over this urgent matter.'

Pausing he looked at Tam intently. 'As a lawyer we believe you to have some knowledge in the matter of criminal-taking.'

Before Tam could think of a suitable response, the prince added as an afterthought: 'As you may require a certain amount of money to make matters more effective, we will provide you with suitable coinage. It is our wish in the absence of John Townsend and, until he arrives, that you abandon your plans to continue your journey and remain here in Brighton. You may proceed with the investigation tomorrow morning.'

Tam bowed. For 'wish', he had already read 'command'.

Chapter Eleven

Much to his surprise, perhaps assisted by the remaining contents of the jug of wine by his bedside, Tam slept soundly, untroubled by either his multiple bruises sustained in the carriage accident or the future of his time-quest. In particular, how he was to return to his own time by the exact same spot at which he had entered the world of Regency Brighton.

*   *   *

He was awakened by the curtains being drawn, the bright sun of another pleasant summer morning, with birds singing lustily in the garden and the silent footman bearing breakfast on a tray. In his train was a servant carrying the cleaned, repaired and generally restored clothes Tam had been wearing as he leapt out of the carriage hurtling down the embankment on the Lewes Road.

Realising that he would have been as helpless to deal with shaving via an open razor as an old-fashioned sword, with results no doubt equally catastrophic, he was greatly relieved by the appearance of a valet bearing warm towels who, bowing, indicated that this task would be his to perform.

Tam accepted gladly and, admiring the man's dexterity, he was soon shaved and dressed, giving some thought meanwhile to where he should begin his investigations into the missing Stuart Sapphire. Weighing the light contents of the purse he had received from the Prince Regent, about two guineas in coin, he calculated that it was enough to provide food and so forth around Brighton for a few days, but certainly quite inadequate to continue that mythical journey into London he had invented. Or, more important, to get him back along the coast to where the dreaded hulks were moored.

This meagre recompense for his services suggested a shrewd assurance that he was neatly trapped or detained during His Royal Highness's pleasure, a sinister overtone. However, it did not take much imagination to realise that the Stuart Sapphire would no longer be in the Pavilion precincts. Whoever had killed the marchioness to obtain it would have decided it prudent not to linger, and at this moment the jewel might be changing hands in London and lost forever to its royal owner.

Remembering his conversation with Beau Brummell, it occurred to Tam that the thief might have in mind a purchaser close to the royal circle, someone who knew its value in the thriving underworld that had grown around the Marine Pavilion.

Having had it described by the prince in some detail as a large, dark blue stone, oval in shape, one inch wide by one and a half inches long, in a thin gold frame, it was striking enough for immediate recognition and, as a gemstone only, it was certainly of less monetary value than the precious gems overlooked by the thief. Its value must lie in its ancient royal associations with the Crown, which would therefore limit the kind of purchaser set on acquiring it.

The more Tam thought, the more certain he became that the known facts indicated that this was no ordinary theft. The dead marchioness, he did not doubt, had had a role to play but was now silenced forever.

The next step was how to get an introduction to the criminal fraternity. That presented a problem. His clothes were modest enough for an upper servant and, looking out of the window, he noticed gardeners at work. A rather unkempt fellow was busy with the roses. His appearance suggested that he might have some knowledge of the less affluent side of Brighton life.

Tam hurried along the royal apartments' corridors, past the ante-rooms, wardrobe and library, where the prince received ministers and conducted official business. Down the grand staircase and across the hall with its continuation of the Pavilion's elegant Chinese theme of wallpaper and decoration, in particular a quantity of large vases from the Ming dynasty. Without being challenged by the inscrutable line of guards, he emerged at the front door and circumnavigated the building until he found his way back to the rose garden.

Opening the conversation with the unkempt gardener with a cheerful 'good day' and adding favourable comments about rose-growing, about which he knew absolutely nothing, he said:

'Ah yes, the very jewels of the garden, are they not? Which reminds me, I am a stranger here and eager to purchase a trinket for a lady. A bargain you know, not too costly,' he added with a knowing wink.

The man barely looked up from his pruning knife. 'A trinket sir, what would that be?'

Tam muttered something about earrings while the man now regarded him, frowning suspiciously. 'I know nothing about such bargains,' he said sharply, 'but there are plenty of shops over yonder—' pointing in the direction of North Street and the Steine. 'Some of them might be able to help you,' he added and turning his back on Tam he returned briskly to his pruning task.

Taking the hint, Tam headed in the direction the gardener had indicated and, after getting thoroughly lost and confused in a maze of twisting lanes, to his enormous relief he found himself outside the Old Ship Inn, which he had visited earlier with Mr Brummell.

Pausing to read a plaque proudly informing visitors that in 1651 a former landlord, Nicholas Tettersell, had been instrumental in arranging the escape of Charles II to France on his coal brig *Surprise*, twenty years later at the Restoration, it was renamed the *Royal Escape*.

Presuming the present landlord shared royalist sympathies, Tam stepped into the gloomy interior from the brightness outside to be confronted by a young lad with short curls. A countenance familiar and one he would long remember.

'Jem! Is it you?' he gasped, delighted at this encounter. 'I have been so worried about you—how did you escape?'

There was no response, only a quick glance, a look of astonishment and terror as the boy slipped past him and darted out into the street.

'Jem! Wait!' Tam yelled and rushed after him. But the boy was even faster moving than he was. The street was deserted and he had vanished into a maze of lanes. Jem, the only link with his arrival in Brighton. And he had lost sight of him.

Tam stood there helpless and stamped his foot angrily. 'Of all the thankless little wretches! I saved his life. Damn him!' Not even a whisper of acknowledgement or gratitude for having saved him from the hulks and from drowning. And what about an explanation for those mysterious smugglers, so keen to rescue the lad that they had thrown Tam back into the sea to drown, after hitting him over the head just to make sure.

While he stood at the door of the inn, frustrated and fuming, he was aware of a shadow at his side. The genial landlord, flicking a duster idly and regarding him with considerable curiosity.

'Something I can do for you, sir?'

Tam swung round to face him. 'That lad who has just rushed out. He works for you? When did you engage him?'

The landlord smiled slyly and regarded him stolidly. 'He came to us through friends. A little young perhaps but recommended as being honest.'

Honest? So he knew nothing of Jem's thieving activities which had landed him on the convict ship with a sentence of transportation to the Colonies.

The landlord gave him a sideways glance, a sigh. 'I doubt that he will be staying long with us. He will soon move on.' A grin. 'To better things, if you get my drift.'

Tam continued to stare at him and he shrugged. 'Too refined, by far. However, sir, if your tastes lie in that direction, there are

128

many more available in the area. Maybe not so pretty or so well-spoken as young Jem.'

And Tam did indeed get the landlord's drift. Perhaps by association with Beau Brummell, whose sexual proclivities seemed doubtful, he was being offered Jem as a male child prostitute.

Speechless for a moment, he turned on his heel and stamped out of the door, overwhelmed by fury with Jem and disgust with the landlord's preposterous assumptions, obliterating even the purpose of his visit—information that might lead to the recovery of the Stuart Sapphire.

'Damn him, damn him and damn the Old Ship too,' he muttered under his breath as, head down, he walked through a tangle of lanes regardless of direction. Tam was trying to sort out how it was that young Jem had managed in the two days since the smugglers took him aboard to find employment in the inn. A remarkable child indeed, this worldly little pickpocket.

He was walking fast, too fast for leisurely Brighton's shadowy lanes, and he cannoned straight into a middle-aged lady emerging from a haberdasher's shop. A scream and her bundles flew in all directions, including her parasol. Her hat flew off and was rescued just in time by the maid at her heels, who shouted indignantly at Tam.

He apologised, and helped gather together

the packages which the maid snatched from him angrily.

Bowing low, again those apologies and, as the lane was too narrow for a carriage, he said weakly: 'May I be permitted to see you both safe home, ma'am?'

The lady was stout but undoubtedly comely, and despite a bosom that was more than ample, she was not unattractive. Expecting an indignant refusal, a tirade of abuse, to his surprise the lady, her balance restored, her gown and hat set to rights, rewarded him with a radiant smile.

'We would be grateful, young sir. It is only a step away—Steine House.'

She continued to regard him as if pleased—which she was—by the sudden apparition on a rather dull shopping occasion of an extremely presentable young man. The kind of young man she had never encountered before. Someone strange, new and interesting, quite out of place in the Brighton she knew so well. There was an air about him she longed to explore.

Tam looked at her quickly. There was something familiar about her too. He had seen a painting, quite famous. Equally entranced, he wanted to know more.

'As there is no one to introduce us,' she held out a firm but dainty small hand, 'and as I am quite old enough to be your mother, there is no indelicacy involved.' She added sternly: 'I am Mrs Maria Fitzherbert.'

Tam bowed, murmured his name. So this was the Prince Regent's legal wife, a twice-widowed commoner and a Roman Catholic, whom all the trouble had been about in 1785 and, quite suddenly, he understood perfectly what the history books had missed. It was there before him. Chemistry was a word not yet invented but Maria Fitzherbert had it all, that rare sexual allure, ageless, untouched by time.

He guessed she was past fifty but, well-treated with respect and a measure of happiness, she would still be devastating at seventy. For this strange enchantment had nothing at all to do with youth and physical beauty. Quite plain women often had it, to the envy of others who had whispered down the ages: 'Can't see what he sees in her. She's quite old really and so ordinary-looking.'

*　　　*　　　*

The short distance traversed along narrow lanes behind a scowling maid protecting her mistress made conversation impossible, but Tam realised delightedly that he was to have his chance of further acquaintance.

At the steps of Steine House, where he expected to be politely dismissed, Mrs Fitzherbert turned with that radiant smile and said: 'Thank you for escorting me, Mr Eildor.'

Then, head on side: 'You are from Scotland, are you not? At least, you sound like a Scotchman.'

Tam bowed and she nodded: 'His Royal Highness speaks highly of you.'

Tam was somewhat taken aback by this considering that he had only arrived two days ago, when, as if correctly guessing his thoughts, she continued: 'I must confess that news runs like wildfire through Brighton, every piece of gossip takes wings and flies through the air.'

Pausing she wagged a finger at him: 'And you, sir, are in danger of becoming a local celebrity already. Snatched from the sea, the only survivor of a sinking ship. What a drama!'

Smiling, she waited for comment, but Tam could think of none.

'Perhaps you would care to have a dish of tea with me, if you are not already engaged.'

Tam bowed. 'I would be honoured, madam.'

Following her into the house, all his anger and frustration at being ignored by the wretched boy whose life he had saved at almost the cost of his own, vanished. And so did the urgent reason for his visit to the town; to track down the thief of the sapphire and the murderer of the Marchioness of Creeve.

He was enjoying a delicious moment of being shown into the salon, a large sunny room with three handsome windows overlooking the sea. Its walls were adorned by

132

charming silhouettes of Mrs Fitzherbert's many friends, side tables here and there were stacked with fine ornaments, while a splendidly ornate French clock bearing a Greek god perched precariously on horseback added a melodious chime in to the delightful room.

Surrounded by a wealth of precious objects on every side, Tam took a seat on a handsome sofa, while he waited for her to return from removing her cloak. That did not take long, and she took a seat alongside him, while her maid attended to the ritual of tea and dainty biscuits.

'His Royal Highness tells me that you are from Edinburgh, Mr Eildor. He is devoted to all things Scottish, particularly to the lives of the Stuart kings. As he did not inherit the throne from them, but in rather less than happy circumstances, I must confess I am somewhat taken aback by this obsession.'

Pausing, she smiled fondly as if referring to a small boy, then, suddenly endearingly informal, she added wistfully: 'You know he takes great fancies to people and causes and is utterly ruled by them, can talk of nothing else. Indeed, every conversation is diverted to include what is for him a new discovery.' She stretched out a hand and patted Tam's knee. 'Like yourself, Mr Eildor—you are the latest in a long line.'

Then, sadly, she sighed, narrowing her eyes

and gazing out at the sea's far horizon as if it might have an answer. A shrug, almost a whisper, 'And a short while later, alas, all are forgotten. Just as if they never existed. Discarded like a child's toy.'

Yet she herself had survived after a period of being discarded. The prince would—Tam guessed, seeing the kind of woman she was—return to this his first real love, who had swept her magic over him and was now his dearest friend.

Turning to Tam, she smiled again. Did that little speech contain a warning that the Prince Regent was not entirely to be trusted, he thought, as with a rapid change of subject she talked of the Pavilion.

'During your visit you must be sure to see and enjoy all the wonders, it is an unforgettable experience. His Royal Highness is a connoisseur of art—from all countries, France in particular, although they have long been our enemies and an invasion from just across the Channel is greatly to be feared. But George thinks they are the very greatest artists in every kind of culture. As for China,' she shrugged, 'a strange foreign land indeed, he has little hope of ever visiting it, but their ancient civilisation is always in his mind—'

As she talked so wistfully, Tam looked around, wondering why she then chose to live in surroundings modest by comparison. As if interpreting his thoughts, she said:

'I am unable to live under the same roof as HRH. There are difficulties. My faith forbids divorce and, in the eyes of God, despite Princess Caroline being regarded as his wife and the future Queen of England, I am still his legal wife. We are bound together until death do us part. The marriage was not of my desire, I knew inevitably that the Prince of Wales, as he was then, must make a dynastic union. But he threatened to take his own life if I refused him. I had no option in the matter.'

She paused and shook her head, as if the weight of remembrance was suddenly too heavy. 'Little joy has come of it for either of them. Right from the outset, a coarse and smelly woman and George is so very fastidious about his person. His accounts of her personal lack of cleanliness were unbelievable. He found her very presence intolerable and he was very drunk indeed on their wedding night when, fortunately for him, Princess Charlotte was most probably conceived. He could not bear to sleep with her again. How he wept, poor dear soul, and shuddered at the very idea. A great pity the little princess had not been a prince, then the future of England would have been assured.

'Charlotte is the very image of her father—in every respect, no use denying paternity. A difficult child, who has sadly been used by her own mother as a pawn in the game of politics,

135

and in any spiteful manner calculated to cause suffering or discomfort to her father.'

Tam decided not to mention his encounter with Charlotte and that he had formed some unfavourable ideas of his own, when again, as if reading his mind, she said: 'You will not have had a chance to meet her, of course.'

Tam smiled vaguely. 'We met in the gardens earlier this morning. Her Royal Highness was on the way to the library.'

Mrs Fitzherbert clapped her hands. 'The library. Ah yes, a very bright child indeed. I see that the idea of a princess heading to the library surprised you. But all is not as it seems. This particular library is the social hub of Brighton,' she added, confirming Brummell's statement. 'We all use it, rich and those who would be regarded as rich and noble, anyone who wishes to be regarded as anyone must follow the rules. It is the first place when one arrives to sign the Master of Ceremonies book, to know who is already here and how to get an invitation to the best social events. The Master is formidable, quite stern about his rules and very forbidding. No one takes liberties with that gentleman. As for the princess—'

Pausing, she gave him a quizzical glance. 'But you have met already,' implied that she was eager for his reactions as she went on: 'Ah yes, and I have a feeling that you will have many more encounters with Her Royal

Highness during your short stay.'

She laughed. 'You see, she is at a very vulnerable age, fifteen years old, a difficult time for a princess when parents' thoughts loom towards a marriage that has also suitable political and financial benefits.' She sighed. 'Poor Charlotte is very confused, for she will never know if young men want her for herself, or for the enticement that one day she will be Queen of England.'

Leaning back a little in her chair, she regarded him, smiling. 'I can well imagine how delighted she will be at the prospect of an acquaintance with a very presentable young gentleman, especially on a brief visit from Scotland, one who has become something of a celebrity and who does not fit into any such category.'

Eager to change the subject, Tam asked: 'Have you any children of your own, madam?' The words were out before he realised the implications.

She glanced up at him sadly and whispered: 'Such dear ones must always live in the shadows, in the background of one's life, never to be acknowledged.'

While Tam was trying to work out the significance of what her vague reply implied, a maid entered, curtseyed: 'Mr Brummell is here, madam.'

Mrs Fitzherbert gave an exasperated sigh. 'On the wrong day. How tiresome.' And to

Tam: 'Have you met?'

Tam rose to his feet and bowed. 'We have indeed, madam, and I will not intrude on you further. My thanks for your kind hospitality.'

She held out her hand. 'And mine too for escorting me home so safely. You must come again.'

'You honour me, madam. I would love to see you again.'

She walked with him towards the door. 'Before you leave—promise!'

'I promise.' Again Tam bowed, thinking this was an easy promise to make to such a charming woman as he walked down the steps and returned to the reality of obeying the Prince Regent's command and the business of tracking down a thief and a murderer.

Chapter Twelve

Maria watched him leave from the window. He moved swiftly, lightly, with such grace. A remarkable young man indeed, quite unlike anyone she had ever met, although on consideration there were faint traces in Tam Eildor of the best persons she had ever encountered and those most dear to her.

Confused by her thoughts, she shook her head. The last hour had been a most extraordinary experience. Here she was, a woman discreet on all occasions, dictated by the delicacy of her role in the Prince Regent's life, positively pouring out her heart to a stranger. Not because of his looks alone. Not really the most handsome man she had ever met, but there was something about his eyes perhaps that seemed to look into her soul and invite her trust.

Dear George, always so very much more susceptible than she, small wonder that he was impressed by Tam Eildor. Yet a future king ready to take this young man to his bosom, a nobody, a shipwrecked survivor, was that not odd? Or was it just the novelty? That sort of thing had a definite appeal to George. Or the fact that Mr Eildor was from Edinburgh and George yearned towards all things Scottish and French, despite the bloody deeds that declared them England's enemies.

Remembering her conversation with Mr Eildor, she frowned darkly at her reflection in the mirror. Was it possible that the Prince Regent nursed feelings of guilt since the Hanoverians had swept away the Stuarts, ignoring their hereditary Divine Right of kings? No, that did not sound like George either.

She sighed. Politics were too deep; not for her, never had been. She found them very confusing indeed, the daily parliamentary battles, the constant sway of power between Whigs and Tories. George had given up in despair trying to explain who was in and who was out, and why? Just as well perhaps that she had never been in any real danger of becoming Queen of England, much as George would have fought parliament and all comers to have her at his side. But she shook her head. She believed one had to be bred to the role, it had to be in the blood.

As her maid did her hair, she found herself thinking rather fearfully that the change in George had begun with the wreck of the *Royal Stuart*. For the past two nights he had slept with her at Steine House. She was used to him staying occasionally but not two nights in succession with the promise of more to come, since he had hinted that all was not going as planned at the Pavilion.

She had closed her mind to the reason for this, seeing that such matters usually concerned the latest in his string of mistresses, although she pretended not to know or care that she had long ago ceased to provide any sexual novelty for the Prince Regent. Even in the heyday of their marriage, he had never been faithful, but he still liked to come to her sometimes and lie in her arms. There he would sleep—and snore dreadfully—with his head on her bosom.

She smiled. He did so love a good bosom, that had always been his boast, and the larger the better. He never did care for flat-chested women.

140

She sighed. They were just like an old married couple, comfortable with each other. But last night was different. She felt that he wanted to confide in her but could not find the words. She knew him well enough to guess that something was preying dreadfully on his mind. He was like a young boy afraid to confess his first love, his first imagined wrong-doing.

When she asked him was anything amiss, he looked at her gravely for an instant. His lips trembled then he shook his head. Quite frankly, she was relieved. His legal wife in the eyes of God, she did not encourage confidences, finding it very indelicate to be the recipient of intimate confidences regarding each new mistress who fleetingly occupied his bed. There had been so many she had forgotten their names and, to be honest, she had to admit she was also jealous, especially as she was losing her looks and growing old and stout. How could an ageing woman hope to compete with young and beautiful women who threw themselves so eagerly at George? Although he himself was no beauty, extremely fat and he had gout, but under the Truefitt nut-brown wigs, worn now for many years, his face remained childishly petulant with traces of his once-good looks. But somehow in a man, in a prince who was one day quite soon to be King of England, no woman seemed to mind that in the least.

Young and even older than herself, all were eager to slip between the sheets of his bed, eager to be his lover, ready to meet his demands however outrageous, since there was much to be gained by doing exactly as he wished, noblewomen ready to behave like the vilest whores and never bat an eyelid, for favours in the way of exquisite jewels and, for the more fortunate, a lucrative income, an insurance for the future when his interest waned in their power to arouse him and excite his lust.

She frowned. Her thoughts flew back to Tam Eildor. There was something amiss in the Pavilion and she felt certain it dated from his arrival.

George was afraid, she could smell fear on him like some stale perfume, and that was why he had arrived so unexpectedly at her home last night, and before leaving this morning he had asked her if it would be convenient for him to sleep at Steine House while the alterations at the Pavilion were in hand.

She had regarded this request with astonishment. Could it be possible that he had tired of the elegance and luxury of his royal apartments, just as he tired of his mistress of the moment? Maria was also taken aback seeing as there were many other beautiful rooms in the Pavilion. However, she did not complain, always glad of his company, docile as the legal wife, that role in which she regarded herself.

Again the image of Tam Eildor came to the forefront of her mind. Had she been wrong about him? Was his strangeness perhaps a little sinister? And George was so impressed by a nobody, as once he had been taken with Beau Brummell who was to have such an influence on his life.

The grandson of a household servant, his father had risen to become Private Secretary to Lord North, and Beau, seventeen years younger than Prince George, had been a mere cornet in the Dragoons when they first met.

Maria sighed, remembering he was waiting downstairs to be received. She rang for the servant. 'Ask Mr Brummell to be so good as to take a seat in the small parlour. I shall be with him directly.'

As she completed her toilette she felt rather irritated. This was an unexpected informal visit or he had mistaken the day. Perhaps there was some urgent piece of gossip he could not wait until tomorrow to pass on to her. For spreading some naughty piece of scandal, some shocking rumour, no woman was Beau's equal.

*   *   *

In this case it so happened that Brummell had seen Tam Eildor sitting by her window. Overcome with curiosity, envy and jealousy,

143

he had quite a tale to tell.

'Madam,' he bowed, kissing her hand.

'You are a day early,' said Maria reproachfully.

A profuse apology. Was his visit inconvenient? A look of astonishment did not fool Maria. 'Now that you are here, pray do be seated.'

Brummell did so, leaning forward eagerly in his chair. 'You have a new admirer, madam?'

So that was it. She smiled. 'More of a brief acquaintance, Mr Brummell. You have met Mr Eildor?'

'Quite so. Mr Eildor is His Royal Highness's new protégé.'

She looked at him quickly. The curl of his lip spoke volumes. It told her that he did not like him. His opinion promised to be both interesting and revealing.

'So?' she said.

Brummell shrugged. 'I should like to know more about Mr Eildor than such scanty information he has seen fit to give us.'

'Information, Mr Brummell? In what way?'

Brummell shook his head and sighed, the very picture of regret. 'I fear, madam, that this—gentleman—is not genuine. He is not all he pretends to be.'

'A spy, you mean?' she whispered. That idea had not occurred to her.

'Quite so, madam. I fear there is a distinct possibility as he is journeying to London.'

Looks were exchanged. The same thought in both their minds. A spy from the camp of the Princess of Wales, George's estranged wife now living permanently in London.

Brummell sighed. 'I fear that His Royal Highness is too trusting.'

Maria sighed, fearing that Brummell, fast losing his place in George's favours, regarded any newcomer as a further threat to usurp him. He was thus eager as any jealous courtesan to inflame the prince's suspicions.

'Do you not agree, madam,' he asked, 'that there is something rather—odd, about this young man?'

'Odd?' Indeed there was, but nothing she could find a word for, so she took refuge in: 'He is extremely good-looking, is he not?'

Brummell laughed harshly. 'Agreed, but he is not one of us. Distinctly not.'

Maria could not deny that. He did not belong to the noble class or the aristocracy at all, the kind of royal circles they moved in. He was quite, quite different. Yet not a common man, either.

Brummell placed the fingers of both hands neatly together and gave her a profound look. 'I think, madam, that we would be well advised to investigate Mr Eildor's background most scrupulously. I have friends in Edinburgh. And if he is a spy—' He shrugged, ardently hoping that would be the case. What a coup! That would surely reinstate him in the prince's regard.

Maria's eyes widened at that. Was he hinting that some secret society, working to undermine the present regime, had sent a spy who threatened dear George, possibly even an assassin? And she remembered uncomfortably that dear Thomas Fitzherbert, her second husband, had been head of an ancient Catholic family who were among the first Catholics to forsake the exiled Stuarts and openly declare their allegiance to the Hanoverians.

As fearful thoughts of espionage and regicide rushed through her mind, Brummell continued: 'An upstart, madam, worming his way into the prince's confidence. A paid spy.'

Was Mr Eildor blackmailing George? Did that account for the feeling she had that George was afraid of something, terrified and unable to talk to her about it? Was his pretended obsession with this new acquaintance masking some deadly threat to the very future of England?

Suddenly she was ashamed, remembering how she had confided in Mr Eildor. Then another terrifying thought occurred to her about his strange luminous eyes. Was he also a mesmerist? And she recalled the evening she had spent in London at the Duchess of Abercorn's supper party. The chief guest was a disciple of Franz Mesmer, the Austrian physician who had used a secret power called animal magnetism by which he could read people's minds and make them do his will.

Maria remembered how he had sat opposite her at the table and, holding her gaze, she had whispered certain secrets of her early life. Unable to resist those strange hypnotic eyes, she had tried to banish the evening afterwards, and had almost succeeded in doing so until now when as she decided it was the mesmerist whose eyes reminded her of Mr Eildor's and held the same strange power.

What had she done? Trembling inwardly, she decided not to share this piece of information with Mr Brummell.

*   *   *

In the Pavilion it was observed by those close to the Prince Regent that he was not himself, and had not been himself, in fact, since the drama of the shipwreck two days ago. Short-tempered, inclined to be forgetful and intensely irritable, even his daily sea bathing was affected. His behaviour had not been his usual roguish, full of fun, shrieks of merriment and boyish glee, playful splashings on bystanders. Instead it was a solemn ritual affair taken more from duty than pleasure.

Around him heads were shaken, there were a few behind-hand whispers too. A tiff with Mrs Fitz perhaps, with whom he had spent the night after the shipwreck, then back at the

147

Pavilion next morning, he had cast a lacklustre eye on the uniforms required for the day. Unable to make his usual prompt decision, and far from his excitement at dressing up for the day, he had stood biting his lip and frowning, his thoughts clearly elsewhere. Very irritable too, shouting angrily at the guiding suggestions of his valets, he had stamped out in a fury.

Lord Henry, who was friendly to everyone in the condescending manner that was familiar to them, nodded vaguely. He could hardly be quizzed about the prince's behaviour, since everyone in the Pavilion, and quite a few beyond it, knew he was yet another favoured royal bastard.

As for the other groom, Lord Percy, he didn't talk much to anyone, kept his own counsel. Very superior, he was. No one knew much about him except that with a wife and children conveniently stowed away in a handsome mansion in Surrey, it had got about that he had a penchant for lower-class female servants and found a maid on her knees scrubbing a floor quite irresistible.

Now, much to his chagrin, Lord Percy was informed that only Henry was to accompany the prince into the royal bedroom.

Closing the door, the prince looked around his once favourite room with distaste. He regarded that massive panelled French bedstead, once so comfortable with its five mattresses, white satin sheets and feather bolster, its five cloud-like pillows, its fine blankets, once the highlight of his nights, and shook his head.

Never, never could he sleep in that bed again, its luxury destroyed forever by memories of the marchioness's murder.

Without a word being said, Henry understood. He did not possess a great imagination, but even crossing the threshold and remembering what he had seen made him shudder. He was not in the least surprised when the prince said:

'We have been thinking, Henry, and we have decided that it would be more convenient to change our sleeping quarters. Have our bedroom downstairs, next to the dining room.' Pausing, he managed a croaky, unconvincing chuckle. 'Easier to fall into bed while the wine is rosy, don't you agree?'

Henry, who would have agreed to anything said by his royal father, nodded nervously. It was becoming increasingly difficult, a considerable effort requiring the services of several of the strongest servants, to elevate the prince's increasingly corpulent frame up the splendid staircase, after a supper consisting of sixteen courses and several bottles of wine before the inevitable final attack on the brandy.

His smile was genuine as the prince waved a vague hand around. 'We will make this the

149

guest bedroom in future.'

Henry cleared his throat, asked somewhat timorously. 'Sire, the stair—into the garden, I mean?'

The prince smiled sadly and shook his head. 'Means will be found, dear lad,' and, tapping the side of his nose significantly, a conspiratorial return to happier days, he winked and repeated: 'Means will be found when necessity arises.'

'Sire, which room would you wish to have prepared while the alterations are being made?' Henry asked.

'Fear not, Henry, arrangements have already been made. Mrs Fitzherbert has been most accommodating. We shall sleep at Steine House—with our legal wife,' he added primly.

Henry withdrew and the prince stood alone, staring at the bed and reliving that dreadful moment he had discovered Sarah Creeve, her body obscenely naked in the cold light of day.

Not only dead, that would have been bad enough—but murdered!

Clutching the bedpost, he groaned. Dear God, would he ever be allowed to forget or would he be haunted forever, that terrible sight indelibly printed on his eyes.

If only her body could be discovered where it lay far away from the Pavilion on the Lewes Road. But there was one last secret that would be laid to rest with her. The identity of her killer who had also stolen the Stuart Sapphire.

150

Chapter Thirteen

Walking through Steine Lane after leaving Mrs Fitzherbert, Tam resumed his investigation into possible shops where stolen goods might be exchanged. He emerged in Market Street, opposite the workhouse, whose occupants had exchanged the cheerless interior for the luxury of being allowed to sit outside in warm sunshine to mend the fishermen's nets, and pick oakum under the watchful eyes of warders armed with stout sticks. That they were prisoners in an institution with little chance of making a bid for freedom was also evident from their brown uniforms.

Beyond Market Street, a glimpse of a scattering of houses on the hilly slopes to the west of the city. Even at that distance they looked little more than hovels, the homes of the poor who knew a lot about pawnshops and the struggle to keep alive. To such unfortunates any comparison with the wild extravagances of life in the Marine Pavilion was an obscenity.

As he walked into the shadowy lanes where his journey had been cut short by his encounter with Maria Fitzherbert, Tam kept a sharp lookout for Jem, rehearsing some harsh words for that young lad as, still bristling with anger and hurt pride, he wondered what excuses would be on offer when they finally met. They had better be good, he thought, diving into the nearest jeweller's shop.

The excuse about the trinket was thin and the shopkeeper soon lost patience when Tam declined to purchase any of the tempting and exceedingly expensive earrings on display. The goldsmith's shop next door exuded such an air of respectability, as well as two ladies dressed in the height of fashion and heavily perfumed that, approaching the counter, Tam lost his nerve, muttered something about the wrong shop and beat a hasty retreat.

The response to his request regarding inexpensive earrings at two further but less assuming shops was equally frustrating but he knew of no other way except the direct approach: Have you by any chance been offered the Stuart Sapphire?' He did not imagine that would meet with much success.

Staring in another shop window and wondering where to go next, he saw reflected in the glass a boy hurrying along the other side of the street.

'Jem!' he shouted.

The boy turned, saw him and ran.

'Jem. Wait!'

But once again Jem took to his heels and darted down a side street and Tam was almost knocked down by a horseman as he tried to cross the road. The man cursed him, as did the occupants of the carriage he was escorting, travelling close behind.

By the time he reached the corner, Jem was almost out of sight, rushing up the hilly street. Tam followed as swiftly as he could to the consternation of pedestrians emerging in his path. As dogs added their angry barks, snapping at his heels, he found himself in an area where the shops were fewer. Ahead lay the poorer houses he had observed earlier.

And there was Jem staring in to a solitary shop window.

Tam rushed over, seized him by the shoulder.

'Got you—at last.'

The boy turned round. Yelling loudly he struggled to free himself from Tam's relentless grip.

Tam looked again and panicked. This wasn't Jem, the only faint similarity was in the shabby clothes. The boy he had accosted was a stranger—and a terrified one.

'Help, help,' he screamed. 'Lemme go, you brute.'

Tam did as requested and, apologising profusely, hurried across the road, narrowly evading being seized by what looked like an indignant mob surging in his direction, urged on by the boy he had accosted.

At last, on the very edge of the town, he found shelter in a tired-looking inn where he ordered a pint of ale, keeping a sharp eye on the door and the window as he drank. The landlord showed no interest in him, and Tam noticed on the opposite side of the road a terrace of identical cottages.

To his question, the landlord said: 'Them's Crown Gardens, sir. Very handsome they are with their own little plots. Better class establishment for this area, they are, built by the prince for servants from the Pavilion and from the royal stables.'

As Tam, refreshed, looked across, he wished he had some excuse to investigate that respectable line of cottages as the thought occurred to him: Had Jem, for it was certainly Jem who ran away from him in the first place, been making his way to the Crown Gardens?

And was it possible that there was some link between Jem and the Marine Pavilion? If that was so, then it was even more important that Tam track him down.

True, there had been little time to find out much about Jem when they met on the convict ship—except for a strange feeling. He was missing something important that he should remember. The fact that the boy's story did not quite ring true and that he seemed remarkably refined and well-spoken for a convicted felon. If only there had been a chance of discovering what circumstances had brought him to the dire necessity of stealing a loaf of bread.

It was a new and interesting theory as he

made his way back through the town, deciding that after the rebuffs he had received regarding his search for cheap earrings for a non-existent lady, he had better rethink the whole procedure and come up with a more positive approach to finding the missing sapphire.

Lured by the warm sunshine in the Pavilion gardens, he decided to linger, certain that his powers of concentration would do better out of doors, especially without possibilities of encountering the Prince Regent and having to confess his lack of success.

Looking for a suitable seat, he took stock of his surroundings. This elegant Promenade Grove had once been open to the public. Acclaimed as a smaller version of the Vauxhall Gardens in London, it was now part of the royal estate, to which the public had only rare access.

Such a pity, thought Tam, this almost deserted park with its flowers, shrubs and grove of elms, the only tall trees that he had seen so far in Brighton. He found a shady seat and closed his eyes. As he was drifting into sleep a female voice said:

'Ha, is it not Mr Eildor, and all alone?'

Tam opened one eye.

'Pray, may I join you, sir?'

The newcomer was Princess Charlotte and Tam groaned inwardly although he managed to stretch a smile across his face. He stood up and, bowing, offered her the seat.

'Nay, sir. I would not disturb you. The seat is large enough—for the two of us,' she added archly.

'Your governess, Highness,' Tam protested, indicating the shadow at the princess's side, but her hand was firm upon his arm.

'Pray, be seated, Mr Eildor. Lady de Clifford is not permitted to sit in the royal presence,' she added, settling herself down and edging close to Tam while the unfortunate governess stationed herself at a discreet distance a few feet away.

Beaming on Tam, her bare arm resting rather too intimately against his own, she whispered, 'We can talk freely, Mr Eildor. Lady de Clifford is rather deaf. She will not admit it and ear trumpets are so undignified and so ageing.'

Tam was very conscious of that lady's discomfiture, as she hovered ever nearer, trying also to keep an eye on all comers. As the princess urged him to tell her about himself, and edged even closer on the small seat, he could almost feel the quivering anxiety of the governess.

And with good reason. Deaf she might be but her eyesight was excellent and should any report be made to the Prince Regent regarding his daughter's outrageous conduct, she would be held responsible.

Tam sympathised as, unable to restrain

herself, she laid a warning hand on Charlotte's shoulder and said: 'His Royal Highness, your father, is approaching.'

The sight of his daughter on a secluded seat talking to Tam could only convey one thing to the prince and that was the dread word: Assignation.

Tam sprang to his feet, he had no desire to be found in any compromising situation with the heiress to the throne. Swift and highly unpleasant visions sped through his mind; the Tower of London looming exceeding large.

Escape might not be too late as the prince, who perhaps did not have such excellent eyesight, was in deep conversation with the man at his side and had not yet observed his daughter's indiscretion.

Charlotte was furious, she clung to Tam's arm. 'Please, Mr Eildor, do remain seated. Pray tell me about yourself—we have much to talk about.'

But Tam bowing, remained standing and took the cowardly opportunity of distancing himself a few feet away.

And not a moment too soon. The prince and his companion were on the other side of an ornate flower bed.

He had been observed. The prince paused in his conversation, glanced across and gestured to Tam to join them. Tam sighed. He was saved. No longer seated at Charlotte's side, her father would presume that Mr Eildor had just encountered the princess as he strolled through the gardens and was merely exchanging a polite greeting. At least that was what Tam most earnestly hoped and that this encounter would not be remembered and used in evidence against him.

'Ah, Mr Eildor!' And Tam wove his way over a rather tricky set piece of flowers surrounded by miniature box hedging which, maze-like, needed very careful negotiation of hopping between the rows.

At last he reached the prince and his companion, a small rotund fellow wearing a rather shabby overcoat that reached to his ankles. On his head, perched at a jaunty angle, was a tall stovepipe hat, no doubt intended to add some impressive inches to his height.

'Mr Townsend, it is our pleasure to present Mr Tam Eildor.' The prince beamed on Tam who gave an inward sigh of relief. Presumably he had not noticed or failed to find any significance in the glimpse of his daughter almost literally throwing herself at Tam's feet.

'Mr Eildor is an Edinburgh lawyer, most accomplished in methods relating to the apprehension of criminals of all description.'

Tam bowed a little uncomfortably at this fulsome addition to his fictional life story, while shaking hands with Townsend, from whose countenance heavily adorned by facial hair, tawny in colour and growing without restraint, a shrewd pair of eyes peered, as if from behind a hedge.

Raising the tall hat revealed a lion-like mane of tawny hair and this extraordinary leonine image was confirmed by hands which, as he walked, were habitually clasped together behind his back, where they waggled expressively, for all the world like a lion's attenuated tail.

'Mr Townsend is a well known thief-taker, a Bow Street officer who has struck terror into the very hearts of London's vilest criminals by hanging the bodies of murderers on a gibbet— a law we firmly believe should be retained.'

And turning to Townsend, he said: 'Pray, tell Mr Eildor how you once gave the magistrate Sir William Scott an excellent piece of advice on the subject.'

Townsend had a moment of looking bashful before saying proudly: 'I told Sir William there were a couple of men hanging near the Thames where the sailors went up and down and one asked: "Pray what are those poor fellows there for?" His companion said: "We will go and ask." They did so and were told: 'Those two men are hung and gibbeted for murdering His Majesty's revenue officers," and so that keeps the warning alive.'

'Capital, capital,' said the prince. 'An excellent deterrent, don't you agree, Mr Eildor?'

Tam considered it very barbaric indeed and was saved the necessity of making any comment as the prince continued: 'We are sure—certain sure, that the pair of you will find, without the slightest difficulty, the vile creature who stole a valuable piece of our Coronation Crown and, no doubt, a like fate can be arranged for them. Good day, gentlemen.'

And with an almost gleeful laugh, he turned on his heel and whistling under his breath, walked away with Henry and Percy who had been hovering at a discreet distance, leaving the newly introduced sleuths in an awkward silence.

How much, if anything, Tam wondered, had Townsend been told of the events leading up to the Stuart Sapphire's disappearance, in particular, the murder of the Marchioness of Creeve?

Chapter Fourteen

As they walked towards the gate of the gardens leading to the Promenade, Townsend was considering this young Edinburgh lawyer, his shrewd gaze born of many years of experience where his judgement of a person had tipped the delicate balance between life and death.

It was Townsend's proud boast to his colleagues that he could sum up a man's character within ten minutes of his company. He would never confess, however, even to himself, that his assessments of a man's standing in society were always accurate. Sometimes, regretfully, they fell far short of the mark and on such occasions the innocent went down with the guilty.

He continued to smile warily at Tam. Now, this young cove was unlikely to fit into the bracket of bawd or pickpocket. Indeed, there were several categories of criminal he could cross without hesitation off his mental list but what about a confidence trickster? Had he lured HRH, who alas was no fine judge of character, into trusting him? That remained in the equation.

A very presentable young man but deuced difficult to slot into any category. In all his years in London, where he had encountered every sort and condition of men and women in every stratum of society, Townsend had never met a cove like this one before. Quite extraordinary eyes. Some ancient Highland strain perhaps?

He sighed. HRH had taken to him, right from that first meeting. However, HRH was always one for the novelty of an interesting newcomer. But they were mostly female, Townsend decided wryly.

As the conversation rattled innocently back and forth between them about weather and the splendid gardens, Townsend was

161

reminded that HRH was particularly partial to Scotland, well aware of his hero worship of the former Stuart kings that the Hanoverians had ousted.

In truth, he found this character quirk quite remarkable. Especially with regard to the bosom friendship of the prince's early years with his uncle, the notorious Duke of Cumberland, better known and despised as 'Butcher' Cumberland, even in France where many Highlanders and their families had sought refuge after the rout of Prince Charles Edward Stuart at Culloden in 1746. Cumberland, not content with the slaughter of the Clans on the battlefield and the English victory, had shown no mercy to any survivors. His policy was to annihilate the Highlands, wreaking vengeance on any who had supported the Jacobite cause.

The Stuarts had not been lucky, and one of the prince's favourite jewels, proudly displayed each day on his many uniforms: the saltire worn by Charles I at his execution. Even for a man from whom extremes of sentiment had long been extinguished, this did seem not only like poor taste, but also suggested tempting fate.

He was aware that the rather formal conversation had drifted into silence. 'Ah, Mr Eildor,' he said and Tam was pleased to note that his voice held a lion-like roar that was in keeping with his physical appearance.

'Now tell me about yourself. How came you to be so far from home?'

This was the second such command Tam had had within the last half-hour, the moment of untruth he dreaded. A blackbird scuttled across his path with a warning cry. Was it a signal to be heeded? since in his experience lies, however white, innocent or face-saving, still had an unhappy habit of weaving themselves into a web, a positive maze in which both entrance and exit are hopelessly confused, and from which only Ariadne's thread might offer release.

'Did I say so-and-so or was it this-and-that?' To be an accomplished liar required an excellent memory.

And while keeping to his sole-survivor story was going to be hard enough, without furnishing any details of being a passenger on the *Royal Stuart*, a true explanation of how he reached Brighton in 1811 from planet Earth in 2250 would probably immediately get him clapped into Bedlam. A raving lunatic in that human circus to be viewed as entertainment, something the whole family could enjoy on Sunday afternoon outings.

Realising he must tread warily indeed, he gave the usual response, which he was almost beginning to believe himself, but vague enough to allow for frequent changes. Legal business in Plymouth and then to London to sort out a family claim for a certain rich

163

Scottish laird.

'Indeed!' Townsend interrupted, the gleam in his eye demanding more details.

But Tam shook his head, indicating that his rich client must remain nameless. 'Discretion, sir, a matter of discretion. You understand?'

'I do. I do indeed,' was the reply as Townsend, dragged away by royal command from a particularly gruesome multiple murder investigation in London, remembered a recent stunning tale of indiscretion in high society that in lesser mortals would have made their hair stand on end and put a friseur out of business for a fortnight.

Townsend's questions regarding Edinburgh were acute and knowledgeable, especially as he had never been there; as an avid reader, his information came entirely from books. Even in their short acquaintance, Tam realised that it would be a serious mistake to underestimate John Townsend as the brain inside that leonine head was continually in operation, observing and assimilating information, then carefully pigeonholing even the smallest detail for future use.

Tam was correct in his assessment, for behind the bluff geniality there were shrewd questions and calculations from which Townsend hoped to learn a lot more about Tam than Tam was anxious to reveal. True, he accepted the prosperous Edinburgh lawyer travelling to England on behalf of a rich

Scottish laird but his curiosity about the *Royal Stuart* was more dangerous, especially as Tam had never been to sea.

However, the tale of seasickness and being confined to his cabin was received with sympathetic groans, but Tam was alarmed to discover that among his many youthful experiences, Townsend had served for a short while on a man o'war.

And then, of course, there was that invented business with the privateer pressing all the crew on to their ship. That was a mistake. As a law officer this was of considerable interest to Townsend who wanted all the details so that he could investigate further and put their apprehension into immediate operation.

A privateer! He had not heard of any such working so close to the south-east coast. Quite extraordinary. As a law officer it was his duty to be always vigilant for any criminal activities.

'One must always be on the sharp lookout!' This remark left Tam feeling sardonically that if Townsend were any sharper, he might be in danger of cutting himself with lethal effect, and he was quick to take advantage of a change of subject as a runaway carriage alerted a sudden rush of onlookers.

He sighed with relief as the *Royal Stuart* hazard was safely put aside for the moment. Long before John Townsend's investigations regarding privateers revealed some glaring inaccuracies in Tam Eildor's dramatic story, and aware that such matters might take several weeks or months, he hoped that this particular mission, which was proving very tricky indeed, would soon be over and he would be safely back in his own time.

As they reached the Promenade, more dangerous waters loomed ahead for Tam than the innocent waves of the afternoon tide.

'This piece of royal jewellery that has been stolen. Very impressive and very important.' He rested an earnest gaze on Tam. 'You being from Scotland will be fully aware of its history, of course, regarding HRH's forthcoming coronation.' A pause and a shake of that leonine head. 'Bearing in mind—and we all must bear in mind—the condition of His Majesty's health, and the daily reports are grim indeed, I imagine that event will be sooner rather than later.'

Giving Tam a moment to digest these solemn details, he got to the main point of discussion. 'I take it that you are in HRH's confidence and that you are fully informed of the circumstances surrounding its disappearance.'

Tam nodded, hoping for something between suitably vague yet at the same time knowledgeable, while Townsend stopped, frowning at the sea as if it might leap up and also reveal some dark secrets, and then turned again to Tam.

'A strange coincidence indeed that the thief

chose the time when HRH was absent watching the shipwreck to steal into his apartments. Very astute indeed, considering that others would also be suitably diverted by such a drama.'

A pause for comment; there was none.

Townsend seemed disappointed. 'We would seem to be dealing with a carefully planned operation. My suspicions are that the thief has long been awaiting such an opportunity, and is well aware of HRH's daily routine in intimate detail. What think you of that?'

Tam shrugged. 'He could hardly have anticipated the shipwreck.'

'We see that, we see that. There must have been several occasions each day most carefully mapped when HRH was to be absent, but this was the perfect opportunity. Couldn't be better. Very convenient, very convenient indeed. Shrewd minds at work, Mr Eildor. Has all the marks of a political intrigue—I imagine that has already occurred to you. The Princess of Wales is well-known as a dangerous intriguer.'

Tam wondered anxiously how much Townsend knew and how much, if anything, the prince had confided in him regarding the marchioness's presence in his bed at the time of the robbery. His heart beat a little faster when, in what might have been a singular piece of mind-reading, Townsend continued:

'I have another reason for this visit. My nephew Peter is in the employ of the Marquis of Creeve at Lewes and I am always delighted at the opportunity of seeing the lad. Especially since His Grace and I have become quite acquainted over the years. We have shared many a glass of port over a game of chess together and I have been privileged to be invited to the annual shoot over at the estate.'

He could hardly keep this boastful allusion out of his lion's roar. 'I have been helpful in tracking down malefactors in His Grace's household. Even saw justice done and made an example of a couple of them by a hanging,' he said with considerable satisfaction. 'A splendid gentleman. Friend of HRH, of course, who introduced us. Lovely young second wife. Bit of a scamp, just between us,' he added with a suggestive wink, which Tam ignored with a change of subject by asking politely where Townsend was taking him.

'The first place to look for HRH's missing jewel, Mr Eildor, is in the very dregs of this fine city.' And pausing to gesture towards the Pavilion, 'Twenty-five years since its establishment and already a thriving den of iniquity clings to those splendid walls.

'Mark my words, Mr Eildor, it's a thing of nature, wherever there is royalty, you get a thriving underworld, royal palaces attract them like a dog attracts fleas. They are the Devil's answer to every criminal and wrong-doer in the vicinity. News of their spoils and success spreads like wildfire and lures their fellow rogues down from London who have failed in their evil ways and are looking for a more hopeful and lucrative future.'

Turning from the refreshing sea breeze of the promenade, he looked back towards the town. 'And so let us set forth. We will begin with the obvious places, inns and fence houses and then the flash houses.'

Pausing, he winked at Tam, giving his arm a friendly squeeze. 'Flash houses, Mr Eildor, for your information, are also brothels. Brothels, sir,' he added with a note of gleeful relish, and as they walked briskly across North Street, with Townsend whistling under his breath, hands behind his back, the gleam in his eye suggested to Tam a more lascivious side of his character.

In the lanes where Tam had been so frustrated earlier, the Bow Street officer was obviously a well-known figure, but one whose presence, Tam decided, must have ensured the rapid disappearance behind closed doors of many of the criminal fraternity.

He was amazed by Townsend's methods of enquiring after lost or stolen property. His interrogation of shopkeepers involved no subtlety of any kind. He did not beat about the bush with overtures of politeness but leaned across the counters in a threatening manner, roaring out a question about their recent acquisitions of stolen jewellery.

Needless to say this approach had no success

and Tam realised that Townsend's manner would reap no more than a brisk denial, whether innocent or guilty. Something else he found blatantly intimidating was that the unpleasant interrogation was quite specific regarding fine pearls and, in lesser establishments, any new acquisition of fur cloaks.

How did Townsend know such details? It suggested that he must be in the prince's confidence regarding the murder.

Tam had a sixth sense of being in danger and, with the promised purse containing only a few coins which doomed any hope of travel, he realised that being almost penniless ensured that he was trapped, since it must have been obvious to anyone less subtle than the Prince Regent that a survivor from the shipwreck of the *Royal Stuart* must have lost all his possessions.

His unease increased as on more than one occasion he saw, out of the corner of his eye, a shadowy figure walking on the other side of the road. Tam had an instinct that he or both he and Townsend were being followed. Their stalker was not a very good actor, nor did he dive swiftly enough back into the shadows to stop Tam's quick glimpse of a tall, heavily built man, not very fast on his feet, who had the look of a prize-fighter.

When he mentioned this, Townsend's eyes widened. Turning slowly, he stared blankly across the road and with one of his rare hearty laughs, murmured that Tam must be imagining things. Tam was not consoled; he wondered if Townsend was speaking the truth. As each day passed he became increasingly uneasy about the reason why he was being included in these expeditions where he had no voice and merely remained a background figure during Townsend's haranguing.

As his presence was quite unnecessary, he realised there be must be some motive behind it, since the prince and the Bow Street officer were a formidable team. The sinister fact for Tam was that, according to the prince, he was only required until Townsend arrived to take over the investigation and then he would be free to leave Brighton.

It suggested that the stalker, whose presence he supposedly imagined, might have instructions to keep a sharp eye on the mythical Edinburgh lawyer. Townsend liked frequent stops for refreshment, for a pot of ale and a pie, and in the area of Ship Street, chose the inn where Tam had earlier seen the convict lad Jem and where the landlord had misunderstood Tam's urgency in arranging a meeting.

Now he had another reason for concern. On constant lookout for Jem, he feared that if they came face to face, and Jem was forced to recognise him, some kind of explanation would be exceedingly difficult, especially as

Tam did not doubt from seeing Townsend's threatening attitude towards reluctant and doubtless innocent shopkeepers, that he would cling to any incriminating theory against Tam with the tenacity of a terrier with a rat.

In the Old Ship he was relieved that the landlord was absent and Townsend's order was taken by a slatternly wench, who nevertheless attracted a lascivious leer and a passing slap at her backside. This was taken in good part, presumably acceptable behaviour from a good customer who also happened to be a law officer.

Meanwhile, in less sinister circumstances, Tam would have relished his enforced stay and the return each evening to the Pavilion's exceedingly comfortable guest house. Overlooking the gardens, with a handsome room of his own next door to Townsend, with servants to look after their comfort, they were provided with a splendid supper.

The reason for Tam's change of venue was that the prince was eager to begin refurbishment of the royal bedroom (with excellent reason, thought Tam) aware that that this arrangement also admirably suited the prince's plan to keep him in a comfortable prison under Townsend's sharp eye until a final decision concerning his fate was reached.

If, after supper, he decided to take a walk in the fresh air, Townsend insisted on accompanying him and Tam was beginning to know the meaning of 'being in a cleft stick'. Allowed little time alone, he once heard a noise outside his bedroom door during the night, and on looking outside it was to confront an armed guard sitting in the corridor.

Mentioning this casually to Townsend, he received a friendly slap on the shoulder. 'Why, sir, we are important guests and HRH is most considerate in seeing that we are well protected and taken care of.'

Still a penniless guest of the prince, Tam observed Townsend dig into his own purse for any expenses needed during their investigations into the seamier side of Brighton life, which necessitated frequent sojourns for food and drink, accompanied by further bizarre speculations from Townsend on the probable fate of the Stuart Sapphire.

For some reason, it evidently pleased the prince to keep his shipwrecked survivor alive. Aware of his danger in being the one person, apart from Lords Henry and Percy, who knew too much about the circumstances regarding the murdered marchioness, Tam was fairly certain that he had not been intended to survive the carriage accident, and that the convenient joint disposal of her body and his would have admirably suited the prince's earnest desires.

Daily Tam was in no doubt that his survival

was but a temporary measure, since it was obvious that Townsend was now managing the investigation himself. It seemed likely that unless Tam was able to produce some special ability to track down the Stuart Sapphire by means of his alleged profession, he would be speedily eliminated.

He was certain one attempt had already been made and only a swift leap on to the path had saved him from a horseman galloping haphazardly down the lane.

Passers-by had screamed but, as he reached safety, Townsend seemed completely unmoved.

'You saw that!' said Tam. 'The man deliberately tried to run me down.'

Townsend shook his head and smiled wryly. 'Mr Eildor, you are imagining things again. Anyone can see how easily accidents can happen. The thoroughfares are so narrow and crowded—and I am afraid these young blades with their fast horses are extremely indifferent to pedestrians; the old are particularly at risk.'

Tam realised there was as little point in arguing about the murderous horseman as there had been about the stalker whom Townsend dismissed as a figment of his imagination. And this attempt first failed, should he meet with another accident, Tam was sure Townsend would not be involved.

The role of assassin would lie with the stalker and Tam had a feeling that he was going to need all his wits about him to stay alive and some ingenuity to escape from Brighton. Escape into yet another hazard. How to find his way back to the convict hulk anchored somewhere along the south-east coast and back to his own time.

Tam would have felt considerably more ill at ease had he known that after he was presumed to be safely asleep and under guard, the prince, when sober enough, summoned Townsend to give a report on the progress of his investigations.

Not only was the Stuart Sapphire under investigation but so too was Tam Eildor. Townsend had to confess that he was baffled. Eildor was a man of mystery and he was having him 'looked in to' by some law officers in Edinburgh.

'This may take a little time, Highness, and in case he turns out to be an impostor and a spy, in league with assassins against the prince's person—'

He left the words unsaid. A pause for dark thoughts regarding the scheming Princess of Wales in Carlton House. 'In Your Royal Highness's best interests, it would be advisable to keep Mr Eildor here. Keep a sharp eye upon him.'

Chapter Fifteen

At last the gnawing terrors that threatened to give the Prince Regent sleepless nights at Mrs Fitzherbert's side in Steine House were almost over. Unable to understand why the dead marchioness had not yet been discovered, Henry's attempts at consolation, that the embankment was off the main road, failed to soothe him.

His thoughts were morbid in the extreme. He dreamt once that he was King of England. Years had passed, her skeleton discovered, the dreadful truth and the shocking scandal revealed and made public.

He had almost given up all hope of an early resolution of that arranged carriage accident, which was meant to remove all association with her death from the Pavilion and, guilt from himself. He was unable to concentrate on the urgent details of refurbishment of the royal bedroom, preferring to put the place out of his mind, even though he knew that to continue sleeping at Steine House would soon invite curiosity and unwelcome comment.

Then, almost a week after the marchioness's murder, Henry rushed in flourishing the *Brighton Herald*. There was rarely anything more exciting than local news concerning the trials of the fishing trade, or some foreign official arriving at the Pavilion. Today however the sensational headline leapt out at them as Henry read:

GRUESOME DISCOVERY.
NAKED CORPSE OF WOMAN
NEAR LEWES ROAD.

Late last night a Lewes man out shooting rabbits was alerted by the excited behaviour of his dog. Upon inspection he found to his horror the naked corpse of a female down an embankment near the Lewes Road. Scattered pieces of a wrecked vehicle in the vicinity, including its wheels, indicated that the dead woman travelling alone was the victim of a strange carriage accident.

The law officers were immediately informed and concluded that the carriage had been attacked by highwaymen, the horses stolen and the vehicle pushed down the embankment. The unfortunate female passenger, who has not yet been identified, was apparently killed in the accident. Her body was then stripped naked, all her clothes and valuable possessions removed by the highwaymen. According to the physician who made the examination, the woman had been dead for several days, her body at the foot of an embankment hidden by shrubbery from passers-by on the main road.

The law officers are anxious to receive information regarding any female missing from her home who fits the following description: aged between twenty-five and thirty-five, fair in complexion and very well-nourished.

The prince held up his hand. 'Ah, a truly gruesome discovery,' he said sadly. His accompanying sigh was not of outrage but of blessed relief. It had all turned out exactly as he had hoped it would. Laying the newspaper aside he smiled at Henry. 'And now we must continue with the business in hand.'

If Henry was taken aback by his father's reaction, he kept it to himself. There were many questions to which he would have liked answers, but as far as the prince was concerned, this was now an unfortunate incident which had befallen some unknown woman, the circumstances of which would be explained in due course to everyone's satisfaction. Once the body in the town mortuary was identified as the missing marchioness, and laid to rest in the family vault at Creeve, the danger would be over, the case closed.

Although there was nothing to link the 'gruesome discovery' with the Pavilion, the unsavoury details of the carriage accident, in which he had been an unwilling participant,

Henry would not readily forget, nor could he share the prince's dismissal of the unpleasant details. There were still hazards ahead which his father chose to ignore, thought Henry, whose nerves were not of the same royal steel nor his conscience so easily placated.

*   *   *

When Tam read the newspaper later that day, his first reaction was also curiosity, as to how the prince would react to this gruesome discovery and, looking further afield to the sensational news when her identity inevitably became known, how he would avoid connecting this fearful incident to the woman who had been his mistress and had been murdered in his bed.

Tam was particularly interested in the fact that she had been found stripped naked. Any mention of a fur cloak and a string of pearls— the murder weapon— had been omitted from the newspaper article and one could only conclude that in this instance 'finders were keepers' and the unnamed man out shooting rabbits who had made the gruesome discovery, had recognised that the pearls and fur cloak were valuable and their disappearance could be listed alongside the missing horses and blamed on the highwaymen.

The mention of highwaymen interested

Tam. Had the law officers thought of that themselves or had someone put the words into their mouths? And as it was unlikely the cloak and pearls would be claimed, had he considered this a just reward for the shock to his nervous system? Doubtless he would console himself that the sale of the pearls would keep himself and his family, if he possessed one, in comfort for the rest of their days.

Tam sighed, awaiting the next stage in the drama. How long before Creeve House was alerted and the absence of the marchioness, whose lifestyle was eccentric to say the least, was noted, questioned by her husband and found significant?

Of more urgency for Tam was planning his own disappearance from the year 1811 before someone did it for him permanently, such as the sinister stalker whom Townsend pretended not to notice. In such circumstances the missing pearls and fur cloak ceased to be of importance, one mystery that he would not be obliged to solve. At the moment he had more than enough with a murderer to track down as well as being on hand to assist Townsend's daily attempts to locate the Stuart Sapphire.

And the intentions of the stalker that only he could see were the least of Tam's worries. He was also being stalked by the very visible and determined presences of Beau Brummell and Princess Charlotte.

On every occasion when he managed to give Townsend the slip, if the Bow Street officer was commanded to attend the Prince Regent, and for a brief half-hour he was relishing the freedom of walking in the warm sunny gardens, it seemed that either Brummell or the Princess had been lying in wait and was hastening towards him.

'Ah, Mr Eildor,' Brummell waved an airy hand in his direction. 'That promised luncheon. If you would have the goodness to spare me an hour of your precious time, I am most interested in hearing more of your life in Edinburgh. Are you by any chance acquainted with Sir Walter Scott, or the painter Allan Ramsay? He has begged me to sit for a portrait. Unfortunately I have had to refuse the honour, since the journey to Scotland is so fatiguing and their weather is dreadful—quite dreadful. As for their roads,' he added, rolling his eyes heavenward. 'And regrettably Mr Ramsay has been quite unable to see me in London—'

And so it went on while Tam realised that he was being quizzed and interrogated. It did not take much imagination to realise that beyond the bonhomie he had made a dangerous enemy in Beau Brummell.

A happier encounter was with Mrs Fitzherbert. Tam had returned exhausted from another wearisome day with Townsend roaring at suspicious persons in the seamier lanes of Brighton in his totally ineffectual pursuit of the missing sapphire. By now Tam realised that everyone, including the thief if he had not already left for London, would be on the alert.

Pleading a headache, hoping Townsend, who suffered from sore feet at the end of the day, would not insist on accompanying him, he escaped to the promenade, and was enjoying a brisk walk with a welcome sea breeze cooling a particularly hot, late afternoon.

He was hailed by a carriage. Mrs Fitzherbert leaned out. 'Mr Eildor, how fast you do walk, sir. Ah, that is youth for you! I thought we should never catch up with you,' and indicating the seat opposite beside her maid, 'Would you care to join us?'

Her radiant smile was irresistible. After conventional greetings regarding his well-being, she said: 'I wonder, did you receive my note, an invitation to a picnic on Friday, if you are free.'

Tam shook his head, he had never received any communication from Mrs Fitzherbert or anyone else.

She sighed. 'Mr Brummell was on his way to the Pavilion to visit George and he promised to deliver it.'

Tam gave a non-committal nod and again she glanced at him wryly. 'I am afraid it must have slipped Mr Brummell's mind or, more to the point, Mr Eildor, I fear that anyone who is favoured in any degree by the prince is a creature to be envied, despised and brought down by Mr Brummell.'

Remembering a conversation she had had with Brummell on the day she had first met Tam Eildor, she said sadly: 'He believes quite wrongfully and not, I fear, very intelligently that this bringing down the ladder of some favoured person will enable him to climb a rung higher and reinstate himself in George's regard.'

She shook her head sadly. 'It is quite pointless. He should be aware of that by now, after all these years. He must have seen many who held favour come and go. And once they go, alas, it is forever,' she added, thinking in particular of the trail of royal mistresses and the miracle by which she herself had survived.

They reached the Steine, and as they parted, Mrs Fitzherbert felt sure that Brummell had been wrong, his speculations about the young man were based on spite and jealousy. She had an instinctive feeling that Tam Eildor was honest, unusual rather than strange and very different from the men of his age she encountered in court society.

Slightly foreign somehow but quite unlike any young men she had met during her travels in Europe, she felt that he was to be trusted, that his word, once given, would not be broken. Certainly he did not seem at all like the dangerous Jacobite spy, the informer from the Princess of Wales' household, that Brummell suspected.

If only she could be sure, could rely on her instincts. And if only dear George was not involved or at risk.

Townsend could not deny Tam the invitation from Mrs Fitzherbert, but he had hastened to tell the prince, who merely smiled and said: 'Mrs Fitzherbert is on our side. She is my wife, after all, and knows where her devotion and loyalty lie. Besides which, Townsend, she is no fool. I trust her judgement. Have always done so and always will.'

The prince was remembering that Maria was puzzled by Tam Eildor and although she could see no ill in him, she too had confessed when closely questioned that he might not be all he pretended to be. But she was sure this had an innocent explanation.

The prince decided not to share these confidences with Townsend, who had enough to do without wasting time investigating Tam Eildor, who would soon be leaving them, one way or another, he decided grimly. Just as soon as the marchioness's body was safely laid to rest.

*   *   *

Most difficult of all Tam's problems was Princess Charlotte and how to evade her, especially as the warm weather continued unbroken and, eager to be free of the claustrophobic interior of the Pavilion, she seemed to frequent the gardens each day with a yearning for fresh air equal to his own.

Observing him from a distance, she would shriek and wave in a most unroyal unladylike way and, lifting her skirts, rush panting to his side.

Tam stood transfixed at this onslaught. He could hardly pretend not to see her, turn his back and take to his heels, quickly launching himself in the opposite direction. Instead, he must stand his ground, wait, bow, and smile.

The princess's conversation did not vary, nor her lingering grasp of his hand. 'It is so good to see you,' and with a sigh, 'I think of you already as my dear and devoted friend, Mr Eildor.'

(Where had she got that idea, Tam wondered.)

'You are so understanding and it grieves me deeply to know that your time with us is so short, fleeting every day, and we have still so much unsaid between us. So much to learn about one another.'

One morning, skimming through the largely local gossip in the *Brighton Herald*, he came across one item of personal interest:

'As mentioned in an earlier edition, Mr Tam Eildor, an Edinburgh lawyer and passenger on the *Royal Stuart*, has been identified as the sole survivor of the wreck which took all other lives.'

The princess mentioned that she had seen it. 'The newspaper is of course circulated each day in the library. Many visitors have read it and the Master of Ceremonies is very keen that you should come and honour us with an account of your ordeal on the *Royal Stuart.*'

Not if I can avoid it, thought Tam, still smiling bravely as on each occasion she presumed a little more, brazenly clinging to his arm and smiling closely into his face, her head touching his own.

Out of the corner of his eye, trying not to wince at her warm breath on his cheek, Tam observed the scandalised countenance of Lady de Clifford and prayed that this behaviour would not reach the ears or the eyes of her father.

That, he realised, would give the Prince Regent an excellent excuse to dispose of Tam Eildor legitimately, on a treasonable charge that he had tried to seduce a royal princess, the next Queen of England.

Chapter Sixteen

In Creeve House, Sir Joseph was reading the newspaper and decided that his dear Sarah would be very interested as she had a somewhat ghoulish taste in such matters, an unfortunate trait in a well-bred lady, but considering the unfortunate background from which he had rescued her, quite understandable.

Laying aside the newspaper and stretching out his hand for the brandy bottle, his greatest comfort these days, he realised that he had not seen Sarah for several days, a not unusual occurrence, for it was their agreement since the birth of Timothy, their only son and heir to Creeve, that his beautiful young wife should be free to live her own life, as was the custom she had quickly observed among other married couples in their stratum of society.

Sir Joseph could not but reluctantly agree, after all he had little choice in the matter. Sarah was his third wife and he had had little luck breeding sons with the other two. The first, chosen by the former marquis, his father, when he was seventeen, was the sixth and last unmarried daughter of an earl. Older than himself and very plain, it was no love match and, preferring horses to men, she had died in a riding accident on the hunting field.

He had no better luck with the second, his own choice this time, a wealthy young widow with a town house in London and an estate some forty miles away. After several miscarriages she had died in the attempt to produce a daughter, premature, and no bigger than a skinned rabbit.

Sir Joseph had tried to hide his disappointment through the years but she had survived, to plague him and his third wife, the voluptuous Sarah Flint whom he met at a London meeting of the Hellfire Club.

Growing old and desperate by now, he realised that even after two marriages, although he knew how one performed to beget children, which in his case was a fumble in the dark under the bedclothes, he was just learning about the more wicked goings-on with a whore, the acts that she could perform for a man, which could take his breath away.

And Sir Joseph developed a new emotion. Jealousy. He could not bear to think of Sarah being intimate, as was her job, with other men in the club. He wanted her all to himself and so he asked, nay, begged her to marry him. Since there were men younger, certainly more handsome than himself in the club, he was surprised and delirious when she accepted.

It wasn't until he got her home to Creeve and unwrapped the parcel that he discovered that Sarah was going to be difficult baggage. He had seen her role as the begetter of sons, but he found that favours had to be paid for. After Timothy's birth, he realised there were to be no more children. Sarah had done her duty and the sensual woman who had teased him in their pre-marriage days was soon little more exciting in his bed, which she rarely graced these days, than his first two wives had been.

Sir Joseph sighed, made excuses and never gave up hope, despite the fact that it was obvious to others that all was not well in Creeve. Sarah soon lost interest in baby Timothy and after the wet nurse's duties were at an end, abandoned him to tutors.

As for the unwanted daughter, Sarah could not abide 'That Girl' as she called her, and her presence became an embarrassment to them both, since Sir Joseph did not dare raise a word in her defence in Sarah's hearing. He had to admit that he had been greatly relieved when 'That Girl' took off for London to stay with her grandmother a month ago.

Refilling his brandy glass, he rang for his valet to ask Lady Sarah to attend him. The valet trudged off and returned to say that Lady Sarah was not at home.

Sir Joseph was considerably ruffled by this, her usual response when she did not wish to be disturbed. After a little insistence and confusion, the valet led him to understand that her ladyship was truly not at home. She was not to be found in the house.

Sir Joseph, the mildest of men, was now feeling aggrieved, since Sarah had not been present at the Masque a few days ago, the event that had been her idea in the first place and which she had carefully planned. But he knew better than to tax her with this omission, since her punishments by withdrawing all

189

favours so reluctantly given could be severe and painful indeed to his pride.

He sighed wearily and dragged himself out of his chair. A hastily penned note was the usual procedure if she was to be absent from Creeve, not out of duty or consideration, but at his insistence. And so he went up to her room which was at the other end of the corridor to his own. Risking her displeasure by opening the door, he was surprised to see her maid Simone sewing by the window.

She sprang to her feet and curtseyed.

'Why are you here, Simone? Shouldn't you be with your mistress?'

Simone blushed. 'My aunt who lives at Whitdean, Your Grace—she was very ill and her ladyship gave me leave to visit her.'

'When was this?'

Simone thought for a moment. 'On Friday, sir.'

'Where was she going?' It was usually London.

'To Brighton, Your Grace, to visit friends.'

A week ago, thought Sir Joseph. 'And who were these friends?'

Simone shook her head warily. 'If it please Your Grace, her ladyship does not tell me their names.'

That was a lie. She knew perfectly well Lady Sarah's destination and her assignations with the Prince Regent but, a simple soul, as Sir Joseph's brow darkened ominously, she was terrified that this interrogation might make her reveal the truth about her mistress's secret apartment.

'I—believe—that she visits the gaming tables—with these friends.'

Sir Joseph's face was growing scarlet. A week in Brighton at the gaming tables, losing his money as she always did. He would have to put a stop to this. Drumming his fingers on the windowsill, he swung round on the now trembling Simone.

Why hadn't she taken her maid with her? Who would unlace her, dress and undress her? An unwelcome vision from the uninhibited pre-marriage days flew into his mind and was speedily banished.

'Did she say when she was returning?'

Simone shook her head, looked at the floor. 'No, Your Grace,' she whispered. 'She did not.'

That was another lie. Because of the Masque next day Simone had expected her mistress to return very early in the morning, as she sometimes did after spending the night with the prince. Arriving in a closed carriage, she entered by the servants' quarters, the door conveniently left unlocked by Simone.

The servants all knew, of course, that her ladyship had been out all night: 'Cat on the tiles,' they whispered and winked behind her back. But this time she hadn't crept up to her room, to take the bath Simone had prepared for her. And there had been no word since.

Simone was a little concerned but not very. She quite understood that her mistress preferred the Pavilion and the prince to any Masque at Creeve House and she was well paid by her ladyship to mind her own business. As well as feeling secretly proud that her mistress was involved with the future King of England, Simone was always glad of a chance to spend another day with her lover, the alleged sick aunt from Whitdean.

Back in his study, Sir Joseph, rereading the details of the gruesome murder story which he had only skimmed, and putting away his fourth glass of brandy, was about to doze off when the footman announced an unexpected visitor.

John Townsend.

Sir Joseph opened his eyes, emerging from the brandy haze with difficulty, and struggled to get to his feet.

'Ah, Townsend. Welcome! Haven't seen you for a while—busy catching criminals as usual. Here to see your nephew, are you? He is doing very well indeed—we are very pleased with his progress. An increase in his wages is on the cards,' he added with a smile.

But Townsend wasn't smiling in return. He looked very grave.

'Bad news, Townsend, someone ill in the family, is that it?'

Townsend gave a deep sigh, shook his head

and said awkwardly: 'Will Your Grace be seated again, please.'

Sir Joseph, who was swaying somewhat, staggered back into his chair. 'What on earth is it, man?' Pausing, he squinted up at Townsend. 'Not the king—not the prince,' he whispered.

'Neither, Your Grace. Worse than that.'

'What could be worse?' The old man glanced anxiously towards the window. He could hear six-year-old Timothy playing a noisy game with his tutor and a new puppy on the terrace. 'Not invasion, is it? Dear God, the French haven't landed—?'

'No, Your Grace. May I beg you to listen for a moment.'

Sir Joseph sat back in his chair. 'Go ahead, go ahead. Let's hear your worst,' and since nothing could be worse than some ill befalling Timothy, or the Prince Regent, he added: 'Though I cannot imagine—'

'No, Your Grace, I am afraid you cannot,' Townsend interrupted. 'I have just come from a most bitter and unhappy experience.' He paused and shook his head, wondering how to continue. 'From identifying the dead woman who was found near the Lewes Road.'

'Oh, that!' said Sir Joseph pointing to the newspaper. 'I have just been reading about that. Wanted to show it to Lady Sarah, she always enjoys a spicy bit of sensational news. Not much usually, is there? Finds life dull here. But highwaymen and the corpse of an unknown naked woman, that would cheer her up.'

Awkwardly Townsend reached out and put his hand on Sir Joseph's shoulder. 'Your Grace, you must prepare yourself for a shock.'

'A shock! How? Why?'

'The body I have just identified in the mortuary—it—is that of—her ladyship.'

Sir Joseph stared at him with disbelieving eyes, then he fell back in his chair and closed his eyes, shaking his head wildly. 'Never— never.'

The study door opened and Townsend signalled Sir Joseph's physician who had been leaving the house after attending to the housekeeper's broken wrist. He confessed that he was also keeping an eye on Sir Joseph's health which would not improve after hearing the Bow Street officer's shocking news.

Coming forward, he whispered: 'Wait outside, Mr Townsend, His Grace may want to have further words. I will give him a sedative—this kind of shock, his heart, you know.'

Townsend didn't know but was glad to have a chance to visit the stables where his nephew was out exercising the Creeve horses for the forthcoming Whitehawk races.

Returning half an hour later, he met the physician, who was just leaving. 'He will see you now, I think, Mr Townsend. I persuaded him to take a rest. Yes, he is much calmer and anxious to know what happened to Her Grace in more detail.'

Townsend cautiously entered the study where Sir Joseph reclined on the sofa. 'I am truly sorry, Your Grace. Please accept my condolences—'

Sir Joseph made a gesture of impatience and in a voice tinged with hope he whispered, 'You are sure—certain sure.'

Townsend took a deep breath. 'I am, alas, Your Grace. I have had the honour to become acquainted with Lady Sarah over the years as a guest here in your house.' He shook his head. 'I am deeply shocked and I can only offer Your Grace my deepest sympathy.'

Sir Joseph nodded wearily. 'Dear God, dear God. On her way home to the Masque—attacked by highwaymen, the newspaper said. That is why she never arrived and I thought she had changed her mind. She does—did—that sort of thing quite often.' He paused, looking towards the window again.

'That carriage accident, going down the embankment like that. And stripped of all her clothes—and her jewels. Left naked—naked! How disgraceful!'

'Disgraceful indeed, Your Grace,' said Townsend as Sir Joseph went on:

'So the highwaymen, those devils, are back again to plague us. I understood we no longer had anything to fear from them in this area.

As a magistrate it did my heart good to see justice done and the lot of them hanged years ago.'

'Nevertheless, Your Grace,' said Townsend, 'the theory is that it was highwaymen or some such disreputable characters, who seized the chance of robbing—a—dead person.'

Sir Joseph sat up, thumped his fists together.

'Then they must be found—and hanged, do you hear? No explanation is acceptable, whoever was concerned must be punished—by hanging. I will put notice out of a reward— a substantial reward—for any information leading to their capture.'

Chapter Seventeen

Not everyone shared the Prince Regent's relief as he wrote letters of sincere condolence to the marquis on the loss of a beloved wife and to his brother Frederick on the death of a close and dear friend.

Mention of highwaymen terrified travellers, especially rich ones, and some carriages had built-in secret compartments beneath the seats where passengers, especially ladies, if they had enough warning could hide their jewels, presenting the highwaymen with 'bad purses' containing a few worthless coins.

The report of a Gruesome Discovery in the

normally mild, genteel and thoroughly boring social news with which the newspaper sought to fill its columns flew like wildfire around the town arousing alarm and despondency.

This was sensational, dangerous and it threatened all travellers. Even those unable to read, and there were quite a few, implored their more literate friends and neighbours for a true account, which regretfully was often given with more relish than accuracy.

Before the dead woman was named, there was some speculation as to her identity and the town's whores were counting their numbers. Unidentified also meant the possibility of being given to the doctors for dissection, a terrible fate. But there was worse to come. The word 'murdered' was also being whispered.

Princess Charlotte did not share the terrors of the female population as she waylaid Tam in one of her accidental meetings. Such was her alacrity that he suspected she must sit in her room which overlooked the gardens, or had maids posted as sentries, to alert her to his appearance.

'Is it not exciting news—and so infamous—the marchioness being the victim?' she said cheerfully, then perhaps aware of Tam's look at her lack of feeling, she took his arm and whispered: 'I must confess, I have never cared for her, so it is no use pretending or shedding false tears. She was a very bad influence on my father. The beastly woman coveted jewels— jewels that should be mine by right—'

Tam tried not to listen to her railing against the marchioness, and leaving her as hastily as politeness allowed, he hurried towards his favourite place, the peaceful promenade. Watching the rollers creeping gently up to the shore, he decided that the Prince Regent still had cause for alarm. He had not been as discreet as he thought, especially if the voluble and tactless princess's gossip reached the marquis's ears.

Townsend had earlier hinted at a number of complications. The marchioness had died a week ago. Her body had lain above ground for several days in very warm weather, and so it had begun to decompose. Its condition was not at all helped by the multitude of small animals, inquisitive predatory crows and insects that had enjoyed a nibble at her flesh, regarding human corpses as an abundant and free access to gatify healthy appetites.

Nor could the funeral be arranged with all the pomp and ritual proper to her position in society. Solemn invitations to members of the royal family and the many aristocratic families to whom the marquis was related, either by marriage or the constant yearly celebration of hunts, shooting parties and weekend house guests, had to be abandoned, and the marchioness laid to rest immediately in the interests of health and hygiene since, even confined to the coolest regions of the mortuary, there were distinct and ominous odours of decay floating upwards.

There was however one further complication. Dr Brooke, who had carried out a meticulous examination of the corpse on arrival, prided himself on his accurate knowledge of the time of death acquired over many years. This expertise told him that the marchioness had not died as a result of the carriage accident and that the highwaymen, whatever else they were guilty of, were not to blame for her death. She had been dead for several days before the carriage journey. And what was more, she had been strangled. Marks around her neck indicated that life had been extinguished by a rope or some other means.

Despite the fact that the funeral should have already taken place and the victim laid to rest, Dr Brooke, a conscientious physician, decided that a solution must be found and the murderer apprehended, tried and hanged for the crime.

This information he eagerly passed on to Townsend whose fame as a criminal catcher and thief-taker had long since reached Brighton and he was therefore the most competent officer to take charge of the case and carry out the investigation.

All of which Townsend dramatically reported to Tam, suggesting that they go on the instant to the scene of the accident and search for clues.

'Dr Brooke knows a thing or two,' he said respectfully. 'Strangling, he says, is not in character for highwaymen, who are brisk about their business. They would not waste time looking for methods of strangling their victims, they might even, with good reason, be superstitious about using ropes, about which they live in dread, but would use the speedier method of pistols.'

Tam, who knew most of the story from first hand, was not confident that they would find anything at all, but at least it was a diversion from the wearisome and futile daily search for the missing sapphire. Even Townsend had to admit they were running out of places to visit and suspicious persons to interrogate.

And so the *Brighton Herald* had another field day. Dr Brooke, eager to instigate a search for the marchioness's foul murderer and, finding the Bow Street officer a little slow to appreciate his observations, took it upon himself to introduce himself to the marquis, thereby risking an attack of apoplexy.

His Grace, however, rallied sufficiently to insist on another reward notice being posted, asking for any information which would lead to apprehending the marchioness's assassin.

This did nothing for the Prince Regent's peace of mind. It was what he dreaded most, all his nightmares come home to roost.

* * *

Townsend decided that Tam should accompany him to the funeral, in the hope that there might be clues to the murderer's identity, a forlorn hope based on a firm belief that murderers often return to the graveside of their victims whose wounds thereupon reopen and dramatically begin to bleed again.

Tam was not quite sure how he was equating this macabre idea with the fact that the victim had been strangled, and failed to share Townsend's faith in such an easy solution to murder.

Approaching Lewes they turned into splendid gates leading down a drive towards a handsome timber-framed building mellowed in time. This was Creeve House, dating from the sixteenth century, where already carriages were lined up, as mourners emerged for the funeral in the family chapel.

Tam wore his black cloak. Townsend retained his long and perhaps his only overcoat but conceded to custom with a black cravat.

At the door a footman solemnly consulted his list. Their names were not there. Townsend explained that he was a personal friend of the marquis but, perhaps considering his informal dress unsuitable for such an occasion, the footman shook his head. No name, no admittance. He added that as the private chapel could only accommodate family and close friends, the gentlemen might wait with the other mourners in the gardens to pay their last respects as the late marchioness was laid to rest in the family crypt.

Townsend, somewhat huffed, returned to the carriage, and informed Tam that as he was sorely in need of refreshment, the inevitable pint of ale and a pie, they might as well adjourn to the Old Bull in Lewes, an ancient establishment once the lodging of Thomas Paine, the reformer and author of *The Rights of Man*, in his time as an excise officer.

Tam was impressed by his first melancholy visit to Lewes, the small county town whose quaint and charming hilly streets enjoyed unrestricted access to the Sussex countryside, its roots sunk deeper into England's history than the Brighton he had just left.

As the carriage rattled along the main thoroughfare, the high street, he had a glimpse of buildings considerably older than the Marine Pavilion, while Townsend eagerly pointed out the site where the Protestant martyrs had been burnt in the reign of Mary Tudor.

Townsend knew Lewes well from his visits to Creeve House, and was eager to tell Tam something of its history. Dating from the Norman Conquest, the castle built by them was deserted in the fourteenth century and eventually disappeared almost completely thanks to later generations using its stones for building purposes.

'Practically all the old mansions you see have something of Lewes Castle in their foundations,' Townsend said, pointing out Barbican House, a sixteenth-century timber-framed building. 'If we had time I'd show you the house Henry the Eighth gave to Anne of Cleves as part of their divorce settlement.'

'One piece of local history you won't know, being from Scotland, is that after the Battle of Lewes in 1264, fought on the Downs out there, King Henry the Third was defeated by Simon de Montfort and the ensuing terms of peace led to the beginning of the English Parliament.'

Leaving the carriage alongside the Old Bull, across the road was St Michael's Church. 'It's been recently renovated but it dates back to the fourteenth century. Very important church, lot of tombs of ancient families. If Creeves hadn't a private chapel, then the funeral would have taken place there.'

They were speedily served and Townsend, refreshed in body and spirit, decided they had given the chapel service a decent interval and that they had best make haste to return or they would miss the best part of the ceremony.

They had left Brighton that morning in brilliant sunshine with few clouds hovering over the horizon, but as they emerged from the inn it seemed that summer had forsaken them.

By the time they were heading down the drive to Creeve House, the mourners were already gathered in the gardens and the distant rumbles of thunder promised a storm violent enough to make the ensuing ceremony at the crypt short indeed, the minister's words were almost inaudible as the coffin, covered with its black velvet pall and the Creeve coat of arms, was placed in the crypt.

Tam watched the marquis supporting a small boy about six years old and, at his other side, a slim girl, clad like the other female members of the family in mourning weeds, a black veil fluttering from her bonnet concealing her face.

As the rain began servants rushed forward with sheltering umbrellas to be held over the mourners as they started to walk quickly towards the house.

The girl hurried past close to where Tam and Townsend had taken somewhat inadequate shelter. Tam was conscious of her eyes watching him from under the veil as Townsend hissed: 'That's the ungrateful daughter who has disgraced the family and broken her poor father's heart. She was no friend of poor Lady Sarah either, I can tell you.'

And indicating another figure hastening along the path, modestly clad in black but without the mourning veils as befitted a servant, 'That is Simone, her ladyship's maid, utterly devoted to her mistress.'

Tam regarded her retreating figure with interest, remembering how, after the prince's dramatic discovery of the dead woman, Lord Percy had been sent to Creeve to bring back Simone but had returned frustrated having learned that she was absent visiting a sick relative.

Lord Percy was also walking with Lord Henry a short distance away. Both had arrived independently and were representing HRH the Prince Regent who was unfortunately (and conveniently) indisposed. Townsend whispered that Prince Frederick, Duke of York, had also been expected to attend, as a close friend of the Creeve family, but was similarly stricken with a mysterious indisposition.

To anyone who knew the true facts, like Lord Henry, these indispositions might have been written off as attacks of conscience. Considering the two princes' intimate relationships with the deceased, it might have made matters somewhat difficult for them to face her bereaved husband.

Although they were getting rather wet, Townsend seemed reluctant to join their carriage and return to Brighton, when a servant carrying an umbrella rushed over and said: 'His Grace has requested that you gentlemen join the other mourners for a glass of wine.'

Townsend, obviously hoping for just such an invitation, was delighted but, as they hurried to join the crowd gathering at the great doorway, Tam thought for a moment he saw the now familiar figure of the stalker standing under a tree.

'Mr Townsend! Look, over there. There's the man who has been following us in Brighton. What on earth is he doing here?'

Townsend turned around and stared with unseeing eyes.

He laughed. 'Mr Eildor—you are imagining things again.'

'He is there, I tell you. You're not looking in the right place. Here,' and seizing Townsend's shoulder he directed his gaze towards the tree.

But even as he and Townsend looked, the man had vanished.

It was Townsend's turn to be remarkably understanding for a change. 'Come along, lad,' he said briskly. 'You're cold and so am I. Funerals are depressing things—especially in weather like this. We'll both feel more like ourselves again when we have a drink inside us.'

And with that Tam had to be satisied, but his ill ease continued. He was certain sure he had seen the Brighton stalker, but what was his sinister purpose in following Townsend and himself to Creeve?

The interior of Creeve was everything its exterior had promised, with its sixteenth-century panelled hall, heavily beamed roof, and minstrels' gallery. Two elaborately carved fireplaces supported by fierce visaged mythical heroes faced each other at either end of a marble floor where doors led to a succession of more practical rooms, including Sir Joseph's study and the library, while a grand oak staircase swept upwards to the bedrooms.

The mourners had spilled over into the salon where Tam was further impressed by the magnificent view over the rolling Downs, taking in an ornamental lake, a pastoral landscape from an ancient painting, including sheep and cows and stately elm trees. Here was a house rooted in England's history, built to stand the test of time, and Tam decided that it made the Marine Pavilion's splendours somewhat tawdry and transient by comparison, as if a bad winter storm might lift it from its flimsy foundations and blow it away across the English Channel.

The girl described as the disgraced daughter was talking to Townsend. Both were staring in Tam's direction as if he was the object of their conversation. The girl nodded and Townsend led her over.

Introducing Tam, he bowed and said: 'Allow me to present Lady Gemma Creeve.'

The girl raised her mourning veil and Tam found himself staring into a face he recognised and had been pursuing the length and breadth of Brighton.

The convict lad he knew as Jem.

Chapter Eighteen

Somehow Tam managed to bow and murmur a conventional greeting. He heard the girl say:

'Mr Eildor lacks a glass of wine,' and smiling at Townsend: 'If you would be so good, sir.'

Watching him retreat towards the tables, she seized Tam's arm and whispered: 'Not a word, please. Not a word. Come with me.'

And, smiling at people she recognised, she led him through their ranks and into the library. Closing the door she leaned against it, trembling.

'I never expected to see you here.'

'Nor I you, Jem,' said Tam grimly. 'Are you going to tell me what on earth that masquerade was all about?'

'It's a very long story, Mr Eildor. I only came back to Creeve when I read of my stepmother's death in the newspaper. Nothing would have induced me to return to the life I had suffered here under her regime—but I

208

thought Father might need my support.'

Pausing, she shook her head sadly. 'It appears that I was wrong. Sarah turned him against me cruelly, even more effectively than I imagined, and I suspect that Timothy is the only one he needs—'

Footsteps were approaching.

'I will explain later,' she added hastily. 'About nine, when the ladies adjourn after supper, the gazebo—the one on the right-hand side of the lake.'

The footsteps departed and Gemma said, 'Safe for a while. The reason I ran away, if it isn't obvious, is that my stepmother hated me and when I refused to obey her commands or reported her injustice to Father, she made him suffer for it. "That Girl must go!"'

She sighed. 'How often I heard those words through closed doors. She never called me by my name, and was determined right from the start to get rid of me. The way most likely to be agreeable to Father was by arranging a marriage—'

'Marriage! You're just a child,' Tam interrupted.

She smiled. 'Looks are deceptive, Mr Eildor. It suited my purposes for the boy, Jem.'

That was true, and Tam realised what an unobservant fool he had been. The young face under its mass of curls, the boyish shape in large, coarse, ill-fitting shirts and breeches was now sheathed in shiny black silk. Close fitting and with the fashionable décolleté neckline revealing small breasts that were undoubtedly female. And, since Tam did not care for large bosoms, extremely attractive.

'You can't be much more than thirteen or fourteen,' he protested, forgetting that such arranged marriages for dynastic purposes between rich families were quite normal.

She laughed. 'You do flatter me, Mr Eildor. I am almost eighteen, ripe for marriage. Some of the girls I knew at school are already married and mothers of infants.'

Tam looked at her. Small, vulnerable; eighteen seemed incredibly young.

'Stepmother found a widower for me—a horrible old man—'

'How old?' asked Tam anxiously.

'Nearly forty.'

Tam groaned inwardly. Less than ten years older than himself, but he remembered that forty was middle-aged in the nineteenth century, as Gemma went on:

'I refused him, of course. The main reason, as well as finding him old and unattractive, was that I overheard him talking to Stepmother and it was quite obvious from their conversation that she had been his mistress at one time.'

With a sudden gesture she took off her bonnet with its veils and threw it on the sofa. 'I am afraid all this mourning is a mockery. We never liked each other, I knew she was unfaithful to Father when she went to London. And she had a little place in Brighton that he never knew about, where she used to entertain lovers. I am sorry for Father, especially when her end was so deplorable, but I cannot weep.'

She paused. 'I feel there is something extraordinary and deeply suspicious about the circumstances of that carriage accident. But I'm fairly sure that highwaymen had nothing to do with it. There's something we haven't—or Father hasn't—been told, to spare him.'

There was quite a lot, thought Tam, as she went on: 'Her maid Simone knows a great deal more than she pretends. They were always thick as thieves and I am certain she is familiar too with these so-called gambling friends and that secret hideout in Brighton. I expect some of them are here mourning her and Simone must be terrified in case the truth leaks out and gets her into trouble, although I expect she was well paid by Sarah to keep her mouth shut.'

There were voices outside and again they were interrupted, this time the door opened to reveal a furtive-looking couple holding hands and obviously hoping for some privacy. As they disappeared, looking very offended, Tam caught a glimpse of Townsend and Lord Henry nearby.

'I had better not be caught with you,' said Gemma, touching his arm. 'Please, Mr Eildor, not a word to Mr Townsend. Promise.'

Tam took her hand and kissed it. 'I promise. And it's Tam, by the way, not Mr Eildor.'

She blushed prettily. 'We'll meet later and I'll tell you all about Jem. How long are you to be in Brighton?' and without waiting for a reply, 'You must try to come to Creeve again—'

Putting a finger to her lips, she let herself out by the secondary door to the library which communicated by a corridor to the kitchens. As she disappeared, the other door opened to admit Lord Henry and Townsend.

'So this is where you've been hiding, Mr Eildor. Admiring the books, are you? We've searched for you everywhere. His Grace has most kindly suggested that we stay the night since it is so inclement for riding back to Brighton. He has heard from the stables that as some of the roads are under water, we should not risk the carriage. Other guests will be staying.'

At his side Lord Henry smiled. 'No need to look alarmed, Mr Eildor, you won't be expected to sleep in the stables. There are at least twenty bedrooms.'

Tam exchanged a glance with Townsend. He suspected that the invitation also included Sir Joseph's desire to have them on hand to discuss further details of how they were to investigate his wife's unfortunate demise.

The supper lasted considerably longer than Lady Gemma had anticipated. There was no sign of the ladies adjourning and they were further frustrated by the storm which had returned in full fury, with thunder and lightning, the windows lashed with rain, the candles guttering in a hundred violent draughts.

Gemma, seated across the table next to Lord Henry, looked frantically in Tam's direction and, catching his eye, gave an almost imperceptible nod, which he hoped was invisible to Townsend at his side, since it indicated the assignation in the gazebo was not to take place. He was amused, meanwhile, to observe that Lord Henry was entranced by Lady Gemma, hanging on her every word.

Could he have had access to Lord Henry's heart at that moment, he would have been even more interested. Henry was in love. For the first time, at past thirty, he had found the girl of his dreams. He had waited a long time for a girl so unique, so completely different to the women he encountered in his father's court. Perhaps it was the prince's taste in heavily bosomed, bewigged and painted, vulgar and overblown women that had stunted his own interest in the sex.

But here at last was the one he had waited for, sitting next to him. What he had seen of her figure he found immensely appealing. A lovely young girl, modest and rather shy, slim and delicately boned, small-bosomed, with an unpainted face under short, curling hair.

He longed to reach out and touch her and claim her for his own. Long before the supper was at an end, Henry had made up his mind. This was the girl he was going to marry. Tomorrow morning when her father Sir Joseph was reasonably sober he would ask for his only daughter's hand in marriage.

That she might not feel the same had not occurred to spoil his dream, for she smiled and was so attentive. And had he any doubts he told himself that he was, although illegitimate, the son of the future King of England.

Observing them, Tam saw that Gemma had only found a convivial table companion who was obviously unaware of the whispers that she was the disgraced daughter of the house. As the wine was passed around once again, some of the solemnity vanished, whispers became louder, and even the hastily subdued merriment increased. Especially as Sir Joseph toppled slowly from his chair, and was scooped up from the floor by his valet and carried up to bed.

'A nightly occurrence,' whispered the man next to Tam.

After Sir Joseph's departure a certain amount of drunken hilarity and levity crept in, turning the sober occasion into a lively wake. More bottles of brandy appeared. Glasses were raised to the late Lady Sarah by many men who, it was soon obvious, had received her gracious favours in the not too distant past, and there were some bawdy regrets at her loss expressed freely in her husband's absence.

Meanwhile Tam, whose toleration of alcohol consumption was limited by a society where drunkenness was almost unknown and, when it existed, severely frowned upon, found himself out of step with the more uninhibited behaviour of the year 1811.

Townsend knew no such inhibitions and it was Tam who finally escorted him somewhat unsteadily up beyond the grand staircase, negotiated with some drunken merriment. Not into one of those twenty bedrooms Lord Henry had predicted, but along a corridor and up some meaner wooden stairs to the attics which were the servants' quarters.

Here they were comfortable enough and had a room to themselves. Townsend, too inebriated to stop singing long enough to complain of this downgrading in status, was glad to put his head on a pillow. There he slept, not at all peacefully, but with a dreadful volume of snoring that, had Tam been completely sober himself, would have kept him from any hope of sleeping.

Next morning, they were awakened by unusual activity. Six o'clock and the servants had apparently been awake and busy with their day's activities for hours. As for Tam, he had some very confused nightmares and, when he awoke, his first thought was that he had dreamt that the convict boy Jem had changed into Lady Gemma Creeve. It was with some difficulty that in those first moments of wakefulness he realised that it was no dream. This was reality and he would no doubt be shortly seeing her again.

A knock on the door and they were informed that they were to make their way down to the study. Immediately.

Townsend, grumbling, with a particularly sore head and very red eyes, had to be shaken awake by Tam and did not receive this summons with good humour. Finally, dressed again in the few outer garments he had discarded including the long overcoat, he accompanied Tam looking slightly less the worse for wear, down to the main part of the house.

Staring through one of the great windows, Townsend said: 'Weather's better. At least we should get back to Brighton today. HRH will be anxious about us. Wanting to know what's happened. A full report.'

At the foot of the grand staircase Lord Henry waited. Looking remarkably sober, he turned a grave face towards them.

'Something wrong?' asked Townsend.

'There is indeed. There has been another death—'

'Not Sir Joseph?' said Townsend, a natural conclusion considering his nocturnal habits of

216

over-indulgence.

Henry shook his head. 'No, not Sir Joseph. Simone, Lady Sarah's maid, was found in the ornamental lake by the gamekeeper out with his dogs. Suicide apparently. Devoted to her mistress—'

Henry had already broken the news to Percy who refused to believe it.

'Someone killed her, because she knew too much. She knew the truth about the marchioness—and the prince.'

Although they were alone, Henry held up a finger to his lips. That was dangerous talk in Creeve and, after all, Lady Sarah was his beloved's stepmother. Such a scandal now made him extremely nervous.

Percy nodded furiously. 'She didn't walk into the lake, that's for sure. We talked earlier and we were to meet—'

'Where?' asked Henry.

Percy looked uncomfortable for a moment. 'At one of the summerhouses by the lake.'

Had they quarrelled, thought Henry, since the story of the aunt in Whitdean suggested that Simone might also have a lover. She was hardly likely to wait around for Percy, since she recognised there was no future for her, a mere lady's maid, beyond a few tumbles in the hay with one of the Prince Regent's grooms, married with a wife and children somewhere offstage in the home counties.

As for Percy, despite his anxiety to find

Simone's killer, he had no wish for anyone at Creeve, particularly Sir Joseph, to learn of their association. He was in blissful ignorance that all the servants who had keen eyes in their heads knew that he was Simone's lover.

'You will stay and help me?' he asked.

Henry said, 'Of course I will.' He had his own reasons for remaining at Percy's request. His mind was racing ahead to that interview with Sir Joseph, when he would formally ask for Lady Gemma's hand and take her to Brighton to meet his royal father.

How the prince would react to his report on the death of the marchioness's maid, he had little idea. Relief, perhaps, that another strand in that nightmare he was most anxious to forget was sealed and made safe by death.

'We must bear in mind, Percy, that there is a distinct possibility that she fell in and drowned by accident.'

Percy was not consoled. He laughed harshly. 'I think not. Someone at the funeral yesterday—someone who is still in this house in all probability—killed her. And I will find them, and bring them to justice, if it's the last thing I ever do.'

Prophetic words, indeed.

Chapter Nineteen

Meanwhile, Tam and Townsend were closeted with Sir Joseph who was similarly distressed and certain that Simone's death was no accident.

'She appeared to be a very level-headed young woman, not the kind who would be so emotionally involved with her mistress that she would feel that life had nothing to offer and she would take her own life. I would like you to remain with us for a day or two and investigate, Mr Townsend, especially as I owe it to my late wife. I cannot dismiss from my mind the fact that Simone's death may well have some connection with her murder. Perhaps she knew more about those gambling friends in Brighton than they wished her to reveal.'

He shrugged. 'Perhaps they were even present last night, sleeping under my roof, and are leaving undetected at this moment.' Beyond the window, where the storm had wreaked havoc with the ornamental gardens, the sound of trotting horses reached their ears from the gravel drive as the carriages of the overnight guests took their leave.

Townsend, following his gaze, gave him a despairing glance.

'Quite correct, Townsend. Of course, I can hardly insist that they all stay and wait to be questioned.'

There was nothing in truth that Townsend would have liked better, thought Tam, than to interrogate distant members of the royal family and the upper echelons of British aristocracy.

'That would present certain difficulties, Your Grace,' Townsend said smoothly. And indicating Tam, 'I should like Mr Eildor to remain to assist me. As a distinguished lawyer he is expert in such matters of detection.'

Tam bowed and smiled at this compliment, considering how little use he had been in tracking down the Stuart Sapphire. They were not one whit further in that investigation, for he was certain, despite Townsend's methods of interrogation putting the fear of God into every shopkeeper or suspicious person they interviewed, that given the circumstances of the robbery, it could only have been carried out by someone inside the Pavilion.

However, he was not too unhappy about Townsend's decision, since it gave him a chance to meet Lady Gemma again and an opportunity to hear the strange story of Jem which had twice been interrupted.

*   *   *

Sir Joseph had given instructions to put at Townsend's disposal one of the minor rooms nearby, a footman's waiting place or large

220

butler's pantry in effect. A long narrow window overlooked the main entrance and Townsend made himself comfortable in one of the two chairs provided. Leaning his elbows on the small table he looked around with satisfaction.

'This will do admirably for our purpose, and we might as well begin by interviewing the servants. If I know anything about domestics, they will know a great deal more about this maid than she knew herself.'

'May I suggest, sir, that we first look at her room,' said Tam. 'There might be some evidence there.'

'Capital idea, capital! You do that, if you please, while I line up the servants,' said Townsend having been presented by Sir Joseph with a long list of names. 'This will take some time,' he sighed.

In the hall, Tam looked around hopefully for a glimpse of Lady Gemma. Disappointed that she was not to be seen at this hour of the morning, he asked a passing servant for directions to Simone's room.

Not this time up the grand staircase but through the long narrow corridors with access to the kitchen, and up three flights of wooden back stairs. A door was opened and he was informed that this was Simone's room which she shared with Bessie, the under-housekeeper.

Tam had expected that the marchioness's

maid would have had the privilege of a room to herself, or at least something more luxurious than the rather dark room under the eaves with its barred windows.

Was that to prevent an easier way of suicide? he wondered, when a voice behind him said:

'What would you be wanting in my room, sir?' A stout apron-clad female had appeared. This was Bessie. With an apologetic smile Tam quickly explained that he was helping Mr Townsend.

'The man from the Bow Street Runners,' said Bessie, dismissing him with a sniff of contempt. 'We know him, he comes here to visit His Grace. But what would he want to know about Simone?'

Tam explained patiently that when someone died unexpectedly, even by their own hand, enquiries had to be made.

'By her own hand, indeed. Never. Not that one! She thought too much of herself. Better than the rest of us, she thought, being her ladyship's maid.'

'Do please sit down,' said Tam hopefully. This encounter promised to be interesting.

'I will sit in my own room, without your permission, young man,' puffed Bessie, but when he smiled at her, she decided she wasn't all that offended after all. In fact, she was quite happy to talk to this nice-looking young man. A pleasant change indeed and there were one or two grievances she wanted to share.

'When did you last see Simone?'

'If you mean when did she last sleep in that bed, it wasn't last night, or the night before that. And when her ladyship was at home, Simone slept in her dressing room. Very proud of that, she was. You can have the room all to yourself, Bessie, she would say. Her ladyship needs me close at hand.'

And pausing for breath, 'She thinks—I mean, thought a lot of herself, did our Simone.' Leaning forward confidentially, she shook her head. 'Now, sir, I ask you, does she sound the kind who would walk into a lake?'

'What do you think happened, Bessie?'

Bessie looked uneasy. 'I haven't made up my mind, but if you was to ask around, you'd find that Mademoiselle Simone Dupres wasn't all that she pretended to be. By no means.' She laughed harshly.

'For one thing, she wasn't French at all. I don't know the language but apart from "yes" and "no", no one ever heard her speak a word of it. Our chef is French and he laughed himself silly about it. Said she had never even set foot in France, never mind being born in Paris. As a matter of fact,' embarrassed for a moment, she cleared her throat, 'we happen to know that she came from up north, Manchester way, and Simone wasn't her real name at all.'

'That is interesting,' said Tam

encouragingly. Interesting but hardly criminal, he thought. There were French ladies' maids all over Britain in stately homes, born in Britain from humble backgrounds, who changed their names to something more exotic than Smith or Jones.

'Did she go everywhere with her ladyship?'

She looked at him and he gave her an almost conspiratorial smile. He certainly was a handsome young man and not a bit snobbish. There was something about him, kind of sympathetic and understanding, that made her want to confide in him, tell him all her troubles.

'No, she did not. We all knew that her ladyship and Simone had lives of their own. For instance, when her ladyship went to Brighton, she had a nice little place there that His Grace knew nothing about, for entertaining her friends. But Simone stayed here. It seemed she wasn't needed there and that gave her time on her own. Her ladyship is so demanding, she would say, and off she would go to that man she had in Whitdean.'

'What man was that, a lover you mean?'

So this was the mysterious sick aunt he had heard about. 'Yes, a lover he was. A married man too, we guessed.'

'Did he ever come here to visit her?'

She shook her head. 'I don't think so. At least not often and I never saw him. But there was another thing. We knew that Simone had

224

someone else.' Pausing for breath, she studied him again. He was smiling, oh, a lovely lad, so nice and friendly, she felt already as if she had known him for ages, someone she could trust.

'She had a real beau, a lord from Brighton. And he used to come and visit her in the summerhouse. He was here at the funeral. Still is, I think. I don't know whether I should give you his name, it might cause trouble.'

He smiled. 'I think I know it already,' and he put a finger to his lips.

Bessie laughed and looked amazed. 'You do know a lot, sir. Here's me telling you about Simone and I bet there's a lot you could tell me.'

'Perhaps there is, Bessie, perhaps there is. Meanwhile I have to look through Simone's possessions, just in case there is anything else we should know about.'

Bessie obligingly indicated a wooden trunk. 'That was all she kept here, her wardrobe as she called it. She kept it locked. She didn't know that I knew where she kept the key,' she added.

Standing on tiptoe she retrieved it from above the window ledge and gave it to Tam. 'It's all right, sir, you won't find anything but clothes. No secrets there. If she had any private letters and things, she didn't keep them here.'

She stood by him while he unlocked the trunk.

'Only clothes, like I said.' It was true. And handing her back the key, he thought she blushed, for his smile also said: As you well know.

A bell rang shrilly on the wall. 'Oh Lord, that's for me. I must go.' And at the door, straightening her apron, she curtseyed and gave him a coquettish glance. 'Glad to have been of help, sir.'

*   *   *

Downstairs in the hall, a selection of servants of various ages and in various uniforms were sitting on improvised benches awaiting their turn to be interviewed by John Townsend. Tam observed one very young and scared-looking maid emerge and he guessed she was thoroughly intimidated by the Bow Street officer's technique of interrogation, as she rushed over to an older, more experienced maid and looked ready to burst into tears.

He followed the next in line and Townsend acknowledged his presence with a nod. Once more he found that, although the questions were conventional, Townsend's manner was threatening, his voice too loud, in that lion's roar which seem to presume severe deafness on the other person's part. He was, by now, well acquainted with Townsend's methods of interviewing possible suspects. He had seen it day after tedious day in the back streets of

226

Brighton.

How long have you been a servant here? What was your relationship with Simone? (Most did not fully understand that this only meant: Did you like her?) Do you know anything, in confidence, of Simone's private life, or of any enemies that would have driven her to suicide or make her a potential murder victim?

The answer was invariably 'No' but it was the word 'murder' that struck terror into their hearts. As one servant was dismissed, Townsend ticked his sheet against that name, whose place was taken by yet another.

'So far,' he whispered, 'can't fault a single one of them. They are all either innocent, know nothing about the maid or are indulging in a conspiracy of silence,' he added grimly.

It was fairly obvious that Townsend's conclusions were justified, and Tam felt that he had done considerably better with Bessie, who had willingly given him information, her assumption correct that Simone considered herself superior to mere domestics and had behaved accordingly, distancing herself from them and from the activities of the servants' hall.

The morning was over when the last of the servants went back to their duties. Townsend threw down his pen and gathered his notes in a gesture of disgust.

'That was a regular waste of time. It's hard

to believe that they were all speaking the truth—' Then, as the stable clock struck twelve, he consulted his pocket watch and brightened considerably. 'Now we might hope for luncheon, but I am afraid Sir Joseph will be disappointed.'

If Townsend had hopes of dining with the family it was he who was to be disappointed, as a servant brought a tray with steak pies, potatoes and roly-poly pudding into the tiny room. Considering the tankard of ale, Townsend looked deeply offended, having hoped for wines from the Creeve cellar, which, he assured Tam, were of excellent vintage.

Tam nodded sympathetically. Townsend was a long way from being treated as the close family friend he bragged about being. But Tam was also nursing a secret disappointment. Lunch in the dining room would have given him another opportunity to talk to Jem, or Lady Gemma, as he had to get used to addressing her.

They were finishing their meal when a knock on the door announced Dr Brooke, who had been called into examine the dead woman.

'I thought you would want to know that she drowned. No doubt about that, her lungs were full of water. But that is not to say that she wasn't pushed into the lake first and her head held under.'

Townsend looked gratified at the doctor's verdict as he went on: 'One thing I did learn was that none of the servants ever heard of her wanting to take the waters in Brighton. She seemed to have an aversion to water in any form; we are given to understand that is a weakness of the French in general.'

Tam looked at him and decided not to mention that Simone was from Manchester. Would Lord Percy make arrangements for her burial? That seemed doubtful in the circumstances, but he hoped that there was enough information about her for someone close to collect her body. Otherwise it would be donated to the medical profession, as was the rule for unclaimed bodies.

As the doctor left them Townsend sighed. 'So we're no further forward,' he grumbled, 'sounds as if she was done in, right enough, but we aren't any nearer finding her killer.'

'We still have the outdoor staff,' Tam reminded him gently and, when Townsend frowned, he added: 'She died outside, after all. What about stable boys, gardeners and so forth?'

Townsend gave him a sharp and rather angry look as if he had rather wished his enquiries to be over for the day. And sighing wearily, he said: 'I suppose you're right. My nephew Rob, he works in the stables.'

This information was given a little reluctantly, Tam thought, guessing that this was Townsend's real connection with Creeve House, not the marquis's friendship he enjoyed boasting about.

'He's an honest, reliable lad so at least we will get the truth from him.'

They were walking across the hall when Townsend spotted Sir Joseph leaving the dining room and heading towards the study. 'Must have a word, he will want to know our progress so far. Just wait here for me.'

Tam waited, enjoying a chance to look at some of the ancient portraits of bygone Creeves that lined the walls, when a footman approached and handed him an envelope. 'This is for Mr Townsend, will you give it to him please?'

When Townsend emerged a few minutes later, he took the envelope and thrust it into his pocket with an impatient gesture. His flushed countenance spoke louder than any words that his interview with His Grace had not gone particularly well.

Chapter Twenty

In the stables, Rob seemed genuinely delighted to see his uncle and looked suitably impressed at being introduced to an Edinburgh lawyer. After the usual preliminaries regarding family matters, Rob said how shocked they all were at the maid drowning in the lake. A suicide, as they had been informed.

'I suppose there must be suspicious circumstances, Uncle John, that we haven't heard about and that's why you're here,' Rob added shrewdly and immediately offered to talk to the lads, to see what they knew.

'Mind you, I can account for most of them last night. We were given the meats and ale left over from her ladyship's funeral and the ten of us had a giddy old time, myself included, and we all went to our beds very drunk indeed. Frankly, Uncle, I don't think any of us knew Simone except for seeing her at a distance walking with Lady Sarah, or on the odd occasion when she was sent to make arrangements for her ladyship's horse to be saddled.'

'Did she ride with her?'

'Never. She was a bit scared of horses.'

'What about her ladyship's visits to Brighton?' Townsend asked the coachman who had joined them and who was eagerly listening to their conversation. 'Didn't she take a carriage?'

'Not from here, sir. Maybe she took her horse.'

'She never did,' Rob replied, and Tam had a sudden unbidden vision of the marchioness clad in nothing but a fur cloak and pearls, riding furiously along the Lewes road. Then sensibly he realised these items were most probably kept in her Brighton apartment to wear on the short step to the secret entrance at the Pavilion.

'His Grace only keeps one carriage these days, doesn't travel much any more. But there are hiring ones available in Lewes. Mostly for rich ladies, widows and suchlike, travelling on their own or for folks who can't afford to keep a carriage and horses. You have to be rich for that, you know.'

The coachman informed them that the gardeners didn't live in and went back to their own homes in the village, starting early on summer mornings.

Townsend had a stroke of luck when the gamekeeper who had discovered the maid's body had seen them walking towards the stables and was waiting in the yard eager to tell his story to the Bow Street officer.

Peters was his name, he said, and he had spotted what he thought at first was an old sack floating in the ornamental lake.

'Gave me quite a turn, it did, when I realised who it was. Yes, I recognised the young lady, she often walked past my cottage near the drive back there, and if I was in my garden we would pass the time of day, very polite she was.'

He sighed and looked bleakly at them. 'Shame it is, smart wench like that taking her own life when she had so much to live for.'

Tam studied him closely as he spoke. He was a handsome man aged about forty, tall, with white hair and a moustache. Tam wondered if Townsend had noticed that he was very well-spoken and had the look of an army officer who had seen better days.

As far as the theory of murders was concerned, the killer was most usually to be found in the ranks of those known to the victim: family or close associates. Or the person who made the discovery and, Tam had reached his own conclusions, deciding that Peters was the prime suspect as he replied to Townsend's question.

'As a matter of fact, sir, I did see a tall man, a stranger—possibly someone who had been at her ladyship's funeral—hanging about near the summerhouse late last night. He wasn't wanting to be seen and was quite upset when my dogs flushed him out. I thought he just didn't want to be sociable, the gentry are often that way inclined, you know.'

Suspect number two, thought Tam uneasily, wondering if the tall stranger the gamekeeper had observed might also be the stalker who remained invisible to Townsend.

As they walked back to the house, Townsend put his hand in his pocket and drew out the envelope which he had forgotten about.

He handed it to Tam. 'I don't have my spectacles. Please read it to me—I don't suppose it is anything important.'

It was a very short note: 'Dear Mr Townsend, I saw you at the funeral. I should like to have a word with you if convenient. (Signed) Simone Dupres.'

Townsend stopped, thumped his fists together. 'There we have it. That is our evidence. Does that sound to you like a note from a woman who was going to throw herself in the lake?'

Handing the note back, Tam considered its significance. There was no point in mentioning that it could have been a note from a woman who had accidentally fallen into the lake.

Continuing to walk with his head down and his hands behind his back in that familiar gesture, he said to Tam: 'How came you by this note, may I ask?'

'One of the footmen gave it to me when you were with Sir Joseph.'

'Oh, that,' said Townsend dismissively at what was obviously an unpleasant reminder. 'We had better find out when the maid gave it to him for a start, and then we can continue our enquiries.'

The note was not as difficult to track down as Townsend had imagined. Tam recognised the footman who said it was left on the hall table amongst the morning's mail.

'I think this makes it fairly obvious that her reason for wishing to speak to me must have concerned something she knew about the death of her mistress,' said Townsend. 'Sounds as if the killer knew and decided to shut her mouth for good.'

Tam realised there was nothing in the note to hint that she was in danger, and it might well have been that she fancied a change of scene, and that the Bow Street officer would have had reliable London connections.

Suddenly Townsend stopped and put his hand in his pocket. 'Dropped my best silk handkerchief. Must have been at the stables. You head on—' he said and hurried back the way they had come.

Which was a piece of fortune for Tam, as at that moment Lady Gemma emerged from one of the adjoining paths.

'I've been hoping to find you,' she said. 'At last!'

She was at his side and looking down at her, longing to take her hand, he was delighted at this encounter, his heart beating unaccountably faster as he remembered those other dreaded encounters in the Promenade Gardens with Princess Charlotte.

'Let's go to the summerhouse over there,' she said. 'We won't be disturbed at this time of day.'

The gazebo was prettily furnished with a comfortable sofa and tables, perfectly adapted, he realised, for assignations since the curtains could also be closed.

'Do sit down, Mr—I mean, Tam, you are making me nervous,' she said patting the sofa beside her and regarding him solemnly. 'We may not have much time so where do I begin about Jem?'

'Why not try the beginning?' he asked dryly.

She laughed. 'As I said yesterday before we were interrupted, life had become intolerable here at Creeve. I couldn't bear it any longer, especially the nightmare prospect of being married off against my will.'

She shrugged. 'From what I have seen of the married state, I would prefer to make my own choice—some day, perhaps! So I decided to go to London to my maternal grandmother who, it is true, I have rarely met over the years. But she has been kind and remembered my birthdays, so I was sure she would understand and make me welcome.

'Alas, I had chosen the wrong time. She was away to Italy, I was told at the door, the house locked up with only this woman, the housekeeper and her husband, as caretakers. I was told, somewhat grudgingly I thought, yes, I could stay the night, but when I got up next morning, I was alone in the house. The two of them had disappeared—so had my luggage from the hall and all my money. In fact, the house had a rather bare look and I suspected that most of the silver and valuable contents were in the process of disappearing and I had interrupted thieves raiding the house.'

She sighed. 'There was I with nothing but the nightgown I was wearing and not a penny to pay for my next meal. I searched through

236

empty cupboards but there was no food, but I did find a shirt and a pair of shabby breeches which had been discarded as worthless, probably by the gardener's boy. Miraculously they fitted, after a fashion, so I sailed forth on London, to make my fortune,' she added bitterly.

'I decided that I would fare better as a boy, trying to get some menial job with enough to live on until my grandmother's return, than a girl wearing only a nightgown. The answer to the latter, I am sure, would have been pretty obvious and street-walking was not an alternative I relished. I wandered about for a whole day and in Covent Garden, desperately hungry, I took a loaf of bread from a stall.'

She sighed. 'From my sheltered life at Creeve, I had no idea of the consequences of stealing a loaf of bread. The woman was furious, called a watchman who was walking by and I was arrested, thrown into a horrible jail where I had to fight off the advances of some dreadful men who were fellow prisoners. Then the very next day, there were trials on the go, and I was sentenced to transportation to the colonies.

'I could hardly believe the injustice of it all. You know the rest. I was put aboard the convict ship in chains but fortunately my ankles and wrists were so thin that I managed to wriggle out of them and get on deck, desperately thinking of a way to escape, as I

237

couldn't swim.'

She stopped and turned to him. 'And then—there you were.'

'Do go on,' said Tam.

She shook her head and said in bewildered tones: 'I was told yesterday that you are an Edinburgh lawyer, a survivor off the *Royal Stuart*, the ship that sank after we were escaping from the hulks.'

Hand on chin, she surveyed him intently, awaiting some comment. When none was forthcoming, Tam staring steadily across the lake, she said softly: 'But that is a lie, is it not, Tam Eildor? You certainly were not a passenger on any ship, you were in the water in that little boat with me when we saw it go down.'

Tam was searching for some convincing but non-committal words, when Gemma continued in a voice that now held caution and a touch of fear. 'Tell me, how did you do it?'

'Do what?' he asked with a smile he hoped was innocent.

'Do what?' she repeated sharply. 'You know perfectly well. How did you get on to the hulks? Just—just suddenly appear like that—out of nowhere.'

She sounded scared now and he tried to make light of it. 'What exactly had you in mind?'

She shook her head. 'I was hiding, carefully

238

watching those two men who had come on deck in search of me, deciding what to do next. There was no one else on that part of the deck—only them and me. Then suddenly there was something—' She frowned, 'like a bit of light, the blink of an eye—and there you were, sitting against the bulwark. It was lucky for me that they were more interested in you and the boots you were wearing.'

There was silence and then puzzlement, and perhaps still rather frightened, she said: 'Where did you come from and how on earth did you do it, Tam Eildor?'

He took her hand, smiled and said: 'It was a trick I learned, I'll tell you all about it sometime.'

'Why not now?' she demanded. 'And why a convict ship, of all places?' she added, pulling her hand free in an impatient gesture.

'Listen, Gemma, I saved your life. You owe me that and all I ask is that you trust me. You didn't seem to do that when we met in Brighton. You took to your heels fast enough, as if you had plenty to hide.'

'And so I had. I didn't want to be sent back to my stepmother's tender mercies.'

'How did you get to Brighton then?' he asked.

'I was going to ask the same of you. An amazing coincidence, wasn't it, us both turning up at the Old Ship like that—'

Looking out of the gazebo, Tam saw

Townsend approaching on the road that would take him past the summerhouse.

'I'm supposed to be helping that gentleman out there solve a murder,' he said briskly. 'Our little talk will have to wait until later, I'm afraid.'

'Don't think you can get away from Creeve without telling me,' she said shortly. 'I have friends in Brighton, too.'

Seizing her hand, he kissed it. 'I wouldn't dream of leaving without seeing you again. You are lovely, dear Gemma—and I much prefer you to young Jem.'

She blushed, and as he was stepping into the garden she asked: 'What do you know about Lord Henry Fitzgeorge, by the way?'

Turning, he said: 'Not a lot. He's the Prince Regent's son. Why?'

She laughed. 'He has just asked my father for my hand in marriage. All based on us having met at supper last night.'

'Are you going to accept Lord Henry then?' Tam, suddenly angry and jealous, was sure he had not disguised the anxiety in his voice.

She looked at him and smiled slowly. There was no mistaking a woman's coquetry this time. 'I haven't really had time to think about it, but I might.'

As he walked quickly to catch up with Townsend, with feelings towards Lord Henry that were far from friendly, he decided that Lady Gemma was learning fast how to

240

become a woman of her time.

Chapter Twenty-One

Tam hurried towards Townsend, his thoughts with Gemma, exquisite in her white muslin dress with its fashionable Paisley shawl. How lovely she was, how could anyone have been idiot enough (meaning himself, in particular) to mistake her for a boy?

So engrossed was he in recriminations, he failed to see Lord Henry who had been lurking about the vicinity of the summerhouse. Hoping to see Gemma and acquaint her with the results of his interview with her father, he was somewhat aggrieved to see her in the company of Mr Eildor, consoling himself that the lawyer perhaps had some legal matter to discuss, a possible legacy from her late stepmother's will.

However, as the minutes passed, sudden bursts of merriment from within the summerhouse suggested less of a lawyer on urgent business than an intimacy based on more than a first acquaintance at Lady Sarah's funeral.

Checking his pocket watch, frowning, with increasing feelings of suspicion, disquiet and jealousy, he strained to hear more than the indistinct murmur of conversation, impatient at being kept waiting since his interview with Sir Joseph had been even more successful than he could have ever anticipated.

Stammering out his request, Henry had found Gemma's father most amenable. Beaming upon him, he had shaken him by the hand in a most sincere manner.

'By all means, young fellow, ask Gemma and if she raises any objections, I think I can deal with them,' Sir Joseph added grimly, certain that no girl in her right mind (but could that be said of Gemma?) would be mad to turn down such a catch.

Besides, he wanted rid of her as soon as possible, any excuse would do. He had allowed himself to be persuaded by Sarah's whispers, tantrums and tears that That Girl was No Good and, having made up his mind years ago, he was not prepared to change it now. But her presence did arouse uneasy feelings of guilt, that he had never ever loved her. She was a blot on his conscience. All his love and devotion belonged to Timothy.

The boy had screamed when Gemma came near him, a tribute to Sarah's influence, and as Sir Joseph heard his bedtime prayers only last night, whispering 'Amen' he said: 'When is That Girl going, Pa? I don't like her much.'

And what Timothy wanted, Timothy got as far as his doting father was concerned. There was another reason too for jubilation at Lord Henry's proposal. As a favoured acquaintance of Prince George, Sir Joseph was selfish enough to consider the social advantages of such a royal alliance, even with a bastard son of the Prince Regent, and, although not greatly endowed with imagination, he could not fail to relish the prospect of a wedding in Westminster Cathedral.

When Henry left, blushing and still stammering his thanks, Sir Joseph had called Gemma to his study. Greeted with a fond smile, he tried not to wince or push her away as she offered to kiss his cheek.

Something deep inside recognised that this was a time ripe for reconciliation but he could not make the right move. He was awkward with her, always had been from the first days when she was handed to him, a tiny bundle of lace shawls. Never knowing what to say or what was expected of him, bitterly resentful with a wife dead giving her birth, when she was not the son he craved. He had never loved her, not even before Timothy.

'Please take a seat, Gemma.'

She looked at him, still smiling, her eyes full of affectionate regard.

'How long are you staying with us?'

'As long as you need me, Father,' she said softly.

He looked away, embarrassed. He did not need her or anyone else in the world, as long as he had Timothy, his joy and his life.

'Have you any plans for the future?' he

asked.

Gemma recognised his embarrassment and said gently: 'Not at all.' That wasn't quite true but she asked: 'How long would you like me to stay?' hoping he would say: 'I love you, my darling girl. I would like you to stay forever, all the past forgotten, we could start anew.'

Instead she saw only his cold face as he shrugged: 'As you wish.' And rubbing his knuckles, a gesture she remembered from childhood when there were disciplinary matters ahead, he said: 'The reason I asked you to come and see me so urgently is because—' Pausing, he took a deep breath, 'because Lord Henry Fitzgeorge has asked for your hand.'

There was a pause from Gemma this time. 'My hand—' she looked at her fingers, clenched her fist. Bewildered, she repeated: 'My hand?'

'Yes, your hand—in marriage,' he said shortly. 'Silly girl, he wants to marry you.'

Gemma sprang from her chair and stared at him as if he had taken leave of his senses. 'But—but I hardly know him. We only met at supper last night—we talked politely—'

'Whatever you talked about must have impressed him enough to ask for you.' Sir Joseph sounded cynical, losing patience rapidly, afraid there might be a trick in this stroke of fortune. It was too good to be true that the Prince Regent's son wanted to marry

244

this skinny, plain girl who had no bosom and looked like an immature boy.

'Well, what have you to say to that?' he demanded.

Gemma shook her head. 'I don't know what to say, Father.'

Sir Joseph drummed his fingers on the arm of his chair and continued to regard her dispassionately. How could any man want to bed this slip of a girl? The thought aroused visions of his voluptuous Sarah and he sighed. He would never find her like again.

'You might at least show some gratitude,' he said huffily.

Head on side she regarded him. 'Gratitude—for what?' she asked quietly.

He stabbed a finger at her. 'Gratitude and honour that the son of the future King of England wants to marry you. That should be enough for any girl. Even for you,' he added sourly.

'So—I'm to be sold to the highest bidder, am I?'

Sir Joseph made an impatient gesture. 'You'll never get such a chance again, I can assure you, if you turn this one down.' He laughed shortly. 'Chance of a lifetime—women all over the country would give their eye teeth to marry the Prince Regent's son.'

'Which would not be a pretty sight,' she said acidly.

He stared at her blankly. It was his turn to

be bewildered and angry. Sarah had been right. He seemed to hear her voice: 'That Girl was born an idiot, an ungrateful idiot after all we have done for her.'

'I will think about it, Father. Now may I be excused?' And with a swift curtsey which somehow seemed more mockery than politeness, she was gone.

*   *   *

Gemma went up to her room, trying to remember the events of the funeral supper, trying to recall anything interesting about Lord Henry's table conversation. All she remembered was smiling and saying 'yes' and 'no' in what she hoped were the right places while all the time watching Tam Eildor across the table and wishing, wishing she had been placed beside him.

Tam Eildor, her rescuer from a watery grave, that intriguing man of mystery. There were a lot of questions with answers only he could provide. Afraid that if she did not see him before he left with Townsend they might never meet again, she had laughed at yet another of Lord Henry's outrageously flattering remarks, of which she had heard not one word.

Obviously she should have paid more attention, for she had in her distraction and anxiety to be polite quickened some masculine desire strong enough to make him want to marry her. Trying now to get him into perspective, all she could remember was her first impression of a resurrected young George, Prince of Wales, from those flattering early portraits. She had thought with some amusement that given the Court lifestyle of over-indulgence in wine and women he would probably run to fat and gouty middle age.

*   *   *

She sighed. That was last night. Today her world had changed, and looking into the secrets of her heart, she knew where her love lay, doomed and too late as, watching Tam striding down the path, remembering their conversation and his angry comments, she gathered up her shawl and prepared to leave the summerhouse.

She found Lord Henry before her, framed in the doorway, bowing and smiling.

He was the last person she wanted to see at that moment and, after a polite greeting, a curtsey and wishing him good day, she expected him to stand aside. But Henry was not in the least intimidated by her somewhat frosty reception, that is, if he even noticed it was a little on the cool side.

He was not to be put off. As she approached him, he grasped her hand firmly; his was cold and clammy, even on a warm summer morning.

Nerves, anxiety, poor creature, Gemma thought with a shudder, remembering other more agreeable hands—Tam's, so warm, so—everything.

Lord Henry was fondling her fingers. How extraordinary. 'You would make me the happiest of men.'

'Indeed!' Gemma said breathlessly, unable to think of anything that would not hint at encouragement.

'I have spoken to your father. I believe he has spoken to you—I have his permission—' All this came out in a rush as he dropped on one knee before her on the dusty summerhouse floor. Those white trousers, she thought, they would never recover from this onslaught.

'Please, I beg you, Lady Gemma. Say you will be my wife and I will be the happiest man in the entire world.'

Gemma stared down on his head. Brown curls, like the Prince's portraits. Not a bad-looking fellow, but about as enticing as Michelangelo's statue of David in Florence. Less really, she thought in a moment's frivolity.

Such grovelling was ridiculous. 'Please, sir, be so good as to take a seat here, and we will talk about this.'

Bounding to his feet like an exuberant puppy he bounced on to the sofa beside her, groping for the hand she had quickly thrust out of sight beneath her shawl.

This did not put him off either, not in the least. He began babbling that she was the most beautiful girl he had ever met. Truly, he had never met anyone quite like her. And he had fallen deeply in love at first sight. If she did not, nay, could not ever return his love, then he was lost forever—

Gemma halted this mid-stream. 'Pray, Lord Henry, I do beseech you—be calm.'

'Calm!' he stared at her wide-eyed as if he had never heard the word before and she had suggested something gross and indecent.

'Yes, calm. It takes two people to make a marriage and two people to consent in the first place. At least, it does in my opinion. I do not adhere to the belief that girls should obey their parents' wishes and marry whoever is chosen for them.' Gemma said this with some feeling, remembering the old widower who had been her stepmother's lover.

Henry said nothing. He looked at her, clearly amazed at this speech, his eyes suddenly rather like a devoted spaniel begging a treat.

Gemma took advantage of the pause— anything was better than the grovelling. 'May I point out, sir, that we hardly know one another. We are mere acquaintances—'

'Our fathers are known to one another—' he began.

'That is not enough for me. We are the parties concerned, strangers to each other, and any talk of marriage between us is quite ridiculous.'

'Ridiculous!' He left her side, down on his knees before her again. 'Do not, I pray, say that. Is there no hope? You who are so lovely, so gentle, do you wish to break my heart?'

She looked at him pityingly. 'Please, Lord Henry, please do not kneel. That is quite ridiculous and very unbecoming to a gentleman.'

He was back beside her in an instant.

'You talk of hearts, well, my heart is also of some consequence for it rules my future life and happiness,' she said.

'I can promise you happiness—such happiness!' he cried. 'Never doubt that.'

Ignoring that promise, Gemma went on: 'I would need to know you a great deal better before I would be comfortable in deciding to spend the rest of my life with you.'

'So there is hope!' he said snatching at straws in the absence of that hand so carefully withheld.

Gemma smiled. 'I can only give you the answer to that when we are better acquainted,' she repeated.

'May I then ask your father's permission to take you back to Brighton with me, suitably chaperoned, of course, to meet HRH, who I imagine you know is my true father,' he added

250

shyly.

Gemma smiled. 'Who could doubt it, sir? The resemblance is very strong.'

It was Henry's turn to smile. It had been easier than he expected to persuade her to return with him. It also fitted in very well with Gemma's plans—Brighton meant the possibility of seeing Tam Eildor again.

'Thank you, sir, for your invitation. I will be honoured to accept.'

So saying, she gave him her hand. He squeezed it and said: 'I will make the necessary arrangements. Perhaps you would care to stay with Mrs Maria Fitzherbert, as it would not be quite proper to stay in the Pavilion.'

As he said the words, he had visions of the lewd goings-on there, of his father's lascivious behaviour and, in particular, the dark remembrance of the very recent fate of one royal whore who was her stepmother.

'If that will not be too inconvenient,' said Gemma.

'It will be splendid, perfectly splendid. And will you please call me Henry—all my friends do.'

Chapter Twenty-Two

Tam caught up with Townsend, realising he should have stayed and heard Gemma's story, in particular how she had escaped from the smugglers who had tried to kill him and how she had arrived in Brighton, still disguised as the convict boy Jem. That omission was his own fault. The idea of her marrying Lord Henry had upset him—he did not dare to put a name to why—and he had left her rather more abruptly than was polite.

Townsend was apologising for the delay. Nephew Rob had remembered all sorts of family matters for discussion.

Tam murmured a reply, but he wasn't really listening, realising that the conclusion of Gemma's story would also involve him in an explanation of how he had travelled from the year 2250 to land on the deck of a convict ship in August 1811. How could he expect her, or anyone else for that matter, to understand?

'There's still a lot untold, and likely to remain so,' Townsend was saying. Tam stared at him but realised he was referring to the mysterious death of Simone. 'But as we are never likely to know the true circumstances,' Townsend went on, 'we might as well get back to Brighton as soon as possible. We still have a jewel thief to track down, remember.'

As they approached the house, Tam guessed that the ending of Gemma's story was also likely to remain untold. Her adventures over, she was back in her own home again, and it was unlikely that he would ever return to Lewes, or see her again. He had a feeling that his time-quest was also drawing to its close and not as successfully as he would have wished. There were too many loose ends.

It seemed unlikely that he would now find out who had murdered the marchioness and stolen the Stuart Sapphire, but his imminent departure from Brighton was timely, since he was disobeying all his own rules by becoming emotionally involved with the characters of history. He recognised all the symptoms. He was not only in danger of losing his own life but also of falling in love with a girl who had been dead for more than four hundred years.

*   *   *

Sir Joseph was waiting for them. Tam listened as Townsend shook his head sadly and confirmed that they were no further forward with their investigations and had drawn a blank with the outside staff too.

Tam looked at him. Surely he had not missed the significance of the gamekeeper as Townsend handed Sir Joseph the note that had been left for him by the maid the night before she died.

253

Sir Joseph scanned it briefly, thrust it back to Townsend and agreed with Tam's own conclusion that it could hardly be regarded as evidence that she had been murdered.

He shook his head. 'That could have meant anything. The woman was quite naturally very distressed and she said to me that as her services were no longer needed in Creeve, perhaps she should move back to London. That note was perhaps only a helpful gesture that you might be able to put her in touch with the right sort of people, Townsend.'

Pausing for a moment, he added: 'I suggest you call a halt to your enquiries which are very unsettling for the servants, and let us all get back to normal as quickly as possible.'

Tam wondered if there had already been complaints from some of the senior members of staff, who had emerged aggrieved and antagonised by the Bow Street officer's questioning methods, as Sir Joseph added: 'The housekeeper has an address for Simone's relatives in this country who will do the necessary, so we can now dismiss the unhappy business as a tragic accident.'

And even if it wasn't, Sir Joseph thought to himself, he no longer cared in the least. He wanted no more scandal, there was a stigma about violent death that families found hard to live down and his beloved Sarah's bizarre and horrible death was more than enough for Creeve to bear. A stain that would remain in

254

people's minds and gossip for a very long time.

He now had a more valid and pressing reason for wishing the Bow Street officer and the Edinburgh lawyer off the premises. The possibility, nay, certainty that his daughter would be persuaded to marry Lord Henry. The royal connection made it of vital importance that the residents of Creeve House should bear careful scrutiny in the Prince Regent's eyes, and that murders and accidental drownings be forgotten as soon as possible.

He was already regretting having offered a reward for information concerning the carriage accident and wondered if it could be withdrawn from the newspaper.

*   *   *

As Tam and Townsend prepared to leave, arrangements were confirmed for their journey back to Brighton. Their carriage from the royal stables was now housed in the Creeve stable block. Walking once more in that direction, Tam realised that the distant summerhouse would also be remembered as the scene of his last parting with Gemma.

Townsend had been very thoughtful and silent since leaving the house, walking swiftly in the lead with his head down and hands behind his back in that characteristic pose.

Tam, who was sensitive to atmosphere and remarkably intuitive, felt certain there was something urgent troubling him which he was not prepared to share.

Suddenly he stopped dead in his tracks. 'Peters—you remember, the gamekeeper!'

Tam looked at him. Had he seen rather too late the significance of the gamekeeper discovering Simone's body floating in the lake?

'Met him earlier on my way back from the stables,' said Townsend. 'He promised me a brace of grouse for HRH. Must collect them.'

If this seemed quaint to Tam, who felt that the prince's larder was always groaning with food, his table overstocked at every meal, to Townsend it was apparently a nice gesture, as he changed direction and plunged through the little wood that led to the gamekeeper's cottage.

Footfalls through the undergrowth, a shout, and Lord Percy emerged.

He was furious. 'Sir Joseph has just told me that the two of you are leaving. That you, Townsend, have decided against any further enquiries into Simone's death—I cannot believe—I cannot believe,' he added, thumping his fists together in an agitated manner, 'that both of you would treat her death in this totally uncaring manner.'

Townsend began to protest, but Percy cut him short. 'It is obvious to me and it must be so to you if you have the least sense of justice in your head, that someone killed her. Someone in Creeve.'

Tam wondered if Percy was right and as the gamekeeper was his own personal choice as prime suspect whether it was a good idea for them to meet. He glanced at Townsend who obviously had no intention of mentioning Simone's note which would have been exceedingly inflammatory to Percy, the proverbial red rag to a bull. Tam observed uneasily that Percy was so enraged, almost completely unhinged by the maid's death, he might well take the law into his own hands.

The gamekeeper was just emerging from his cottage with a gun and his two dogs as they reached the gate. He greeted them cheerfully and, darting inside, came out again flourishing the promised brace of grouse.

Lord Percy hung back, breathing deeply. Townsend was about to introduce them when Peters said coldly:

'We have met.'

The two men glared at each other and bowed stiffly. No love lost there either, thought Tam, wondering what earlier encounters had brought that about. Peters accompanied them, chatting to Townsend as they headed in the direction of the stables, and left them at a fork in the path, heading towards open fields.

'Checking my snares, see if I've caught

anything,' he said saluting them cheerfully.

As they walked on through the wood on the narrow path, which was rough underfoot, Percy, in the lead, turned occasionally to shout over his shoulder and revile Townsend about going back to Brighton when he had work tracking down a killer here in Creeve.

Percy was like a hound with a rabbit, Tam thought, he just wouldn't let go.

Townsend refused to argue any more, he said smoothly that he realised how Lord Percy felt and while he was completely in sympathy with his natural distress, Lord Percy must understand that the Bow Street officer was not his own master. He was answerable to the highest authority in the land.

'I beg to point out, sir, that the search for the Stuart Sapphire is the very reason for my presence in Brighton and I was called away, most reluctantly, from investigating a particularly important and gruesome murder case in London to obey HRH's command.'

Tam noted that there was no mention of Mr Eildor's journey to London similarly being cut short. And then he remembered grimly that he was dispensable and, walking between the two men, a few steps ahead of Townsend, he had the uncomfortable feeling that there was someone else there, following them.

The faint crack of a branch underfoot, a bush that moved when there was no wind, a frightened cry as a disturbed bird took up in to

258

the air.

Danger, danger, his instinct alerted him. And then it was worse. Suddenly they were surrounded by an army of buzzing insects, feeding on the corpse of a long-dead rabbit underfoot and bitterly resentful of this human intrusion to their grisly feast.

One of them flung itself angrily into Tam's face.

As he jerked his head aside, the shot rang out.

A cry and, in front of him, Percy fell to the ground, a deep, dark red rose of blood on his head.

Tam leapt back, past Townsend who stood still, his mouth open like one paralysed, and headed in the direction of the pistol shot, moving with his usual swiftness, his feet hardly seeming to touch the ground.

Seconds later he had the fleeing assassin in his grip and stared into the terrified face of the Brighton stalker.

The man was burly, built like a prize-fighter, but no match for Tam's litheness and speed. As he tried to escape that relentless hold, the pistol fell to the ground. Both tried to retrieve it and the man, using his extra weight, shouldered Tam off balance and hurled him against a tree.

As Tam slithered down against the tree trunk, Townsend appeared. One glance took in the scene.

'Tell him who I am, for Christ's sake,' shouted the stalker. 'Tell the silly bugger I'm one of you.'

At that, Townsend calmly bent down, picked up the double-barrelled pistol, took aim straight at the stalker's head. The man screamed: 'You bloody devil, Townsend— you—' and was silenced by bloody death.

Townsend paused, calmly turned and regarded Tam lying against the tree trunk. It seemed to Tam that there was a moment's indecision. Perhaps this was to be his death scene too. Then, calmly pocketing the pistol, Townsend held out a hand to help Tam to his feet.

'Not hurt, are you? Good. Saved us a hanging. Let's see to Lord Percy.'

They raced back along the narrow path where Percy lay still on the ground, bleeding heavily from his head wound. As Townsend bent over him Tam watched horrified and sickened by the scene before him and the execution he had just witnessed.

It was now perfectly obvious that the stalker had been one of the Bow Street men brought secretly to Brighton, perhaps to protect his master by remaining invisible, or to follow and annihilate Tam Eildor. Today in the wood, Tam had been the target and a buzzing angry insect deprived of its feast had saved his life, for the bullet that hit Percy in the back of the head was meant for him, of that he had not the slightest doubt.

Henry rushed towards them. 'What's happened? I heard shots—anyone hurt?'

He saw their grave faces and Percy lying bleeding on the ground. With a groan, he bent over his friend. 'An accident—oh God, we must get him back to the house.'

There were other voices. The gamekeeper appeared, said he had also heard pistol shots, seen smoke arising from the wood. The shots had also been heard by two of the estate workers, and as Townsend and Henry carried Percy into the summerhouse where Tam dragged down some of the drapery to staunch that terrible flow of blood, one of the men was sent up to the house to summon Dr Brooke.

It seemed like hours before the doctor appeared. He had been leaving Sir Joseph after his almost daily visit. Now he was panting along the path by the lake, followed by two footmen bearing an improvised stretcher to take the unconscious Lord Percy back up to the house.

Tam was still in a state of shock and could hardly bear to look at John Townsend, who was saying to Sir Joseph:

'Apparently there was a stalker,' and looking at Tam, he bowed. 'Mr Eildor, whose eyes are younger and sharper than mine, thought he spotted the man yesterday at her ladyship's funeral. I wish I had seen him too.'

'And who was this man?' demanded Sir

Joseph.

Townsend shook his head sadly. 'We have no idea, sir. Never will now. Possibly a madman of some sort, lurking about. Perhaps someone with a grudge against Lord Percy.'

A shrug and he continued: 'It seems quite likely now that Lord Percy was right after all and that he did push the maid into the lake. Perhaps she rejected his advances.'

And spreading his hands wide: 'But who knows the tangled thoughts in a madman's mind? Anyway, sir, there's nothing more to fear from him, you can sleep with an easy conscience in your bed. He's dead now, back there in the wood. Shot him myself,' he added proudly, 'with his own pistol. Trying to escape. Saved the law a hanging and we saw justice done.'

Did we indeed? thought Tam, standing mute listening to this pack of lies, chillingly aware that the plan to kill him had failed. Had it been successful, Townsend would have chased a little way after the stalker but would never have caught him.

An unfortunate accident, Mr Eildor killed, is how it would have been reported. And he wondered how that piece of news would have been received by the Prince Regent. Probably with another shrug of the royal shoulders, content that, apart from Henry, who was entirely trustworthy as became a son, the last of those who were a peril to his future, since they knew the real facts regarding the death of the marchioness and the bungled carriage accident, had had their mouths effectively closed forever.

Perhaps there would even be a whisper: 'Well done, Townsend, well done.'

Tam realised that the count was growing almost daily. There had been three failed attempts on his life. There would undoubtedly be another.

And it was increasingly obvious that he must use all his wits and ingenuity to escape from Brighton and back to his own time before an attempt on his life was successful.

Chapter Twenty-Three

Lord Percy was carried upstairs and laid down in a bedroom, with Dr Brooke in attendance and Henry hovering anxiously at his side.

Tam, still in a state of shock at the enormity of the whole incident and his own narrow escape from death, lingered in the corridor outside, staring out of the window and hoping for a glimpse of Gemma, hoping to satisfy the urgent necessity of picking up those loose ends of what had happened to her when she was taken aboard the smugglers' boat and he was hit on the head and left in the water to die.

After what seemed like a considerable time, the doctor emerged and shook his head. 'I fear there is nothing more to be done. The bullet lodged too close to the brain to be extracted. We must prepare ourselves for the worst. He will not survive the day.'

Dr Brooke was followed by Henry, who joined Tam at the window. He looked close to tears. 'He is dying, and he wants a priest. Roman Catholic, you know, born and baptised, somewhat lapsed in recent years. Kept it dark, wouldn't do for a groom of the bedchamber to be Catholic, not after all that fuss about Mrs Fitzherbert and HRH. People remember.'

Pausing, he added, 'Percy wants to see you, Mr Eildor.'

Tam was mystified as Henry added, 'Has something to say to us both.'

Tam followed him into the room. Even with the curtains drawn, it was obvious that Percy was near death, his bandaged head on the now bloodied pillow unmoving.

Perhaps they were too late and he was already dead. Henry thought the same. Drawing a sharp breath and with a frantic glance at Tam, he leaned over the bed.

'We're here, Percy.'

His eyelids stirred. 'The priest? Is he with you?' he whispered.

'He is on his way. Mr Eildor is here, as you asked.'

The eyes opened wide, stared up at the ceiling. 'Good. Have to confess, need a priest.'

'He's coming, Percy. Be here very soon.'

An exhausted sigh. 'Good—get him to hurry. Not much time.' And groping for Henry's hand. 'You are my old friend, Henry. Have to tell someone—is Mr Eildor still there? Good—want him to hear this as well. Need a witness.'

He paused, weak and still for a moment then drawing a deep breath that seemed to rattle through his whole being, he said in a clear voice:

'I have committed a mortal sin, Henry. I killed Lady Sarah Creeve that night.'

Henry shook his head and exchanged a startled glance with Tam. And grasping Percy's hand, he said softly: 'You didn't, old chap, you're imagining things.'

'No, this is the truth, Henry, as I shall soon stand before my Maker. I killed her. I didn't mean to, but she led me on, you know. I wanted her from the day we first met and she hinted that she loved me too. That night when HRH was watching the shipwreck, I knew she was in his bed next door to us.'

A faint smile touched his ashen face. 'Such a perfect opportunity. Remember, Henry, I left you watching the ship going down and went back. She was lying there smiling, waiting for me but when—when we—started—I got nervous, bed curtains drawn. Couldn't see for sure, but thought I heard someone else, moving about in the room. She pushed me away, called me a fumbling idiot, said I was useless as a lover. I tried to—to make her—'

Another pause. 'But she wasn't having any. She tried to get up, away from me. I got angry, I seized her by those damned pearls, pulled her back on to the bed. I was beyond reason, I would have her, whether she wanted me or not. Then I realised I had tight hold of the pearls and she wasn't breathing any more. I had strangled her. It has been terrible, terrible—living with this nightmare.'

As he said the words, the priest arrived to administer the last rites. Henry stayed, still holding Percy's hand, and Tam left them to wait outside. To wait for what? he wondered.

The marchioness's murder which had troubled the Prince Regent so deeply had been solved at last, her killer one of his own devoted grooms.

There still remained the theft of the Stuart Sapphire. It seemed unlikely that Percy had stolen that. But his dying words had thrown new light on it. Whoever he heard in the bedroom moving about had undoubtedly also known of the marchioness's weakness for jewels and, having in all probability seen her wearing the sapphire that evening, had taken the opportunity when the prince was absent to steal it.

Tam had no great satisfaction in knowing

that he had been right all along and that Townsend's wearisome interminable interrogations in the sleazy dark corners of Brighton had been a waste of time. The theft had been committed by someone inside the Pavilion, someone close to the Prince.

He looked out of the window and was rewarded by the sight of Gemma, in a green velvet riding coat, throwing a ball to Timothy's new puppy in the garden below. He must speak to her. Only she had the knowledge to help him retrace his steps back to the hulks and make his exit from Regency Brighton.

Once she shaded her eyes, looked up towards the window where he lifted a hand in greeting, but she did not see him after all. He was considering dashing down to see her, when someone signalled from inside the house and she disappeared.

She was so beautiful, Gemma was life itself, he thought, turning to look at the bedroom door closed fast on its scene of tragic, unnecessary death. And as he counted the minutes, he knew that not many men in this world could owe their lives to the flight of an angry insect. Had it not chosen to fly at his face that instant in the wood, he and not Percy would have been lying dead. And he remembered, as if in some nightmare, seeing Townsend over and over calmly shooting the stalker, whose name and secret business only Townsend knew.

Perhaps Townsend did not fully realise that Tam, lying against the tree's trunk with the breath knocked out of him, had heard what had passed between them. But he also realised that his knowledge and witness were dangerous indeed and, now that he knew too much to live, he must be very wary about turning his back on the Bow Street officer.

The door opened and Henry came out and sat with him on the windowsill. He said nothing, just shook his head sadly, close to tears. Below them the sunshine in the garden had hardened and grown cold. Gemma and the puppy had disappeared, their place taken by heavy, grey mist. In the distance the ornamental lake looked dark and forbidding, as if biding its time for yet another tragedy.

'He was my friend,' said Henry. 'All these years we have been together serving the prince and yet I realise I hardly knew him at all.'

He sighed. 'I hoped he would be best man at my wedding, now he doesn't even know that I am in love and have found the girl of my dreams.'

(And my dreams too, thought Tam.)

'Instead of going back to Brighton to my father full of joyous expectations, it will be to tell him this grave news and send someone down to Surrey. Percy's wife and children will have to be informed, arrangements made for his—him to be buried in the family vault.'

268

He put his hands to his face and sobbed. 'Dear God, it is terrible, unbelievable that just a few moments before we had been talking. What cause had a madman with a gun to kill Percy, a stranger to him? Townsend believes he killed Simone too. Why on earth should such a thing happen?'

Tam could have told him the truth—that Percy had been killed by mistake—but that would only have made his grief even harder to bear. He said: 'Percy's wife—she will be heartbroken.'

Henry sighed. 'Not for long, I fear. There was no real love there. An arranged marriage when they were both young. There are children but Percy was never faithful. They had their own lives to lead; it is the way of this world we live in. But poor Percy, I felt, was always searching for someone to love who would love him in return.'

Again he sighed. 'That way of life is not for me, never has been. I have waited a long time and I will be faithful to my beloved, and no other, until I die.'

That will make a change from your royal father, that is something you did not inherit from him, Tam was tempted to say, but he did not want to hear all about Henry's love for Gemma, and instead he asked:

'Was all that true—back there? Did you have any idea what happened that night when Lady Sarah died?'

'I only know that when we went into the attics to view your ship sinking, Percy only stayed a couple of minutes, said he was feeling unwell, his stomach was troubling him, said he must go urgently to what he called the house of easement. When I went back downstairs again, about half an hour later, he was in bed. I remember he asked me if it was all over. I said yes and was he feeling better now. He said he was, yes, but he hadn't felt like watching a ship go down.'

Henry paused, shook his head sadly. 'Poor old Percy. He must have been in an agony of remorse and terror of what he had done.'

'And yet when the marchioness was discovered, you never suspected him.'

He laughed bitterly. 'Never in a thousand years would I or anyone else have ever suspected Percy. He never had any luck with women, always, it seemed, infatuated with someone who didn't want him.'

'Did you know he felt like that about the marchioness?'

He frowned. 'When I think about it now, he did seem rather taken with her—but so did most men. They were easy targets; she was that kind of woman, always flaunting herself. I must say, the last thought in my mind would be his poaching on the prince's preserves, as one might say. Certainly his behaviour has been a bit erratic lately, about Simone, who like her mistress must have rejected him. But I still can't believe that he killed Sarah, even by accident.'

He stopped, looked at Tam earnestly and said: 'Promise, I beg you—promise you won't tell anyone else, Mr Eildor.'

'You have my word upon it, sir.'

'Not even Townsend,' Henry insisted.

Tam said firmly, 'Not even Townsend,' wondering how much the Bow Street officer was already in the Prince Regent's confidence. 'What good would it do to blacken Lord Percy's name when he is dead and cannot defend himself?'

Henry smiled sadly. 'You are a good man, Tam Eildor, a very good man and I feel privileged to have known you and to shake you by the hand.'

They shook hands solemnly and Henry said: 'My father will have to be told the truth, of course. He will be sad about Percy but no doubt relieved in a way that Sarah's killer has been found.'

And the truth laid to rest, silenced permanently by death, thought Tam grimly, as Henry continued: 'That was a terrible morning when we found her, the worst in my whole life—until now. Poor Percy went away to vomit and I thought it was just the sight of a dead woman that had upset him.'

They were interrupted as the priest left the room and Dr Brooke appeared with Sir Joseph to have a word with Henry.

271

Tam went downstairs, feeling a need for fresh air. As he stood undecided at the front door, wondering if those pleasant gardens were any longer a safe haven to wander in, a man, obviously a stranger, came up the steps and said:

'Excuse me, sir, I have urgent business with Sir Joseph.'

'If you ring the bell—' But the footman was already there. The man bowed, looked at Tam intently and disappeared inside the house, leaving Tam with a curious feeling that he had met him, or someone very like him, recently. However, before he could pursue the idea, Henry joined him once more and they were approached by Townsend who had been at the stables.

Putting aside his pipe, he was ready with condolences for Henry on the loss of a dear friend. Tam listened unmoving and thought how Townsend would have reacted had the fatal accident befallen himself, as was intended. And how very difficult it would have been to trace any family of the late Mr Tam Eildor in Edinburgh or elsewhere.

Turning to Tam, Townsend said: 'All the arrangements have been made and we need not delay ourselves any longer. I have asked the coachman to bring the carriage round, if you are ready to leave.'

'I have much to do,' said Henry. 'HRH must be told as soon as possible and the sad news

272

broken to Percy's family.'

And regarding the approaching carriage: 'Might I accompany you back to Brighton, if that is convenient, and you have room for two extra passengers?' He indicated Gemma who had emerged from the front door, a footman at her heels carrying a small trunk.

'Lady Gemma is also going to Brighton on a short visit. She is to be the guest of HRH,' he beamed proudly, 'and will be staying with Mrs Fitzherbert.'

Gemma smiled kindly at Henry as he handed her into the carriage. They took the seats opposite Townsend and Tam, whom she greeted with a smile and a polite nod, before devoting her attention to staring out of the window.

It proposed to be a silent journey, no one in the mood for polite conversation. Henry occasionally darted fond glances at Gemma which were not returned with much enthusiasm.

She was remembering her parting conversation with her father. He had been quite frank that unless she decided to take Lord Henry Fitzgeorge she would not be welcome back at Creeve. He would, however, give her an allowance to go to London and remain there with her grandmother, indicating that whatever arrangements she made for her future were no longer any concern of his.

In a state of shock at the enormity of this

statement, Gemma realised that she was being politely disowned, abandoned by her father. Then he added that if, however, she made a favourable decision, the one of which he so heartily approved, she would be most welcome to return to the family home. She would then be married from Creeve, all past bitterness forgotten.

As for Tam, aware of the preoccupied expression which made her face even lovelier, he knew only delight at her unexpected presence. Unlikely ever to set foot in Lewes again, the possibility that they would be able to meet again in Brighton was more than he could ever have hoped for.

Chapter Twenty-Four

They were within a mile of Brighton when a fallen tree across the road blocked their path. The coachman took a circuitous way which emerged near the promenade.

As Tam wondered what lay in store at the Pavilion, Henry said to Gemma: 'Steine House lies over yonder, an excellent opportunity to meet Mrs Fitzherbert. She is my dear friend.'

Gemma smiled wanly and as they reached the house, Mrs Fitzherbert appeared on the steps in outdoor attire. Seeing Henry in the

274

carriage, she smiled radiantly and, as he stepped out, she embraced him fondly and kissed his cheek.

Drawing her aside and indicating Gemma, there followed an urgent whispered conversation, since he had had no opportunity to ask her if it was convenient for Gemma to stay. A moment's hesitation and he received the answer he needed. The prince was sleeping in the Pavilion again.

Handing Gemma down from the carriage, Tam caught a glimpse of Mrs Fitzherbert's curious expression, delighted as they were introduced and Gemma curtseyed prettily.

'Lady Gemma, Henry's friends are always most welcome in my home,' she said.

A cautious response and most diplomatic, Tam thought, and as their carriage was about to move on, he was suddenly noticed.

'Mr Eildor—how very nice to see you again. Will you not join us?'

And to Henry: 'My outing was quite unimportant, my dear, a mere breath of sea air—and I should like very much to take this opportunity of receiving Mr Eildor's company before he leaves,' she added with one of her radiant smiles.

With such a warm invitation Tam could hardly refuse to descend from the carriage and kiss the hand she offered. Not only would he enjoy meeting her again but he was curious to see how she received Lady Gemma, this guest thrust upon her without the least warning.

'You may drive on, coachman,' she said.

Townsend, a silent witness to this charming encounter, was obviously dismissed as a servant travelling with them. Feeling slighted he leaned forward and said stiffly:

'Madam, if you will please excuse Mr Eildor on this occasion. He and I have urgent business at the Pavilion which will not wait.'

Nodding to Tam, Henry replied: 'I will join you shortly.' His expression was grave, with all laughter gone, as he remembered his own urgent business, to report the death of his friend.

Mrs Fitzherbert smiled at Tam. 'Remember your promise to me, Mr Eildor.'

Assuring her of his intention to do so, Tam hoped this was one promise he would be able to keep as he returned to the carriage and watched her with a hand tucked into Henry's arm going indoors once more.

There was something about that little scene that remained with him. It struck a note of intimacy and it suddenly occurred to him to wonder if Lord Henry was in fact one of those children who she had said so wistfully 'could never be acknowledged'.

The Pavilion loomed ahead, its splendour more transient-seeming than ever, after the harsh reality of the two days at Creeve. As the carriage dropped them at the entrance to the guest apartments, Townsend said:

'I have matters to discuss with HRH and then we will resume our investigation.' This was not quite the excuse he had given to Mrs Fitzherbert, Tam thought resentfully, but merely a ruse to keep an eye on him since he was not to be included in that meeting with the prince.

As for the investigation, since Townsend had left no stone unturned, what possible further venues could he have in mind? Tam would have been mightily interested to hear Townsend give the prince an account of the events at Creeve.

Which version would the prince be told of Lord Percy's death? At least any account would save Henry that heart-rending and highly emotional task of breaking such tragic news.

Again he was curious to know if Townsend had been told the truth about the marchioness's murder, and that as all witnesses were to be eliminated, the death of Lord Percy was a plot that had failed, with Tam Eildor as the intended victim.

*   *   *

As he walked towards his bedroom he hoped to have some time on his own, and was looking forward to the sight of clean linen spread out on the bed.

It was not to be. He opened the door, and there, spread out on the bed, was Princess Charlotte.

'What on earth are you doing here, Highness?' In his anger he even forgot the customary manners, the bow and smile.

'Dear Mr Eildor, I saw the carriage approaching from my window over there and so I decided to welcome you.'

'Please get up, Highness,' said Tam shortly in no mood, after all he had been through, to humour this tiresome girl.

She lay back against the pillows. 'We will not be disturbed. My governess is having her afternoon rest. Be assured, I left her fast asleep. She will not rise until four—'

Tam interrupted this assurance with an impatient gesture. 'You cannot stay here. Please go, Highness.'

Instead she snuggled down into the bed. 'No one will disturb us,' she repeated softly. 'I have waited so long for such an opportunity. Why cannot I stay—'

'You cannot stay because I say so and because, in case you have forgotten, you are the Prince Regent's daughter.'

She laughed a little coarsely. 'Oh that! He has a different woman in his bed every night of the week, no one even notices. It is the general rule.'

Tam was not prepared to argue that point, in terror that a knock on the door would herald

Townsend's return and such a scene as he would witness would give any man, even one with a less suspicious nature than the Bow Street officer, all the wrong impressions.

He regarded her grimly. 'It is not my general rule, Highness. Besides you are just a child.'

That made her sit up indignantly. 'I—am—not—not—a child. See for yourself,' she added angrily tearing down the bodice of her gown.

Averting his eyes hastily from plump breasts, he realised to his horror that she was wearing only a nightgown. At two o'clock in the afternoon—was it also the custom in the Pavilion to disrobe for the afternoon rest?

'I am a woman,' she repeated, as if some doubt might still remain in his mind.

'I can see that,' he said coldly. 'Now cover yourself up in case you catch a cold.'

'Do you not find me attractive?' she pleaded.

To be candid, Tam did not. Not in the least; a lumpish young woman with plump feet and hands and a stout bosom had never been to his taste. Less than ever since he had the vision of Gemma Creeve's slender frame firmly imprinted in his mind.

'You'll do well enough when the right man comes along,' he said.

'I won't—I won't!' Had her feet been on the ground she would have stamped them indignantly.

Conscious that he was on the road to nowhere and that he must get rid of her as soon as possible, Tam decided to humour her. He sat on the very edge of the bed as far away from her as possible.

'Now listen to me,' he said sternly. 'You have to marry, you know that.'

'I hate marriage, I won't—won't be like my mother and father—I will have lovers instead, that I can quickly dispose of when I get tired of them.'

'As you would tire of me,' Tam said softly.

She shook her head vigorously. 'I would never tire of you. I would want to keep you with me forever.'

'You are very kind, Highness, and I will be honoured to be your friend.'

'Even when I am Queen.'

'Even when you are Queen.'

Tam got up and said: 'That's settled then. Now will you please go back to your own rooms, before your governess wakens and sounds the alarm.'

She looked at him doubtfully. 'Promise me you'll be my friend.'

'I have said so.'

She slipped out of bed and, as she did so, Tam observed a uniform jacket hanging on the back of the door. It had not been there before.

He looked at Charlotte, suddenly realising that she could never have found access to the

280

guest apartments from the Pavilion wearing only what he now saw was a flimsy nightgown. She must have worn the long jacket as a hopeful piece of anonymity.

As he helped her into it, keeping as much distance between them as was physically possible, there was a sharp reminder—a very significant fact from the night of the marchioness's murder.

A piece of valuable information stored away at the back of his mind.

'How did you manage to escape from Lady de Clifford?' he asked.

'I told you, she was asleep.'

'I don't mean now, Highness. I mean the last time you wore that coat.'

'I just borrowed it,' she said carelessly. 'It is quite inconspicuous, there are so many guards about the Pavilion that no one ever gives them a second glance. Especially as I'm tall enough. I can wander about and it's the perfect disguise, isn't it?'

'Highness, I am not referring to this afternoon and your visit to me, I am talking about the night that the Stuart Sapphire disappeared from your royal father's bedroom. The night I was rescued from the shipwreck.'

Aware too late of the trap he had set for her, she stammered: 'I—I don't—know—know what you are talking about, Mr Eildor,' but her heightened colour gave away the lie.

'I think you do. As a matter of fact, you were seen by the duty guards.'

'Oh, no!' she squealed. 'They didn't tell—him—did they?'

'No, they told me, when I was asking if they knew anything about its disappearance.'

Looking alarmed now, she asked anxiously: 'What did they say?'

'Only that a guard rather casually dressed in uniform was inspecting some problem to do with the prince's apartments.'

'But they didn't recognise me!' she laughed. 'What a relief!'

'You are aware, Highness,' Tam said sternly, 'that the missing sapphire we are talking about is the reason Mr Townsend is here from London?'

'Oh is it really?' she said casually. 'I had no idea—no one told me. He comes quite a lot to see my father.'

'Well, this time he is here searching for the sapphire, all over Brighton, and I have had to accompany him.'

She giggled, put a hand to her mouth. Then seriously, as she realised what this conversation implied, she said defensively:

'It is mine, you know. Father promised to give it to me, so that I could wear it when I reviewed his Dragoons. Then when that—that—odious woman started coming to dinner, he broke his promise. She was there displaying it proudly on her huge bosom—the cheek of her. She was awfully rude to me, never gave me the respect due to a royal princess, just treated me like a silly child. She was wearing it that night—' She stopped.

'Go on,' said Tam.

She shrugged. 'I guessed she would be sleeping in—his—bedroom. When I left them all watching the shipwreck, I knew my father would be there for ages. I came back, put on one of the uniform jackets from the guard room and slipped along the corridor to his bedroom. I muttered something about light sconces being checked. Wasn't that clever of me?'

'Very clever,' said Tam as was expected of him. 'Do go on.'

'I opened the door and the bed curtains were drawn, I hoped she was still asleep but I heard creakings and sounds like deep breathing. I could smell her awful perfume too. But the jewels were on the little table by the window and there was enough daylight to see my sapphire. I snatched it up and went quietly out. Back the way I came. The guards were playing cards—they never even noticed me leave—'

But Lord Percy heard you, Tam remembered grimly. And that interrupted lovemaking behind the bed curtains cost Lady Sarah Creeve her life.

'I am glad she'll never be coming back,' Charlotte continued. 'In fact I wasn't sorry at

283

all to hear that she had been killed going back home to Creeve. She deserved it. She was greedy and horrible.'

'Where is the sapphire now?'

She gave him a sly look and said softly: 'What will you give me, if I tell you?'

'I won't give you anything, since it is not my property and you had better give it back to your father. He is quite distraught at its disappearance, you know. I gather it is part of the Coronation Crown—'

Momentarily sulky, she shrugged then suddenly brightened. 'If I tell you where it is, will you give me a kiss?'

'I might,' said Tam warily. 'One kiss.'

She came close, leaned against him, closed her eyes and opened her lips. As he gently covered them with his own, she seized him tightly, forcing his lips apart.

Struggling free, resisting the desire to wipe his hand across his mouth, he took her face in his hands and gently pushed her away.

'One kiss, I said, Highness. Not my face washed.'

She sighed, clinging to him again. 'But I love you—I love you.'

'I know you think you do, but you must understand, I shall be leaving here, probably tomorrow—'

'No—not so soon—please,' she begged.

'Yes, Highness, and so you must not waste your love on me. You will find a fine prince worthy of you someday.'

Shaking her head, she looked ready for floods of tears. 'No—never.'

There were sounds in the corridor outside and Tam froze. 'You must go.'

'Please—when you leave—take me with you.'

The footsteps had receded and Tam took her firmly by the arms. 'Highness, you are one day to be Queen of England. I am a nobody—'

'You are an Edinburgh lawyer.'

Tam shook his head. 'For what it's worth, I am a commoner. You know nothing about me. So please be sensible. Even if we were in love with each other, it could never be.'

'What about my father and Mrs Fitzherbert?' she demanded.

'Yes, that should be a lesson to you. How difficult your people would make such an arrangement to say nothing of parliament.'

'I would risk it—I would risk anything if you loved me!'

'Maybe you would, but I'm not ready to risk being hung, drawn and quartered.'

'But—'

'Highness—you must go—now. Remember you made a promise, one kiss and you would show me where you hid the sapphire.'

She pouted her lips. 'Another kiss, and I'll show you.'

'Very well.' He kissed her gently, listening for those footsteps returning.

He had to humour her, so near now to finding the hiding place of the sapphire, but what would it be like if her governess had missed her and she was found here alone with him in his room, wearing only a nightgown?

Sure that men had been incarcerated in the dungeons of the Tower of London and forgotten for the rest of their lives for less, he found himself sweating as she tried once again to make the kiss linger, pressing herself against him.

As a last resort, he pretended to be seized by a fit of coughing. Forced to release him, he breathed again and said: 'Highness, the sapphire, if you please, where is it?'

She put her hand deep in the pocket of her jacket. 'Here it is, isn't it lovely?' she said cheerfully. 'I carry it with me everywhere.'

'May I see it?'

Tam took it from her. A dark blue stone, no larger than a miniature or a lady's locket.

'You have no idea the trouble this has caused,' he said. 'The weary hours Mr Townsend and I have spent—days at your royal father's command searching every jeweller's shop, every thieves' kitchen the length and breadth of Brighton searching for it. You have been very naughty, Highness.'

She shrugged. 'I had no idea. I am sorry.'

He believed her. It was hardly surprising that her father had not told her that it was missing with so many other things on his mind.

His mistress murdered in his bed and how to get rid of her body so that he would not be involved.

'He never talks to me, you know,' she said sadly. 'Avoids me whenever he can and, if he has anything worth saying, he gives it to messengers or Lady de Clifford to deliver.'

Tam's annoyance evaporated in sudden compassion for her loneliness and rejection. The reason she stole the sapphire was that she could not ask as any adored daughter would, knowing it could be wheedled out of a doting father.

'Will you do something for me?' he asked.

'Anything,' she said hopefully. 'Anything.'

'Do you want to get into your father's favour again—have him think you are a wonderful, clever girl that he is proud of?' he added, realising he was asking a great deal from the little he knew of the Prince Regent.

'Do you really think he could feel like that?' She sounded hopeful, although she could never love her father. Too late for that, but it was interesting to consider the possibilities of what might be in this for her.

'As I told you he has been distraught at the sapphire's loss and if anyone—particularly yourself—were to—find—it, then he would be so grateful I am sure he would grant you anything you wish.'

'Let me keep it, you mean?' she said eagerly.

'As it will be yours one day to wear in the

Coronation Crown, I am sure he will let you look after it until it is needed officially.'

She frowned and gave a little shiver. 'But he will be furious if I confess that I took it,' she said nervously.

'I realise that. I think you should—perhaps find it—somewhere. In the garden or even better maybe in the bedroom he is having refurbished, in a crack in the floorboards perhaps. If he thinks it has been there all the time, he will be too relieved to be angry even though it might have been the first place he looked.'

She brightened. 'I am so sorry,' she repeated. 'I don't care about Townsend, don't like him much. He is not important. But I do apologise for all the trouble I have put you through, searching the town for it.' And standing on tiptoe, she kissed his cheek.

Closing the door on her, he felt no great satisfaction that the mystery of the Stuart Sapphire was solved.

Only deep despair. Charlotte would be the most surprised girl in the whole world to know that she had been indirectly the cause of two deaths. Her theft of the sapphire had set in motion a train of events that had ended in Percy's death.

And had she not been in the prince's bedroom that night and interrupted Percy's inept lovemaking, Lady Sarah Creeve would still be alive.

Chapter Twenty-Five

Going over to the window Tam saw Lady Gemma walking past. She was alone and he rapped furiously on the pane to alert her attention.

Turning briefly, she nodded and, although he mouthed 'Wait!' she hurried on. Exasperated, Tam rushed out of the front door and across the garden almost knocking over Townsend walking towards the entrance to the Pavilion, in deep conversation with a stranger.

Hastily apologising, he noted that Townsend's companion was the man he had seen briefly on the steps as he was leaving Creeve House. It must be very important business and a fast horse that had brought him so swiftly to Brighton, Tam decided, as he rushed on in his headlong pursuit of Gemma.

He had to talk to her and he no longer cared who saw them together. Now that the Stuart Sapphire had been found and the marchioness's death solved, he was well aware that his own death knell had sounded.

He was expendable. Beneath the genteel splendour of the Pavilion, the executioner's pistol was poised in readiness.

Gemma was walking swiftly but he caught up with her and instead of slowing down she merely acknowledged his presence with an angry glance. 'Your visitor has left, has she?'

Tam stared at her, shook his head. How did she know about the princess?

He was not long kept in doubt.

'Henry took me to meet his father. It was very brief. I cannot say that HRH was very impressed. He was polite but he indicated that he wished to speak to Henry alone. I was dismissed. Henry was so embarrassed I decided that instead of waiting around in the corridors with various courtiers seeking an audience, I would come in search of you.'

Tam smiled at her. 'I am so glad you did.'

There was no answer to that smile. 'Outside your door, I heard voices, one of them was young and female. So I decided not to wait, that you might be some time and put out by my unwanted presence. Now if you will excuse me,' she added coldly.

Keeping pace with her, he put a restraining hand on her arm. 'No, I won't excuse you. Gemma, please—please listen!'

Even as he said the words, he thought, what reason has she to be angry anyway? She is going to marry Lord Henry.

They had reached one of the shaded arbours with a secluded seat. The gardens were almost deserted on a dull afternoon, with a chill breeze off the sea. 'Let us sit down—for just a moment,' he pleaded.

She didn't refuse and sounding mollified,

said: 'What is it all about, Tam?'

'You might well ask. I am being pursued—relentlessly.'

She bristled at that. 'Not by me—I assure you,' she said hotly.

'Would that it were, Gemma,' his smile was tender. 'Now will you please listen. Princess Charlotte has got it into her silly young head that she is in love with me. When I got to my room, looking forward, I might add, to being on my own for a while, a little peace and quiet, there she was, waiting for me. It seems that I cannot escape—'

'How sad for you,' she said mockingly and rose to her feet. 'Do not let me detain you a minute longer. I cannot compete with a royal princess.'

He stood up, took hold of her arms and throwing caution to the winds, he whispered: 'Just say that again. Do you want to compete?'

She blushed, looking almost tearfully into those strange luminous eyes gazing down into hers. 'Of course not, Tam,' she said hastily. 'A mere slip of the tongue. I thought—I just thought that we were—friends,' she added lamely knowing that this was the thinnest of excuses.

'We are friends and you are going to marry Lord Henry,' he said firmly.

'Am I? Then you know more than I do. I would point out that I have not accepted his proposal yet. I still have to make up my mind.'

'Then what are you doing here in Brighton at the Pavilion as the prince's guest?'

'It was an excuse, any excuse, I am afraid, to get away from Creeve, I mean.'

'Is that the truth?'

She looked up at him again, shook her head. 'No, it is not, Tam Eildor, only part of it. I wanted to see you again. It was the perfect opportunity. I might never have another. I knew that,' she said sadly.

And jabbing a finger in the direction of his chest, 'I also want to know the truth—about you. About your magic appearance on the hulks that day. I am plagued by an enquiring kind of mind and I simply cannot work it out.'

He laughed. 'And I want the truth too. Of how you escaped from the smugglers and turned up at the Old Ship Inn.' He indicated the seat. 'So let's sit down and pray that this time, the weather will be on our side and we won't be interrupted yet again. This might be our last chance,' he added grimly. Taking her hand, he went on: 'You first, Gemma.'

Taking a deep breath, she said: 'When I was hauled aboard the smugglers' boat, I had a bit of unexpected luck. Their leader was no stranger. I had known him most of my life. A regular and most welcome visitor at Creeve, he provides Father with fine French brandies and wines, all duty free. He used to bring me lace and French dolls. I thought he was wonderful.

'He had another use now, he was able to keep his men at bay, from laying hands on a pretty boy, the pretty fish they said they had caught. I thought you were dead, that you had drowned,' she said sadly, and went on:

'They were too polite to ask what Lady Gemma Creeve was doing in the water in boy's clothes and presumed that I wanted to get back to Creeve. But then I told old Davy Jones—yes, that was his real name or so he said—my sorry tale about running away from my wicked stepmother. It seemed that even the smugglers had heard about Lady Sarah. I said I was never going back and that once I had enough money I would go back to London and proceed with my ambition—to be an actress. I had met Mr Sheridan and I was sure he would give me a part in one of his plays.

'Old Davy immediately offered me money, but I said no. I was not willing to accept his charity. It had to be my very own money that I had earned for the first time in my life. He thought for a while, looking me over, as it were, and said that perhaps I could give a hand, become one of their band for a while, going back and forward to France. He explained that it was very lucrative.'

She paused. 'Have you any idea how much they earn?'

Tam shook his head and she continued: 'Half a guinea for a day and a night's work, plus expenses for eating and drinking and a horse found for land travel. They also got profits of a dollop of tea, thirteen pounds in weight, which is half a bag. Their total profit is about twenty-four or twenty-five shillings a time and they sometimes make two journeys a week.'

Again she paused, frowning. 'I'm sure you can do your sums as well as I can, Tam. Very tempting, when common working men, labourers, are lucky to earn twenty pounds a year and, when they are out of a job, a handout from the parish.'

'That's the good side,' said Tam. 'What happens if they are caught?'

She shuddered. 'Condemned to death and hanged in chains as a grisly warning. I didn't fancy that much and there was another slight problem. I get dreadfully seasick, as I discovered being transported over to the hulks—so what use would I be to anyone on a stormy Channel crossing? However, I was tempted; just one successful voyage would be enough.

'After they put me ashore they were going back to France that night so I promised to think it over and they left me in the Old Ship, where incidentally the landlord had worked in the stables at Creeve as a young lad. So luck was with me once again; I had fallen among friends.

'When I saw Sarah's death in the newspaper,

I decided to give Father another try. He would need comforting. I hoped he had missed me and wanted me home again. How wrong could one be,' she added bitterly.

'Why did you run away from me?'

'When you came into the Old Ship, at first I thought I was seeing a ghost. The smugglers thought, and so did I, that they had killed you and, seeing you alive and well, I guessed that you would be furious, believing that I was responsible—for what happened—being hit on the head and thrown back in the sea. I was scared—'

'Scared of me, when I had saved your life?'

'In a word, yes. There was another reason. The more I thought about your miraculous appearance on the hulks, the more convinced I was that this was something beyond my understanding. A trick—but sinister and very frightening.'

She stopped and smiled sweetly. 'But that is what you are going to tell me about, is it not?' At his reluctant expression she said: 'I want the truth, Tam Eildor. Are you a magician, or an alchemist? Something like that.'

Tam shook his head. 'I wish it was that easy to explain.'

She put a hand on his arm. 'Whatever it is, please—please Tam, I must know.' She paused. 'You're not the Devil, are you?'

Tam laughed out loud and bent his head: 'Look—have a search. No horns. No cloven hoofs either.'

'An angel then?' she said solemnly.

'An angel—me? My dear Gemma, you do me too much credit!' And touching his chin ruefully, 'Have you ever heard of an angel in need of a shave?'

Ignoring that, she said rather crossly: 'I have heard they come to earth sometimes.'

'Indeed—well, I have never met one, so you can cross that assumption off your list.' And, taking her hand again: 'Dear Gemma, I will tell you all that I can, but I can hardly expect you to believe me.'

'Try me,' she said firmly. 'There are lots of things I cannot see and touch that my religious belief insists I have faith in, like angels and being raised from the dead and having everlasting life.'

Tam hoped she wouldn't ask him about God since even in 2250, despite all efforts of the scientists, the jury was still out on that particular mystery.

'You believe that the past exists then,' he said, 'what about the future? Can you believe in the world that will exist for centuries after this one?'

'I hope so.'

'Can you imagine this world, this place we are now, what it will be like, say, four hundred years from now?'

She frowned looking towards the distant line on the horizon that was the English Channel.

296

'I can imagine that a lot of new things will be invented, science we are told is just at the beginning.'

'And if I were to tell you that carriages will run without the aid of horses, and vehicles called trains will run on lines across the country carrying passengers from town to town, the length and breadth of the land.'

Pausing he pointed upwards. 'And there in the sky above us, machines will fly like birds and we will be able to talk and see other people in other countries and planets on screens in their own homes. And that future man will not only have made all these marvellous inventions but will have conquered travel beyond earth, through space and time, so that he can choose to visit past worlds. And there will be one universal language; people the world over will understand one another.'

He couldn't expect her to understand that at birth a microchip in a child's brain made that possible.

She had listened patiently, now she said calmly: 'So that is your answer, Tam. You are telling me all this because you came here from the future.'

'You believe me?' Tam was surprised at her fearless, unquestioning acceptance of what he had dreaded trying to explain.

'I don't think you would tell me a lie about something so important,' she said simply. 'Especially as this is the answer to why you are

297

human like the rest of us, yet so different. I have never met anyone like you, nor has Mrs Fitzherbert. She is similarly curious, I can tell you. She is very impressed by you but said the same thing when your name was mentioned.'

Smiling, she said: 'Tell me what brought you here, Tam.'

And as briefly as he could, realising that at any moment they might be interrupted, Tam told her how he had chosen this time-quest in Brighton during the prince's Regency, only to be landed by some coastal erosion over the centuries, in the wrong place on the hulks. And how it was vital that he got back to that same place before he could return once again to his own time.

Pausing for breath, he waited for comment. There was none beyond a mere nod.

'I have to get back soon, Gemma. My time here is running out. I'll spare you all the details but I have been helping Mr Townsend the Bow Street officer with his enquiries. Tracking down your stepmother's murderer and a jewel robbery at the Pavilion.'

'You think the same person was involved in both?'

Remembering Princess Charlotte's confession, he said: 'Perhaps I am getting too close as there have been a number of attempts to kill me.'

'Oh, Tam,' she clasped his hand. 'How dreadful. I could get you money to go to

298

London—'

He didn't ask how. 'I don't want to go to London, I have to go as near as possible to where the convict ship is anchored, the stepping-off place to my own time.'

Gemma was frowning, silent for a moment. 'These attempts to kill you, are they connected to Simone and Percy's deaths?' she asked shrewdly.

'Percy was killed in error. The pistol shot was meant for me.' He owed her that part of the truth and he heard her sharp intake of breath as she clasped his hand more tightly.

'And so you see it is vital that I leave, and you are the only person on this earth that can help me. Your smuggler friends could perhaps be persuaded to take me out to the hulks. In the dark I can climb aboard, find the exact spot—'

'And then you will vanish again, just as you first appeared.' She sounded doubtful. 'It is going to be very difficult to arrange all this, Tam. I do not even know how to get in touch with Old Davy beyond leaving a message at the inn. Besides, when I was not there they would presume that I had gone back to my old life at Creeve. They could hardly be expected to wait around while I made up my mind about joining them.'

Pausing, she asked: 'Is there no other way?'

In answer he rolled back the sleeve of his shirt and showed her the star shape in his wrist containing the microchip.

'I can use this in an emergency. I have only tried it once when we were both in the sea, but it might be different on land. I don't know.'

'Oh Tam, try it. And take me back with you.'

'I can't, Gemma.'

She sighed and said: 'Don't you want to?'

'I think you know the answer to that, Gemma. In the interests of time of which we have so little, to put it simply, I love you. If that is what you want to know. But there is no way I can transport anything or anybody from 1811 into the future.'

She knew it was true, and leaning over she kissed his cheek. 'I love you, Tam. What is more, I think I will always love you,' she added sadly.

It was the answer he already knew. For one brief moment they had looked into the depths of one another's souls where there were no secrets.

'There is not the least possibility of meeting anyone like you ever again.'

This revelation did not make Tam rejoice. No longer jealous of Lord Henry, he wanted above all things for Gemma to forget this brief time when the paths of their lives had touched and to be happy. But in common with taking her forward in time, her future was beyond his powers.

'We cannot rely on Old Davy. If I told him the truth he would think he was dealing with a madman—and however hard-headed smugglers are, they do cling to sailors' superstitious nonsense about the sea.'

She thought for a moment. 'There is another way. Henry and I left immediately after you, he to see his father, so I came to tell you that Mrs Fitzherbert had arranged to meet friends on a picnic along the coast. It was agreed that Henry and I should accompany her suitably chaperoned, and quite fortuitously, having just met you again, she thought perhaps you would like to join us.'

She laughed and gave him a coy glance. 'Please say yes.'

And Tam realised that the shadows were darkening ahead.

Looking at Gemma with time ticking away into hours only, this would be their last leave-taking.

As if she read his mind, suddenly practical, she said: 'I am glad we never had the chance to be lovers, Tam. I do not think I could have borne the sadness of having made love, being yours for a brief hour, then having to face the rest of my life without you. And because I would never forget you, your ghost would stand between me and any other man.'

*   *   *

The sun had come out again and there were people walking in the gardens. Tam wondered idly if Charlotte had produced the sapphire for her father. Once the prince knew that Percy had killed the marchioness, the two mysteries solved would also signal his death knell, his immediate execution.

Tam Eildor the expendable would be eliminated.

Footsteps near the arbour, voices. Gemma said: 'I must go back to Steine House. Henry will be looking for me.'

In what might be their own farewell, Tam took her in his arms, held her for a moment and they kissed, not deeply or passionately but as loving friends. Releasing her, she laughed: 'At least you are real, Tam Eildor.'

'Real enough.' Real enough for my heart to break, Tam thought. A few more moments like that and I would be the one staying in her time. He had never felt such strong emotions, but he recognised the potential dangers.

He walked with her the short distance to Steine House. Bowing over her hand, she curtseyed, and they parted as polite strangers.

Turning, Tam walked briskly towards the Pavilion. The world seemed suddenly empty without her. The pain was so great, he wondered if next time he took on a time-quest, was there some way he could leave his emotions behind, become a mere detecting machine?

He didn't like what he had found in 1811 and the sooner he returned to the future the better. As for Gemma, she would forget him and marry Lord Henry. There might even be a mention of it in the history books, if he could bear to read about it.

He saw Henry walking across the gardens. He looked anxious and preoccupied. Greeting Tam, he said: 'I am searching for Lady Gemma. Have you seen her?'

'I believe it was she I observed heading in the direction of Steine House.' Something of a lie, but he was not sure how the lovesick Henry would take that long tête-à-tête in a secluded arbour.

Henry nodded briefly and, about to continue on his walk, he turned quickly and said: 'Do take extra care, Mr Eildor. If your work with Mr Townsend is at an end, I would advise you to resume your journey to London as soon as possible.'

Without awaiting any reply, he bowed briefly and hurried on.

Tam watched him go. Was that the remark of a jealous lover? Did Henry suspect something and want rid of the competition? Or, more charitably, had he some knowledge and was this a deadly warning?

Chapter Twenty-Six

It was indeed a deadly warning.

Henry's interview with his royal father had

not gone at all well. It was obvious to him, and he feared also to Gemma, that although polite, the prince was somewhat taken aback at Henry's sudden decision to wed and at his choice of a wife. Such a slip of a girl, plain and not a bit of flesh on her, no bosom either. Just a bag of bones in bed.

Henry could almost read his father's thoughts as Gemma took her leave from the royal presence and he could hear that Townsend was forestalling him with the sad news of Percy's death, Townsend's own carefully edited version.

'A stalker, you say, Townsend,' the prince had said; 'How very odd. He should be closely questioned.'

And the prince was not well pleased that this would not be possible since Townsend had shot him on the spot. Listening to this graphic account, the prince interrupted:

'How very unfortunate. He might have had useful information.' A hard glance at Townsend's face and he said smoothly: 'Perhaps it was an accident, do you think, Townsend? Perhaps he killed the wrong man.'

Townsend barely suppressed a sigh of relief. 'As your Royal Highness suggests, it is possible,' was his vague reply and the glance they exchanged and the prince's brief nod confirmed that Eildor had to go and Townsend was now the man for the job.

It remained a question of once the sapphire

was recovered, and the marchioness's killer apprehended, that would be the right time.

Listening respectfully to the prince's sympathetic noises over the death of a loyal servant, the necessity of getting a speedy messenger on the road to inform Percy's wife and family, who the prince had met only once, Townsend felt that perhaps he was secretly relieved that yet another witness had been permanently silenced, a royal scandal averted.

They had been interrupted by the arrival of Henry and Gemma. After the brief introduction both she and Townsend were dismissed.

Henry was upset as the door closed on Gemma, keenly aware that she had not made the right impression on his father, as he had hoped. But that must wait. There were other matters, as the prince said:

'That was a sad business indeed about Percy. Most unfortunate. He will be sadly missed.'

'He was my good friend, Sire—' Henry began.

'Indeed, indeed, and you will no doubt miss him. But have you any suitable person in mind who might most easily fill this vacant role? I am sure there are many with the right qualifications—'

His manner was urgent, and as Henry listened politely to the required qualifications of background and breeding, he was taken aback by this impersonal requiem for Percy's long years as a trusted and loyal servant.

'I have not yet had time or even desire to consider such matters. I beg pardon, Sire, but so many things happened all together: Lady Sarah's funeral and my meeting with Lady Gemma. I had just asked Sir Joseph for her hand a few hours before—before—Percy—' Overcome with emotion his voice trailed off.

'Quite so, quite so.' Mention of the funeral reminded the prince that the identity of the marchioness's killer was still lacking.

He frowned. 'Matters are not progressing, indeed not at all, in that direction, or the urgent recovery of our missing sapphire. We are disappointed in Townsend—most deeply—I had imagined he would have had the solution by now.' And shaking his head sadly, 'Our faith in him is quite destroyed.'

Henry forbore to point out that just a week had passed and that such matters might take some time.

'You are quite sure, Henry, that the man who killed Percy is not the one we are looking for?' the Prince said hopefully.

Townsend had been a little too rash in executing the fellow. Had he been kept alive a confession might have been obtained before his hanging.

'I am certain sure, Sire.'

The prince looked at him and Henry knew that he must be told the truth however distressing.

'Percy confessed—before he died.' Pausing, Henry took a deep breath. 'He confessed that he had in fact killed Lady Sarah.'

The Prince's eyes widened in shock and he sat down hurriedly.

'He—WHAT!'

'He strangled Lady Sarah with her pearls—it was an accident—'

'An accident! How could such a thing be an accident?'

This was going to be very difficult indeed. And embarrassing. 'I am afraid, Sire, that in your absence—that night, Lady Sarah—er, led him on—'

He paused, waiting uneasily for his father's reaction.

'Led him on—did she now? Now there's a thing.'

Henry suppressed a sigh of relief. At least he did not have to spell that out.

The prince gestured impatiently. 'And did he also confess to taking the sapphire?'

'No, Sire, he did not.'

The prince shrugged. 'A pity.' And with a wry smile, 'Percy and Lady Sarah, eh? We would never have guessed that Percy had it in him, Henry. Poaching on the royal preserves, was he? By heaven, he could have been most severely punished, most severely.'

'He was punished, Sire.' And in as few words as possible Henry related all that Percy had confessed, including without graphic details

Percy's suspicions that someone else had entered the bedroom.

The prince's head jerked upwards. 'Ah, our jewel thief no doubt. How unfortunate that Percy was so occupied at that moment. He might have intercepted the villain and that would have saved us—and Townsend—a great deal of trouble and time.'

Pausing, he sighed deeply. 'So we have a murder solved but we are no nearer to finding the stolen sapphire.' Another sigh. 'Who else was present?'

'Only myself and Mr Eildor. The priest came later.'

'Mr Eildor, eh?'

'Percy wished to have a witness, Sire. He trusted Mr Eildor.'

The prince looked grim. Townsend was right. Although he knew nothing of Percy's deathbed confession and had been a singular failure in recovering the sapphire, the Bow Street officer was right about Eildor. The man knew far too much, more than was good for his survival. He would have to go.

He looked at Henry and said lightly, as if making a joke of it: 'We suspect that our present difficulties might have been solved this very instant if—if the stalker had killed Mr Eildor instead of Percy. Is that not so?'

Henry shook his head. 'How so, Sire?'

'Surely that is obvious, Henry. Why, it would save us having to recommend several unpleasant measures.'

Henry stared at him, there was no mistaking those grim words. 'You intend, Sire—' He could not finish it as a lot of things became clear at that moment. Tam Eildor was to be the next victim and Townsend would put a gun to his head in the same manner as he had despatched Percy's unknown assassin.

And the thought came unbidden, suddenly spoken aloud. 'Was it Eildor and not Percy who should have died, Sire?'

The prince evaded his gaze, stared out of the window. 'We believe that was the intention. Might as well be straight with you, Henry. The so-called stalker, we have reason to believe, was one of Townsend's own men. Came from London with him to keep an eye on things.'

Henry took a backward step. 'Sire, that is dreadful, dreadful.'

And as he thought of his dying friend, he also remembered the carriage accident to dispose of the body of his father's mistress. The four guards disguised as highwaymen had been his own idea but he had not intended Eildor's death.

'Sire, could he not go to London as you promised him?' he pleaded.

The prince smiled thinly. He raised one eyebrow. 'You are very tender-hearted, Henry, about enemies of the state.'

'Have you proof of that, Sire?' Henry

demanded sternly.

The prince shrugged. 'A matter of time before Brummell's enquiries in Edinburgh reveal something to Eildor's discredit, or Townsend's independent enquiries reveal him as a spy.'

'A spy! Never—I refuse to believe such a thing,' said Henry indignantly.

The prince smiled indulgently and wagged a teasing finger at his son. 'As I have said, you are very soft-hearted these days, Henry. We are surprised at you. But love is surely to blame; first love, especially, does that to a young man sometimes.'

Henry wondered if that sudden shadow across his father's face was a recollection of how he had threatened suicide when Mrs Fitzherbert refused to marry him. Emotional blackmail, which had succeeded.

'Makes him think that all's well with the world and that everyone in it is his friend. But it does not do for rulers of great kingdoms to be tender-hearted. We cannot afford such luxuries if we are to keep the people happy and keep our heads firmly upon our shoulders.'

And giving this a moment to sink in, watching Henry's expressionless face, he said, 'Mr Eildor is a danger to the state, to England and to ourself—can you not see that, my dear lad?' he added patiently. 'If he were allowed to talk, the scandal regarding, er, what happened here that night, could be exceedingly unpleasant for many innocent parties involved.'

He frowned, considering his brother Frederick's reactions to the knowledge that George was his mistress's secret lover. Worse by far, his own lack of popularity with the parents who despised him.

Suppressing a shudder, he went on: 'This knowledge could be exceeding dangerous in the wrong hands, it might well overthrow us and, indeed, unseat the whole government.'

As Henry continued to shake his head obstinately over Eildor's fate, his father sighed and patted his hand. 'Indeed, it is as well for England, dear lad, oft as we have regretted it, that we cannot acknowledge you as our own son, and heir to the throne.'

Not at all put out by these remarks, having been in silent agreement with that decision for most of his life now, Henry begged to be excused and went in search of Gemma.

Chapter Twenty-Seven

Walking towards Steine House, Henry knew that he was also at a crossroads in his life. Much had happened since Tam Eildor's arrival and the events of the past two days had made him aware that he no longer wished to stay as one of the grooms of the royal bedchamber.

The prince's almost casual dismissal of Percy's death and the necessity of finding a replacement for their years of friendship, he realised, was the final straw.

In a few years his father would be King and Henry knew that the amoral, extravagant life in the Pavilion replaced by Buckingham House was not for him either.

His meeting with Gemma had changed his outlook on life dramatically. He had outgrown life at Court and, after a long wait, for the first time in his life he believed he had found a love that could last forever, instead of the frantic couplings that went on in the Pavilion and in the society in which he lived.

He needed a wife.

*　　　*　　　*

He found Gemma and Maria Fitzherbert cosily seated by the window deep in conversation. They looked completely at ease, like old friends who had met regularly through the years.

Gemma looked up at Henry shyly. 'I have a lot to tell you,' she said.

'You have made up your mind,' he said eagerly.

She shook her head and laughed. 'Not yet,

Henry. Do please give me time.' She gave a helpless look in Maria's direction who smiled:

'There is much to consider, Henry.'

In answer he said: 'Then pray tell her, I am quite a good fellow.'

Gemma laughed. 'No need. She has been singing your praises,' and quickly changing the subject, 'What is this you have to tell me?'

'Shall I leave?' Maria rose to her feet.

'No, stay. It concerns you too,' said Henry, touching her arms and smiling at her tenderly. 'But I trust this will help Gemma make her decision.' Drawing a deep breath, he said: 'I have decided to leave Court. I have held my position for more than twelve years and with Percy gone, and the necessity of sharing my tasks with a newly appointed stranger, I feel it is time I had a place of my own.'

Pausing, he looked at Maria. 'As you know, I have a small estate in West Sussex given to me by the prince on my 25th birthday. An apology, I suppose, that he could never acknowledge me.'

Gemma intercepted a deep and understanding glance between the two as he turned to her and taking her hand he said: 'I wish to live there as a country squire. I have a fancy to try my hand at dabbling in local politics, perhaps giving my tenants a model village.'

'Bravo,' whispered Maria. 'A very wise choice. You were never meant to be a courtier, Henry dear. Always too honest.'

He bowed and turned again to Gemma. 'What do you say?'

Gemma smiled. 'I think it's a wise decision too.'

Again he bowed. 'All I ask of fate is a loving wife to share my new life with me,' he said gently.

She looked at him intently. 'Once you said you would do anything, anything if I would marry you.'

His eyes were full of hope as he whispered. 'You have my word.'

She frowned. 'This may seem a rather odd request. But I know someone whose life is in terrible danger—'

'You wish me to break the law,' he said sternly.

'No, there is no law for this particular person, just people who want him dead.' She paused. 'People, alas, known to us.'

He looked uncertain, then she said: 'Henry, will you help Mr Eildor to get safely away from here? There is very little time.'

He stared at her. 'How did you know? I have just realised, talking to—to the prince, that he is in mortal danger.'

Gemma did not ask the obvious. How the prince could not intervene.

'There is a way,' said Maria. 'I have a planned excursion, in a few hours, a moonlight picnic to meet friends at a little cove along the coast. We can take Mr Eildor with us, no one will be surprised at that, and put him on the coach for London. By the time he is missed, he will be safe and can make his own arrangements to return to Scotland.'

All three agreed that this was an excellent plan, the best that they could think of at short notice. But Gemma, who knew the true facts of Tam's desperate and quite unique situation, realised that only the fact of being close to the sea might make Tam's emergency exit possible.

Henry decided that he should go in search of Tam immediately and tell him of their plan. In sight of the Pavilion, deep in thought, he heard his name called and saw Townsend heading rapidly in his direction, accompanied by a stranger he was eager to introduce as Mr Watkins, a Brighton resident.

'Tell his lordship your story, sir.'

Mr Watkins bowed. A modest grocer, he was rendered rather tongue-tied at having to address a member of the royal court at the Pavilion. His tale, confused with 'ers' and 'ums', was likely to take some time, and as Townsend was not a patient man, he interrupted several times to speed him on.

Then, exasperated, he pushed Mr Watkins aside. 'Excuse me, sir, if you will,' and to Lord Henry: 'It is like this, sir. Mr Watkins claims that he stopped a carriage on the Lewes road the other night. He was misinformed by his

315

friends after a somewhat hilarious evening and had taken what he believed was a short cut back to Brighton—'

Henry listened horrified, all too familiar with the carriage involved.

'Mr Watkins reported this to Sir Joseph and was sent to me to investigate the facts. There is as you know a substantial reward involved.'

'Indeed,' said Henry vaguely. 'Then do not let me delay you.'

Townsend looked at him slyly. 'Just thought you might be interested, connections with Sir Joseph and so forth.'

All of which suggested to Henry that Townsend was in full possession of the facts of the carriage accident and knew that he was also personally involved. Townsend continued: 'HRH might also care to know of this matter, being a close friend of His Grace and very keen to see justice done. However, he is dining and cannot be disturbed. I thought that in the circumstances your lordship might care to report to him—'

Henry waited no longer. Murmuring reassurances which he did not mean, excusing himself he went in search of Tam. His room in the guest apartments was empty and borrowed clothes on the bed suggested that he had already left.

Hastily he retraced his steps to Steine House and to the footman said:

'Mr Eildor? Is he here?'

He was informed that Mr Eildor had arrived only five minutes ago and was at present in the small parlour waiting to be received by Madam.

'I do not need to be announced,' said Henry and crossing the hall he found Tam staring out of the window. 'Thank God, I got here in time.' And closing the door: 'We are in a pretty fix, Mr Eildor. I have just met a Mr Watkins from Brighton—'

And proceeding to relate Mr Watkins' experience on the Lewes Road, he gave Tam a despairing glance. 'The worst is to come. Mr Watkins claims that he also recognised you as the gentleman he met on the steps of Creeve House when he was about to call on Sir Joseph and claim his reward.'

Pausing for breath, he said wryly, 'Thankfully he did not also recognise the coachman muffled up to the eyes as the man who was now listening to his story. But he also recalled that there was a lady inside the carriage. She was very silent, her eyes closed, very pale and ill-looking. She ignored his excuses for interrupting her journey and was asleep or, as he now realised—dead!'

This was bad news indeed, a piece of ill luck. 'How did Sir Joseph receive this information?' Tam asked.

'Very profoundly. Gave him half the reward on account, sent him off to find Mr Townsend with instructions to begin an investigation. He then told Mr Watkins that he would receive the remainder of the reward once his story was proved and led to the arrest of Her Grace's killer. Mr Watkins, advised to act upon these instructions, was told that Mr Townsend was in the employ of HRH and most likely to be found at the Pavilion. Which is where they were both heading when I met them.'

He put a hand on Tam's arm. 'Mr Eildor, you have been recognised. Before long Townsend will be on your heels, tracking you down. It would be most unwise for you to linger here. We are in terrible danger.'

Tam smiled. 'Not you, sir. There is no way I would ever divulge the coachman's identity. You have my word on that.'

Henry shook his head. 'My concern is for you. You must leave this place immediately, with us in Mrs Fitz's carriage. Do not on any account return to the guest apartments. That was the first place I looked for you and no doubt Townsend will be lying in wait.'

Tam had delayed only long enough to change into the shirt and breeches he had been wearing when he landed on the hulks. Over them he threw the borrowed cloak which he would discard, along with the borrowed shoes.

Henry said: 'You must stay here until we are ready to leave. You will be quite safe and should Townsend come in search of you, the

318

servants will have instructions to keep him at bay. Fortunately HRH will be in no condition to interview Townsend, or anyone else for that matter, until tomorrow morning,' he added wryly.

*   *   *

An angry Townsend was soon to learn the truth of Henry's words. Frustrated by his attempts to find Tam, who was no longer in the guest apartments, although his clothes suggested that he was not far away, he thought for a moment and felt it imperative that the prince be told the latest developments involving the carriage accident. At the Pavilion he was informed that the prince was dining with important guests and had given orders that on no account whatsoever was he to be interrupted.

As Townsend tried in vain to stress the importance, it was even more maddening to hear the prince's loud guffaws. Swearing under his breath, he decided to take the law into his own hands, as he had done so many times in his life and with great success.

Summoning two of the personal bodyguards who knew him, he informed them that there was a wanted man in the Pavilion whose immediate arrest was of vital importance to HRH. They regarded him with suspicion, shook their heads and said they took their orders only from the Prince Regent himself.

Townsend thereupon assured them that the criminal was a thief that HRH was most anxious should not escape, adding a promise that should anything at all go wrong, and HRH decided that he had overstepped the mark, then he would take full personal blame. However, if they succeeded in capturing the criminal, then he would also make certain that they were well rewarded.

To his chagrin they remained unimpressed. Who was this man—a mere Bow Street officer—to order them about?

Mr Watkins, patiently waiting and trembling considerably in an anteroom, was summarily dismissed, armed only with promises of the rest of that reward in due course.

Townsend watched him go regretfully.

What an opportunity missed! If only he had been allowed to bring him face to face with Tam Eildor, to be brought before the prince and dramatically presented as the man in the carriage, whose identity would be made public after he was safely behind bars as the Marchioness of Creeve's murderer.

What a sensation. What a personal triumph!

Of course, Townsend was aware that the prince knew that it wasn't true. But a scapegoat had to be found. Perhaps Eildor should be allowed to escape from his prison and get shot trying to evade the law, thus silenced forever.

It did Townsend's temper no good at all as he marched out of the Pavilion to hear sounds of music and merriment issuing from the dining room.

* * *

The Prince Regent had excellent reason for merriment as he gazed across the vast dining table at his important guests. His adviser on paintings and furniture had newly returned from France armed with negotiations for a Rembrandt to add to the royal collection.

Lord Yarmouth was the son of Lady Hereford, for some years the prince's mistress, a middle-aged lady who had little that was obvious to commend her as a beauty and whose presence at Court had long been a gift to the caricaturists.

Yarmouth, however, had brought with him a delectable young widowed countess from Paris. Regrettably, only a short stay, he was informed, but her eyes meeting those of the Prince Regent boldly across the table promised that a great deal might be achieved as his guest for a night or two.

Another conquest. He was greatly relieved that his new bedroom, although not yet completely decorated to his satisfaction, was ready for immediate occupancy.

Aware of Prime Minister Perceval seated as far away as possible and scowling at him from

321

the far end of the table, he ignored the issues that had brought him to Brighton; to urge the Prince Regent to return to London immediately. Echoes of the Regency Bill of 1810 still threatened the smooth running of parliament with stormy debates between not only Whigs and Tories but also involving his own brothers.

Tonight at his side, seated very proudly in her prettiest gown, was his daughter Princess Charlotte, the unlikely source of his additional good humour. This was indeed a surprise to many of the prince's more intimate guests, well aware of the uneasy relationship between the two. The servants too were taken aback, since the princess was normally excluded from dining even informally at the royal table.

Chapter Twenty-Eight

Just an hour earlier, Princess Charlotte had sought out her father, timidly tapping on the library door where he was frowning over those beastly tiresome State documents to be discussed with Prime Minister Perceval.

He looked up, saw who it was and was very short with her. What did she want? And could it not wait?

'Papa—sire—this is—is—quite—urgent.' As always her father's presence brought back that childish stammer, the feeling of inadequacy and disappointment forced upon her from birth.

'Papa—I—I found—this.' And with a trembling hand she laid down the Stuart Sapphire on his desk in front of him.

With a cry of triumph he seized it. Even clutched in his hand, he could hardly believe his eyes. 'Where did this come from?'

'From—from your bedroom, Papa—wh— which you have just—vacated—upstairs.' And aware that he was not going to shout at her as usual, growing bolder, she added: 'Actually, Papa, I rather like it—I was wondering—'

He held up an impatient hand. 'Yes, yes, by all means, you can have anything. But tell me about this!' Waving the sapphire, 'Where did you get it?' A sudden dark frown. 'Who gave it to you?'

'No one, Papa. I—I was looking around your—your old bedroom—thinking I might like to have it for my stay sometime—I dropped my shawl, and when I was picking— picking it off the floor, I saw jammed in between the boards, something—something shiny. And there it was—'

She stopped, giving him a wide-eyed innocent look. 'I did not know that it was lost, Papa. I would have been most—most upset had I known.' She took a deep breath. 'Seeing that you had always promised it to me,' she added reproachfully.

But her father was no longer listening. Relief flooded over him. All was well, his kingdom steadied again, no longer rocked to its foundations.

What a day it had been! The marchioness's murder—solved. Poor Percy, but it did serve him right, just a bit! The missing Stuart Sapphire—solved. And waiting for him later this evening, if he could remain sober enough to enjoy her, that delightful creature, the French countess.

His cup of joy overflowing, he realised that now at last he could be rid of Mr Eildor. He would tell Townsend to get on with it. And now that the sapphire had been recovered, he might return to London immediately.

Yes indeed, he would summon Townsend first thing tomorrow morning, tell him that his services were no longer required. A gracious thank you and small reimbursement for his troubles should be sufficient.

But tonight there were even more important matters.

He smiled at Charlotte, warmed to her for a moment of gratitude. 'Thank you, my dear. There is a young man we should like you to meet. Prince Leopold of Saxe-Coburg-Saalsfeld is coming to London shortly. Meanwhile, perhaps you would care to join us at dinner this evening. A little experience at entertaining our important guests—'

Charlotte did not care in the least about any

young prince, but to be invited to one of her father's banquets! She rushed forward, round the desk:

'Oh thank you, Papa, thank you.'

For a dreadful moment he thought she was going to kiss him, but it was just a brief hug instead.

*   *   *

Townsend had, with some difficulty, completed his search of the Pavilion, assured by guards constantly on duty that no, they had not seen Mr Eildor.

He was certainly not on the premises and of course they would recognise him. But not even Mr Eildor, or Mr Townsend for that matter, they told him sternly, would be allowed to enter the royal apartments unchallenged.

Had Mr Townsend tried the guest apartments?

He had, as well as a thorough look around the gardens, so where could Eildor be hiding? He would hardly be wandering around Brighton, seeing that he had no money and no friends.

Then Townsend had a sudden inspiration. Remembering that conversation with Lord Henry and Lady Gemma when they had arrived from Creeve House, Eildor might well have taken refuge with Mrs Fitzherbert.

325

Hastening to Steine House, he was informed by a footman that he had missed Mrs Fitzherbert. Madam had left half an hour ago in her carriage. No, he did not know Madam's destination nor the identities of her companions. But should Mr Townsend care to leave a message?

Walking down the steps Townsend realised the significance of the carriage. Eildor would already be on the outskirts of Brighton, ready to catch the London coach. As he stood on the Steine, wondering what to do next, he saw a rider approaching from the promenade, heading towards the Pavilion.

By a stroke of luck it was one of the Dragoons guards who knew him well. Attracting his attention, Townsend explained that he was in pursuit of a dangerous criminal and asked if he could possibly borrow his horse? The man looked doubtful until Townsend insisted that this was an urgent mission and vital to the safety of HRH. So, agreeing somewhat reluctantly, and saying this was a very fast horse, he dismounted.

Watching Townsend ride off, as he made his way back to the Pavilion, the officer wondered what all the fuss was about, as neither he nor any of his comrades had heard of any threats to their royal master.

Townsend was jubilant. Riding a good, fast horse he should easily overtake a leisurely carriage, and he was now quite confident that

Eildor's destination was the coaching inn some four miles down the road. There he would lie in wait, and arrest Eildor. Having failed miserably to locate the Stuart Sapphire, perhaps some of that failure would be forgiven and forgotten when it became public that he had solved and captured single-handedly the Marchioness of Creeve's murderer.

The fact that Eildor would be shot trying to escape would also, he felt sure, be the wisest and most agreeable solution to any scandal threatening the Prince Regent.

* * *

As Mrs Fitzherbert's carriage came in sight of the coaching inn, Tam realised that this was indeed journey's end. They had travelled almost in silence, preoccupied and anxious, for even he suspected Maria Fitzherbert knew that there was more at stake than whether it would stay fine for a moonlight picnic.

Alighting from the carriage, Tam was relieved to see that the inn was on the cliff road, within sight of the sea. Following them into the inn, he made his decision. He must take his chance on the sea being at hand and trust that the microchip would see him back to his own time, and not leave him stranded in some dread limbo of past or future.

Making his excuses in the already

overcrowded inn with no chance to say lingering farewells, no chance to grasp Gemma's hand or kiss her cheek, he slipped the coins Henry had given him for his coach fare into her reticule and announced that he would take a look outside as there were other travellers gathered to board the London coach.

Alone, he walked the short distance to the edge of the cliff, appearing just as a casual observer. He heard the horn and the vibration of the horses' hooves announcing the imminent arrival of the London coach.

Turning, he thought he saw Gemma's face at the window of the inn.

Raising his hand in farewell, at the same instant his name was called.

'Mr Eildor!'

It was Townsend on horseback.

'A word with you, sir. A word, if you please.'

This was it. 'Goodbye, Brighton. Goodbye, Gemma, dear lovely Gemma, be happy,' he whispered.

Townsend had dismounted. 'You cannot escape, Mr Eildor. I have you now!' he said triumphantly.

He heard a noise, a vibration like air being sucked out of the world around him and the place he had seen Eildor standing just yards away was empty.

Empty? Damn the man, he had escaped, he had jumped off the steep road down on to the stony beach.

'Come back! I'll have you yet!' he yelled.

He ran to the road's edge, his pistol cocked at the ready, but there was no sign of Eildor. Or of any living soul, the shore deserted as far as the eye could see, an azure line on the horizon, the sea at ebb tide.

Had Eildor slipped past him, and joined the coach? Impossible that he could not have seen him, and as he walked back to the horse, he almost tripped over a black cloak and a pair of shoes. All that remained of Tam Eildor to show that he had been there at all.

Townsend felt suddenly quite ill. It was a magician's trick, of course, no one in his experience had ever vanished into thin air. But how the devil was he going to explain all this to the Prince Regent? Or to himself?

He had quick look in the coach, which was about to leave. Eildor was not among the passengers.

Going into the inn, just to make sure, he fought his way over to a table where Mrs Fitzherbert, Lord Henry and Lady Gemma were taking a little refreshment.

Approaching them, he bowed and stating the obvious: 'Mr Eildor is not with you?'

He was told: 'He left just moments ago for the London coach.'

They were smiling, laughing at him, three conspirators.

Damn them, damn them. Ordering a pint of

ale and a pie he went to another table and there he tried to work out logically what had happened.

Was it possible that Eildor had somehow slipped by him and hidden on the coach? Surely he was not journeying to London in his bare feet? He might have dropped the cloak by accident, but he would never have abandoned a good pair of shoes. That took a lot of explanation.

The three conspirators had their backs towards him, Lord Henry in casual conversation with Mrs Fitzherbert, and Lady Gemma looking intently out of the window.

They heard the coach leave. 'Got away all right, has he?' asked Henry.

'Just perfectly,' said Gemma who knew the truth and had seen Tam vanish from the cliff road. Fighting back tears and smiling at Henry, she realised that someday he must be told.

But not, of course, until they were married.

Epilogue

The events portrayed in this book are entirely fictitious and I have taken certain liberties with the historical characters, based on biographical accounts of their lives.

The Prince Regent became George IV on the death of his father 'mad' King George III in 1821. His hedonistic lifestyle continued with overindulgence in food, wine and mistresses until his death in June 1830.

Maria Fitzherbert, abandoned by the prince, continued to live in Brighton until her death in 1837 and lies buried in St John the Baptist's Catholic Church.

John Townsend, most celebrated of Bow Street officers, thief-taker for thirty-four years, continued his colourful career working for the Bank of England and for individual prosecutors.

Beau Brummell finally fell from royal favour and in 1813 fled to Calais to escape his creditors. Continuing a life of dissipation and gambling debts, he died in a pauper's lunatic asylum in 1840.

Princess Charlotte found true love at last. In 1816, aged twenty, she married Prince Leopold of Saxe-Coburg-Saalfeld, a brief happiness and romance which presaged that of Albert and Victoria, his nephew and niece, a generation later. In 1817 she sadly died after giving birth to a well-formed but stillborn son.

The Stuart Sapphire, to be viewed to this day in the Queen's crown, was returned by Charlotte's heartbroken husband to the Prince Regent, who, in company with the rest of Britain, mourned her with all the passion he had lacked in loving her during her short life.

Had Charlotte and her son survived, however, the Georgians would have continued to rule over us and we might never have known the Victorian age.